ONE DEADL
Second E

ONE DEADLY SECRET

Marie Sibbons

Chapter One

Lara's eyes fixed on the dark wooden door in front of her. Behind it was the answer to a question, the question that had dominated her life for so long. After twenty years of extreme emotions, she had no idea how she would feel when the door finally opened. When it did, her emotions remained buried deep inside.

He was just as she expected him to be. He did not turn his scrawny face to look at her when she walked into the small room where he and several suited men and women were sitting. How could she tell if he was truly remorseful when she couldn't see into his eyes, the windows of his soul? As if reading her mind, he lifted his head and turned his cold, beady blue eyes to meet hers. There was no remorse; she could tell that immediately. Yet he had convinced the parole board to the contrary.

The man dressed in the least expensive suit, who had guided Lara into the room, sat down next to her. With his softly softly approach he'd persuaded Lara to contribute to the deluge of information that the Hugo Boss suits had to consider. Those men and women would need to decide the extent of the risk the convict posed to the community he would be going back to after twenty years. What had prison life been like for him? Twenty years was a long time to be well-behaved. And did he now regret the heinous crime he had committed all those years ago?

Her hands were shaking as she unfolded the statement that she was dreading reading out. It was brief, like the time she'd had with her sister. All she could say was that she missed Bella and grieved for the future relationship that they'd both been robbed of. It didn't matter to the panel. That she could also tell. They feigned sympathy but they had already made their decision. Tom Bailey would be released.

Outside the courtroom, Lara thanked the victim liaison officer and hurried back to her car. Bailey would be back on the streets within weeks, but at least he wouldn't be anywhere near her. That was the first and last time she would have to see him.

Then the realisation slammed into her like a steel bar - she had seen him before, those cruel blue eyes, that smirk, the tiny scar on his left cheek. Suddenly, it was clear - he didn't feel remorse because there was nothing to feel remorse for. He didn't kill Bella. Someone else did.

One month later

Why was it so unfamiliar? The hedgerows that lined the road weren't there before; nor were those trees. Or were they? Plants grow, just like most people ... but not all people. Bella stopped growing. Cut down like a weed in a flower show her roots were already withered, and her name forgotten. She would be forty in a couple of years with a husband and children and a house filled with family photographs, her own family that no one could take away from her.

Lara pulled down the sun visor and looked at her face in the mirror. Her long dark hair hung limply against skin that was far too pale to look healthy. Lines were visible around her dark brown eyes, eyes that had lost their brightness over the last year. Was that the face of a thirty-year-old woman?

A car horn sounded, and Lara snapped out of her thoughts just in time to avoid a head-on collision, a collision that would have been her fault. However, the taxi had already vanished from her rear-view mirror, and she realised how fast it had been travelling. Where were the speed cameras? If there had been more cameras when Bella was alive ... concentrate Lara!

The road was a continuous slalom bending left and right, with little view of whatever was ahead, and she knew it symbolised her immediate future. The lack of turnoffs meant that her companion had little need to speak allowing Lara to ignore its presence. She preferred roadmaps anyway.

Although driving back to the place of her birth, Lara felt no nostalgia as she, at last, glanced at the various landmarks – flat fields, tiny lakes, and solitary houses. No nostalgia but there was recognition. She knew she was approaching her destination.

As soon as she saw the hotel, Lara recognised it. The ugly Victorian house looked just like many family homes except for the sign hanging from a wooden post reading *Six Ways Hotel*. There were no cars in the narrow driveway, and Lara wondered if there were any other guests.

The sound of the car on gravel announced her arrival and within seconds, a woman of about seventy appeared in the doorway. At nearly six feet tall and with white hair cut into a sharp bob, she looked more like a retired headteacher than the owner of a tiny hotel.

'Hello, dear. Have you booked a room?' The kindness in her voice belied the sternness of her appearance.

'Yes. I booked online. I hope there hasn't been a mistake.'

'Oh no. It's fine. My daughter deals with all the computer bookings. She doesn't always tell me about them, however. Please come in.'

Lara followed her statuesque hostess through a dark hallway dominated by an austere grandfather clock. It looked at least a hundred years old. The clock's pendulum matched the rhythm of Lara's footsteps as though it were observing her.

'This is the breakfast room,' the hotel owner said.

They had entered a square-shaped room somewhere at the back of the house. Like the hall, it was also dark despite the large sash window in the far corner. Four small tables had been squashed into the middle to make room for an oversized sideboard holding an array of crockery, cereal boxes, and a large hot water canister.

'Breakfast is self-service, but each morning there will be fresh orange juice and hot water for tea and coffee.'

'Do you serve evening meals? I haven't eaten much today.'

'You are welcome to make yourself toast for no extra cost,' she said, pointing towards a small, battered-looking toaster poking out from behind a box of Cornflakes.

Lara took that as a no. 'Is there a takeaway near here?'

'There's a fish and chip shop in the village, but I'd appreciate it if you did not bring any back here. The smell lingers for hours.'

Deciding that toast would suffice, Lara was shown to her room.

It was like stepping into the eighties. A radio cassette player rested on an ugly wooden cabinet – the extent of the In-room entertainment. It had probably been there when she last visited the hotel. She sat on the edge of the lumpy, single bed covered with woollen blankets, then took a velvet bag out of her handbag. It had been sent to her by Bella's foster parents who'd had a clear-out before emigrating. It contained the remnants of Bella's belongings.

There were several photographs of Bella looking angelic in some and surly in others. One photograph stood out. With a tear down the middle and held together by tape, it was the last one taken. It pictured Bella in the final few hours of her life. Laying it down on the bed, Lara reached back into the bag and brought out a miniature diary, the clasp of which was broken.

The lock was still intact when it reached her, but Lara felt that she was entitled to share her sister's secrets. When she first read it she'd quickly lost patience with the abbreviated names and coded words. But after the parole hearing, she'd returned to it, searching for a clue that would justify her doubts about the conviction. And there it was on the last page of writing:

"I'm so excited. If I get the two hundred pounds tonight, I'll be in London tomorrow. If I don't, I'll tell everyone what I know. I don't care anymore."

That was the clue and the justification. Lara put the diary back in her suitcase. She wasn't ready to share Bella's secrets with anyone else just yet.

As it turned out, the uncomfortable bed gave Lara the best night's sleep she'd had in a long time. It was probably due to the heavy blankets preventing her usual tossing and turning through the night. Feeling refreshed, she fought back nerves as she entered the small breakfast room. Expecting it to be empty, she was surprised to find two tables occupied by several burly men.

'It's self-service, luv,' one said.

'Yes, I know. I'm just putting my things down,' Lara replied, hating herself for blushing.

She walked over to the table nearest the window and sat down with her back to the rest of the room. All the other guests were male, and Lara assumed they were builders. She wondered what they made of the miserly breakfast on offer.

Every now and again a young woman dressed in a maid's outfit checked the supply of orange juice, milk, and bread. Not feeling like toast again, she settled on a bowl of Shreddies and a cup of tea, and then pulled out the notebook and pen that served as imaginary companions to deter unwelcome conversation.

Eight chimes sounded from the hallway and the four men departed, leaving Lara by herself. She took out the contents of the envelope once more and focussed on one thing. Pictured in the photograph were five girls wearing party dresses. At least they looked like girls but Lara knew they were seventeen or eighteen, that awkward time of life that fell between the constrained boundaries of childhood and the responsibilities of adulthood. She looked closely at each figure.

The girl in the middle was struggling to fill out her light grey satin dress but was ridiculously pretty with long blonde hair. Two were plainer but more developed and wore their dresses better. The other two girls could have been sisters with their identical black hairstyles, but it was obvious which one was Bella. She was standing slightly away from the other four, wearing a far more modest outfit enhanced by a pretty bangle. There was something special, almost magical, about the way she looked.

'Can I get you anything else?'

Lara jumped out of her thoughts and looked up at the young woman who was now holding a dishcloth and spray. She was very pretty even with her long black hair scraped into a bun but couldn't disguise her boredom.

'No, thank you. Sorry if I am holding you up,' Lara said, looking around at the other empty tables.

'There's no need to rush,' the young woman said kindly. 'It's a change to have a woman staying here.'

'Was that your grandmother who I met yesterday?'

She laughed. 'No, that's my mother but I appreciate the gesture. She's a late sleeper so I do the morning shift, not that there's any other shift to do.'

Lara smiled. 'I'm sure there's more to running a hotel than serving breakfast. For a start, there's all the bedding to make and wash.'

'Yes, I know and I'm no good at laundry. I still don't understand what synthetics are,' she said with another laugh. Then, after noticing the photograph she looked at Lara with intrigue. 'Are those members of your family?'

'No,' Lara replied, then quickly changed the subject. 'Your mother said that there is only a chip shop in the village, so I wondered, if I brought back a microwave meal tonight, could you heat it up for me?'

'Yes, of course. I tell you what, I'll bring the microwave in here after I've cleared up. We don't really use it ourselves. I suppose my mother has laid down the law regarding fish and chips.'

'That's okay. If you have a minute, I wonder if I could ask you something …'

'Flora. My name is Flora.'

'Thanks, Flora. Have you lived here all your life?'

'Yes, why?'

'Do you recognise anyone in this photograph?' She lifted the photograph so that Flora could view it properly.

Flora squinted at the tatty picture held together by Sellotape. 'Oh, it's not in good condition. It's quite

9

old, isn't it? But that looks like the woman who works in the Spar,' she said, pointing to the tallest girl in the group who resembled Bella. 'I don't know her name, but she's in the shop most evenings.'

Lara jotted the information down in her notebook while Flora looked on with curiosity.

'What about the other three?' Lara asked. 'Have you seen them before? They'd be twenty years older of course.'

'So, are they old schoolmates of yours?' Flora asked, without the tact of her guest.

'No, not exactly. I'm just trying to trace my family history, and this photograph has always fascinated me. Do you recognise the others?'

'I don't think so. The one in the middle with the blonde hair looks familiar though. I think she could be the new owner of the café on the seafront. It's only just opened. I think her name's Jenny.'

'Is it far?' Lara asked, after writing in her notebook.

'It's about a mile from the village. If you turn right outside, the village is about a half-mile walk, then the beach is further on in the same direction.'

'Are there any buses? I don't feel like driving again just yet.'

'There's a bus that goes to the village, but you'd have to walk the rest of the way. It's not that far really. You could stop in the shop to break up the walk.'

'Do you know the name of the café?'

'No, but you can't miss it. It's the only one there.'

Situated between a boarded-up shop and a forlorn-looking newsagent the café looked relatively new with its freshly painted walls and clean windows. As Lara opened the door, a bell rang causing the only two customers to briefly look up from their ice cream. Behind the counter, a youngish woman, seemingly oblivious to all around her, was leafing through a magazine. There was a mixture of glamour and sophistication in her dress and demeanour that was slightly out of place as a café worker, even if she was the owner. She looked up and, on seeing Lara, her face paled.

'Are you Jenny?' Lara asked, even though she knew the answer.

The woman on the other side of the counter simply nodded, causing strands of blonde hair to slide from her stylish bun.

'I'm -'

'Bella's sister?'

'Yes. I guess I must resemble her.'

'For a moment, I thought I was seeing things. You look so much like her. Anyway, what can I do for you …?'

'Lara.'

'What can I do for you, Lara?'

'A cappuccino and a bacon sandwich please.'

'Not quite what I meant but if you take a seat, I'll bring them over when they're ready.'

Lara walked over to the table furthest away from the young couple and immediately placed her notebook on the table. The smell of bacon filled the café, at which point the young couple paid for their ice cream and left.

'I hope I didn't scare them off,' Lara said, laughing.

'I don't care if you have. They've been taking up that table for over an hour. And who eats ice cream at this hour?'

Lara wondered if the café had had any other customers that morning, but she replied with tact. 'It must be really annoying when that happens. I'll try not to outstay my welcome.'

Rather than leaving Lara alone to eat her sandwich, Jenny joined her at the table.

'I'm sorry I didn't remember your name, Lara, but it's been a long time.'

'Don't apologise. My parents changed it when they adopted me. I suppose it made me seem more like their child. Anyway, I suppose you're wondering why I've come to Weston,' Lara said.

'Not as much as why you've come to see me.'

'I'm writing a book about my life as an adopted child and want to find out more about my sister. I never really knew her you see.'

'Yes. You were still in primary school. Bella didn't really know you much either. I remember her refusing to see you when you came back that day. It was heartbreaking. But what do you want to know exactly?'

'What she was like. Did you like her? Who were her closest friends?'

Jenny's expression changed as if a thought had just occurred to her. 'How did you know about me? Have you spoken to anyone else about Bella?'

'Not exactly.' Lara produced the photograph from her bag and passed it to Jenny. 'I showed it to Flora, the girl in the hotel, and she thought she recognised you. And she definitely knew her.' She pointed to the tallest girl.

'Ah yes, that's Tanya. She works in the local Spar.'

'I know,' Lara said. 'Flora told me that too.'

'So, you've already spoken to Tanya?'

'No. I called in on my way here but couldn't see her.'

'Yes, of course. Tanya works the later shift.'

'So, after I left the shop, I came straight here to talk to you. Can you tell me about the other girls in the photograph? I take it Bella is the one on the end.'

'Yes,' Jenny said sadly. 'That's Bella. You look so much like her. the same thick black hair, dark eyes, creamy skin. She was beautiful.'

Lara found herself blushing. She never knew how to react to a compliment, so she did what she always did and ignored it. 'Why is Bella standing away from the rest of you?'

'We hung around together as a group, but really, I was Bella's only friend.'

13

'Didn't the others like her much?'

'Tanya got on all right with her. Hanna was too quiet to say what she thought. Simone, next to me in the photo, didn't like Bella much at all, I'm afraid to say.'

'Was there any particular reason for that?'

'I'm not sure. Simone said she was a troublemaker, but I think she was just jealous of the attention Bella got from the boys.'

'Did Bella have a boyfriend?'

'No, but she was very popular that way.'

Lara didn't really know what "that way" meant, but before she could ask yet another question, Jenny asked her own.

'Where did you get this photograph?'

'It belonged to Bella and was amongst her things that were given to me.'

'Oh, yes. My mother sent it to Bella's foster parents. She never knew if it reached you.'

'It was good of her to do that but I only got it last year. They've recently emigrated so were having a clear out. I suppose they ripped it in two by mistake thinking it was rubbish.'

'At least you've got it now,' said Jenny, putting her slender hand on Lara's shoulder. 'I'm sorry but I can't stop as I've cakes in the oven. It's lovely to see you again, Lara. Give me your number, and I'll ring you as soon as I've got more time.'

'Okay. I'll look forward to it,' Lara said, ignoring the absence of any smell of baking.

The young woman sitting on the ground didn't look up at any customers entering or leaving the Spar, but that didn't mean she hadn't noticed them. Of course, beggars clock everyone who walks past them, but Lara always gave on the way out just in case.

It was a small supermarket with far less choice than what she was used to. The man in front of her in the fresh food section seemed to be undecided about his meal choice. Lara mentally crossed her fingers as his hand hovered between a solitary macaroni cheese and various curries. Why was he taking so long? A sixth sense caused her to look up. His eyes were fixed on her, and they were not friendly.

'Excuse me. Can I just grab something?' she asked.

Without taking his eyes off her, he picked up the macaroni cheese and stood back. 'It's all yours.'

The queue for the till was stationary. A scruffily dressed woman at the front was causing the cashier problems, and eventually, a colleague stepped away from her shelf stacking to serve the other customers. Lara couldn't help but stare at the scruffy woman who had dropped her bags onto the floor, along with a packet of cigarettes, a lighter and a bag of coins.

'Do you want a carrier bag, or not?' asked the exasperated cashier, clearly used to the difficult customer.

The customer nodded and was handed a carrier bag that she probably didn't need. After picking up the bag of coins, she took out ten pence and handed it over in exchange for her purchase. Before leaving, she turned to meet Lara's gaze, and, for a moment there was a flicker of recognition in her otherwise dead eyes. Then it was gone. Lara shivered. What kind of dead-end town had she returned to?

'Next customer, please.'

The piercing cry of the cashier snapped both women out of their mysterious bond, and Lara walked up to the till and handed her frozen pasta dish to the cashier. She was clearly the woman from the photograph, with the same towering figure and black hair which was now glittered with silver strands.

'That'll be three pounds twenty. Do you have a loyalty card?'

'No,' Lara replied, as she handed over a ten-pound note.

This method of payment seemed to irritate the shop assistant, clearly preferring the less effort-demanding contactless card, and she glanced at Lara with disapproval. Then her expression changed. 'Do I know you from somewhere?' she asked suspiciously.

'No, but I think you knew my sister, Bella.'

'You're Bella's sister! Oh my! You are the spitting image of her.'

'I know. You were her friend, weren't you?'

Tanya nodded before putting Lara's change on the counter. 'Nice to meet you. Next customer please.'

As Lara walked out of the shop, she picked a pound coin out of her change, but the woman who had been begging was no longer there. Lara left it in her coat pocket ready for the next time she saw her. If she saw her again.

Chapter Two

'What's the hotel like?'

'It's small and old-fashioned but okay for what I need.'

'Is your room warm? Do they serve evening meals? What are the other guests like? I cannot understand why you're staying in that hotel. I bet it hasn't changed in twenty years. Copston has far better places to stay.'

'Everything's fine, Mum, and Copston is not the place I want to be. This hotel is perfect for me. I would send you some pictures if you'd only go on Facebook like I told you to.'

'I don't want pictures, Lara. They won't answer my questions. And I have been there before as you know. How much longer are you staying?'

'Give me a chance. I've only just arrived. I'll be here at least another couple of days.'

'I don't understand why you wanted to go there in the first place. It's not like you were there long, and there's no one there to visit.'

'It's just something I need to do.'

'Well, ring straight away if you need us to come and get you.'

'Thanks, Mum. Of course, I will.'

Lara had not told her mother about the diary and photographs because they involved a part of her life that was separate from the people who'd adopted her when she was five years old. They'd chosen to cut Lara off from her blood sister as the elder sister was regarded as "broken" with no hope of recovering from the abuse she had suffered from her father. Lara was spared the torture as their father had died just after she was born, followed by her mother three years later. After two years of foster care, Lara was adopted and her name, along with her life, changed. Bella remained in foster care.

Lara wondered how different her life would have been if she hadn't been taken in by a kind, middle-class couple who had no children of their own. It had been a quiet upbringing, but Lara had loved her home and the security her new parents offered. Although knowing about her estranged sister, she had never felt the need to reunite with her. Now she wondered why.

She looked at the information she had gathered thus far.

• Jenny was Bella's close friend. She recently came back from London and now owns a café. She seems friendly enough but didn't want to talk for long.

• Tanya works in the local shop. She did not want to talk to me but it might have been because she was at work.

And that was it. A whole morning's investigation had led virtually nowhere. Throwing her pen onto the carpet in frustration, she began to agree with her mother that no good could come of the visit. Should she give up now and save on hotel rooms? Jenny had not really been that helpful, and Tanya could barely look at her.

Lara had thought she could turn up in Weston, meet everyone who knew Bella, and then work out which one was the real murderer. Now she felt silly. All she had were some photographs and a few words from her sister's diary. Maybe there was nothing untoward about the money that was mentioned. Or perhaps Bella was going to steal the two hundred pounds from somewhere but was killed before she had the chance. Was her sister a blackmailer or a thief?

Suddenly, her mobile beeped, displaying a message from an unrecognised number. With a sense of anticipation, she opened it.

Hi Lara. Sorry, I couldn't spend more time with you earlier. I'm meeting Tanya and Hanna for a drink tonight. Do you want to join us? You could interrogate them too. x Jen

The ping of the microwave attracted the attention of the hotel owner, Mrs Parsons, who came marching into the breakfast room.

'Is that your microwave?' she asked curiously.

'Er, no. It's yours. Your daughter brought it in here for me to use. She said that you never use it.'

'Well, no, but I wished she had asked me first because I would have cleaned it. It's fine for you to use it. Are you in for the night?'

'No, I'm going out with a few friends. I'm meeting them in the local pub. I take it there's only one.'

'Yes, and a right den of thieves it is too,' Mrs Parsons replied.

'What do the youngsters do around here? Is there a nightclub?' Lara asked, taking the opportunity to find out more about the area.

'No, there isn't. Thank goodness! The young people usually get taxis into Copston then stagger home any way they can which is usually through the crop fields.'

'I went there once but I was very young at the time. What's it like?'

'Nothing to write home about but it is our lifeline so I shouldn't complain. It serves all the coastal villages for miles. We couldn't survive on the pathetic shops we have here.'

Lara thought that was a small price to pay to live in such a spectacular part of the country. However, she wasn't sure if she could live in such a quiet place herself. Weston had a population of less than two thousand, and there were few tourists to bring in more life.

'Well, I can't stand here talking all day,' Mrs Parsons said. 'And I suppose you need to get going. Who are your friends?'

'Well, they're not actually my friends. They are my sister's old friends so I only know their first names. There's Jenny who has a café on the seafront, Tanya from the Spar and someone called Hanna.'

'Who is your sister? You didn't mention that you had a sister living here.'

'Lived. She lived here a long time ago but not now. You might remember her. Her name was Bella Young.'

'Oh, I see. Yes, I do remember her.' The older woman was silent for a moment as if considering her next comment. Then, with a look which made Lara shiver, she said, 'Be careful. You don't know those women. Not all friends can be trusted.'

The large gathering of bikers outside suggested that The Royal Oak attracted people who came from far and wide, not just Weston. Until recently, her father would travel around the country on the motorbike which was his pride and joy. She told herself that these men were just like him and wouldn't even notice her.

Unfortunately for Lara, all the bikers were standing around their vehicles, and she cringed as she swerved her way through the metal, rubber, and leather that blocked the entrance. An unwelcome wolf whistle resulted in sniggers and jeers, and she was relieved to step inside the dingy bar.

After a quick scan of the room, her heart sank on failing to see the women she was supposed to be meeting. Was she too early? She looked around again for an empty table but changed her mind. If she sat by herself, it would look like she'd been stood up, and what if any of those bikers saw her sitting alone? But the thought of having to walk back through the bikers made her overcome her embarrassment, and she approached the bar. Then, just as she was about to be served, an unfamiliar face appeared next to her.

'Hi. It's Lara, isn't it? We are sitting over there. What can I get you?' The woman was not even looking at her.

'Er, a glass of red wine, please. Shall I help you carry the drinks?' Lara asked, but the frumpily dressed woman was now talking to a tall blond man at the bar, so she went in search of the other women.

Jenny and Tanya were sitting at a corner table behind a pillar and showing little sign of looking out for Lara. She greeted them meekly and sat down on an empty chair.

Tanya smirked before saying, 'So, is Hanna getting you a drink Zara?'

'Yes, and it's Lara.'

'I do apologize, Lara,'

'Don't worry. I've been called Tara, Cara, and Sara too. Thanks for inviting me.'

'No problem. You are Bella's sister and Bella was our friend,' Jenny said. 'I hope Hanna isn't long. Was she being served when you left her?'

'No. She was talking to a man at the bar.'

'Wonder who that is,' said the other two women at the same time.

'Did you use to come here with Bella?' Lara asked, not interested in the mystery man at the bar.

'Sometimes, but the landlady was too strict to serve us without ID. When she wasn't here, we'd smuggle ourselves into the corner, and the boys would get our drinks.'

'The boys?'

'We did have boyfriends, you know,' Tanya said. 'Apart from Simone, of course.'

'Did Bella like any of the boys you hung out with?' Lara asked, remembering Jenny's earlier comment about Bella not having a boyfriend.

'She never said but I think she secretly had a thing for Ben. She hung around with him a lot,' Jenny said.

Tanya laughed out loud. 'Oh, come off it. Why on earth would she have liked him? He was a weirdo. He still is a weirdo for that matter.'

'Don't be mean. Ben's shy that's all,' Jenny said. 'Anyway, Lara wants to know about her sister so I suggest that she asks us questions, and we answer where we can.'

Lara smiled awkwardly and took out her notebook again, saying, 'I hope you don't mind if I make some notes, as I have a terrible memory.' She also took out

25

the photograph and placed it in the centre of the table.

'Was this taken the night Bella was murdered?' she asked bluntly.

'Is that us?' Hanna asked, viewing the photograph from upside down as she put down the tray of drinks. 'I don't think I've seen that photograph before. Look at those awful dresses.'

Jenny said, 'You have seen it before, Hanna, because I gave you a copy about a year after.'

'Well, I never got it. My mother probably destroyed it because she hated Bella. I'm sorry Lara, but I can't pretend I liked her either.' Hanna was constantly turning her bangle around her slender wrist as if she was nervous.

Lara was shocked. 'Why didn't you like her? Did she hurt you in some way?'

Hanna shrugged her shoulders and said, 'Nobody liked her because -'

'Come on, girls. Let's have a selfie. It's been years.' Jenny said as she held her phone to capture the image of the three old friends.

Lara felt embarrassed as she watched the three women from the other side of the table. Even when they were sat down, Tanya towered over the other two women. Her demeanour was that of the friends' protector. Hanna's look was the opposite. She was petite and almost childlike except for the silver strands in her light brown hair. She looked nothing like the plump teenager in the photograph. Her body language revealed a timid woman who felt uncomfortable in the present company or, at least, in Lara's company. And in the centre sat Jenny just like in the photograph. She was still the queen bee.

The three women giggled at the new image, seemingly ignorant of Lara's presence, but she was determined not to be put off. She returned her focus to the woman who had been so rude about her sister.

'Hanna, did you ever get on with Bella?'

Hanna glanced at Tanya before answering. 'She was nice enough at school but she changed near the end. One minute she was a choir girl, the next a bully. It was like she suddenly resented everyone around her.'

'What did she do though? She must have done something to make you hate her?' Lara said, with growing frustration.

'It's really none of your business,' Tanya snapped. 'Bella was out for what she could get. She was a -'

'I liked Bella,' Jenny interrupted. 'She was funny and a good friend to me. I was devastated when she died. You got on with her too, Tanya. Don't pretend you didn't.'

'Yes, I suppose I did but that's because I wouldn't take any of her nonsense. Bella could be cruel if she didn't like you. She was mean to Simone, wasn't she?'

'That's not fair. Simone was horrid to Bella too,' Jenny said. 'They just didn't get on, that's all.'

'Did they fall out that night?' Lara asked.

'Yes. They had a huge row,' Jenny replied. 'You see, our parents had paid for a limousine to take us to the school ball, and Bella started smoking on the journey there. The driver went mad and refused to pick us up afterwards so we had to find our own way home.'

'And how did you get home?'

Lara noticed the three other women looking at each other as if wondering who should answer the question. It was Tanya who finally spoke.

'We began to walk home, then Tom Bailey, a local lowlife, pulled up and offered us a lift. But we told him to get lost. A young couple stopped soon after and dropped us off near the village. Then Bailey showed up again. You screamed at him then, Hanna, didn't you? He was really angry when he drove off. He threatened to get us when we were on our own. It got worse when we split up. Jenny left first and he tried to attack her, but we heard her screaming. After that, he must have seen Bella walking the rest of the way home by herself.'

For the first time, Lara realised that Bella's friends might have their own unpleasant memories about that night. 'That's terrible, Jenny. I'm so sorry.'

Jenny seemed unaffected. 'Luckily for me, I can't remember anything about it, but I'm so grateful to the others for rescuing me.'

'Did he face charges for that? I don't recall hearing about a sexual assault.'

'No, because I didn't want my name dragged through the mud. The others made sure everyone heard about it on the grapevine, though.'

'So how did she end up on the coastal path? Her foster home was nowhere near there,' Lara asked.

'That's what we couldn't understand,' Hanna said. 'We stayed together for about half an hour after that.'

'Why?' Lara was getting confused about their journey home but knew it was important.

'We were just chatting about the night,' Jenny said.

'But I thought you were drunk, Jenny.' Lara gave a confused expression.

'That didn't stop her talking though,' Hanna said.

'Then, Bella left us. We assumed she went home, but she couldn't have unless Bailey saw her and dragged her in his car,' Jenny said. 'He'd just failed to get me, so he must have gone looking for another victim.'

'And when did the rest of you split up?' Lara asked.

'About fifteen minutes later,' Hanna said. 'Jenny was too drunk to walk the rest of the way home, so she stayed with Tanya. Simone, and I walked the rest of the way home, alone.'

'What time was it when you got home?'

'We left the party at about eleven o'clock. We got home not long after twelve. We all noticed Bailey's car driving away from the coast at about ten past twelve. The police think Bella must have been killed at around twelve.'

'All of you noticed Bailey's car even though you weren't together,' Lara said, trying not to sound dubious.

'It's a tiny place if you haven't already noticed,' Tanya replied.

Lara couldn't help but feel that they were skimming over things when what she wanted was detailed information. 'How come you were the only one drunk? Jenny.'

'I drowned my sorrows after being dumped at the ball.'

'Oh!' Lara found it difficult to imagine any man finishing with Jenny. 'Were there any other suspects?'

'Not once Tom's alibi was found to be false. Until then, the focus was on an older student. He was known to like young girls too,' Tanya said.

'Oh, that's not fair. He was just trying to help Bella,' Jenny said.

'What was his name?'

'John -' Tanya was nudged by Jenny before she could complete the name.

'Do you think they were involved in some way?'

Tanya glanced at Hanna before saying, 'Perhaps. I think she was involved with someone, but she was so secretive about things. You can even tell from her face in this photograph that she is hiding something, maybe many things.'

For the first time, Hanna picked up the photograph and looked carefully at each figure until her eyes fell on the dead girl. For about a minute she was silent, deep in thought, before shaking her head. To everyone's surprise, she threw the photograph down as she stood up from the table.

'I just need to speak to someone,' she said, before disappearing into the crowd.

Tanya and Jenny gave each other a confused look before an awkward silence descended on the table. Then the two old friends began talking quietly as if to exclude an embarrassed Lara. She wished Hanna would come back. Finally, she did.

. 'I don't feel well so I'm going home.' Hanna's cheeks were moist.

'Don't go yet, Hanna. Give me time to finish my drink and we'll leave together,' Jenny pleaded.

'I'm sorry to spoil the night but I've got a headache. But you all stay and enjoy yourselves. I'll be fine. There are plenty of taxis outside, so I'll jump in one of them. It was nice to meet you, Lara.' And with that, she rushed out.

There were a few seconds of silence before Tanya turned to Lara. 'Why are you dragging all this up? It's only opening old wounds. Bella's dead so you've no business here. Go back to wherever it is you came from.'

Lara fought back the tears as she packed up her things and left the pub. This time she barely noticed the bikers as she rushed through them. Nor did they notice her, except for one who continued to watch her as she walked out of sight.

Tears streamed down Hanna's face as she walked along the road leading out of Weston. As soon as she'd left the pub, she'd realised that the only taxi was booked. But she couldn't face returning, not after seeing that photograph. What if it came out that she'd helped send an innocent man to jail? But he wasn't that innocent, she reminded herself. She'd never regretted doing what she'd done, and she'd never really cared whether Tom Bailey killed Bella or not. But now she wasn't so sure. Now she would have to go over everything that was said at the time.

But there was nothing she could do about it tonight. It was too late to call anyone, and she didn't want to go to the police yet. It was still early, so if she walked along the main road, a bus might pass and stop. Were there buses this late?

The worst thing that could happen would be that she had to walk the four miles home. It wasn't cold but it was quiet so she decided she would run as much of the way as she could. She always ran when she was in a lonely place because it made her feel safer, as irrational as that feeling was.

The route home was not quite as Hanna remembered it, and after an hour, she found herself faced with a dilemma. A new bypass cut across the road, so she would either have to walk through an underpass or turn back. She stopped and looked around, knowing how risky it would be to walk through a dark, underground tunnel on her own. Yet, the alternative was to walk all the way back into

Weston, or at least until a taxi stopped for her. If she kept her head down and ran all the way she would be across the other side in less than a minute, she thought.

Looking around one last time, she stepped down the steps and turned right into the tunnel, surprised at how short it was. However, when she emerged from the other side, she found that, rather than being on the other side of the road, she was still in the underpass which branched off in several directions. It was dimly lit, and parts were hidden by large shadows. The bypass was clearly bigger than she had realised. Suddenly, she lost her nerve and walked back down the short tunnel and up the steps.

Seeing the darkness surrounding her, she now regretted leaving the pub early, but what she saw in the photograph had been the last straw. The night had been bad enough anyway with that woman asking questions. Images flashed through her mind: Bella's laughing eyes. Bella's cruel face. Why did her sister have to show up after all this time? They all thought the secret was dead and buried.

To her relief, Hanna noticed a footbridge further down the bypass which would save her from turning back. All she needed to do was go down a side street until she reached it. Relieved, she hurriedly zigzagged her way through a couple of streets of student-type houses until she reached the footbridge. Looking up, she thought she could see someone walking ahead of her. It looked like another woman which reassured her.

She ascended the steps up onto the bridge and was surprised to see that the woman was still only at the midway point, the same place she had been when Hanna first spotted her. Feeling uncertain, Hanna slowed down so as not to catch the other woman up, but however slow she walked, the distance between her and the woman got smaller and smaller. Something did not feel right.

The driver could not have been concentrating on the road ahead or he would have stopped, regardless of it being too late. It was too late as soon as the woman hit the ground, even before the long-distance vehicle had driven over her. In spite of the devastating injuries to the body, a preliminary identification was possible due to the discovery of a handbag on the footbridge twenty feet above the bypass.

'Looks like suicide, Sir,' the uniformed officer said to his plain-clothed colleague, even before the arrival of the pathologist. 'Walking into the sea would have been a cleaner method.'

'She won't be popular with the Saturday morning shoppers,' said the detective. 'Not that she'll care. I'm assuming it is a she.'

'Yes. This handbag was found on the footbridge above. Here's her driver's license.'

The detective took hold of the small plastic card, and after holding it up to the streetlight, he frowned. Has the next of kin been informed?

'We're checking who that is now.'

'No need. I know her.'

Chapter Three

The leaves were beginning to change into a glorious swansong of colours which Autumn always brings. But there were only two colours in the graveyard – green and grey.

After walking the length and width of the yard, Lara finally found the gravestone. It was the one closest to the willow tree, already beginning to weep leaves; the first to live and the first to die. She brushed away the pointy leaves that had fallen on the neglected memorial and then touched the empty metal vase. Looking around, she could see that most of the other plots were also in a sorry state. Only those that lined the path to the church door had been tended recently.

A few feet away, a sombre-faced couple walked up to another grave, one that looked new. She felt a pang of guilt taking over her body as she watched them. It had never crossed her mind to visit Bella's grave herself as she had been all too ready to leave her past behind. When she was adopted by a loving couple, it was like all her Christmases had come at once. But the parole hearing had put an end to the blissful ignorance of her sister's life.

'It's sad to see a neglected plot, isn't it?'

The voice seemed to come from nowhere but when Lara spun around, she saw a man wearing a dog collar standing on the path. She had never spoken to a vicar before, and she found herself engulfed in a feeling that was either intimidation or awe. She remained silent until the vicar spoke again.

'Are you a friend or family member?' he asked curiously. 'I don't believe I've seen you here before.'

'Yes,' Lara said, at last. 'This is my sister's grave, but I live so far away that I haven't been able to visit until now.'

Did Lara imagine the vicar's doubtful expression as he stepped off the path and joined her at the grave? After leaning down and brushing away the cobwebs and old leaves from the granite stone, he looked pensively at Lara for a few moments. Then he said,

'It was the saddest funeral I have ever conducted. The church should have been filled with mourners, not half empty. She was so young and her life so tragic. I don't remember you there but I suppose you must have been young, and children don't tend to go to funerals.'

'I wanted to go but my parents wouldn't let me. They didn't go either, but they did pay for everything. I suppose I should add that they are my adoptive parents.'

She wondered if the vicar was critical of her parents because he did not respond to her excuses.

'Did you know my sister?' she asked, moving the topic away from herself.

Lara's question appeared to snap the vicar out of his contemplation, and he fiddled around with his dog collar before answering.

'She was in the church choir for a while. Her voice was like an angel, and she could have won awards, but then teenage life took over and we did not see her anymore. Such a shame.'

He looked as though he had returned to the deep recesses of his thoughts, and Lara watched as he walked away merely nodding his head in acknowledgement.

Then he added, 'You should not feel guilty because you were only a child. I'm sure she knows you are here now.'

His words had made her feel even sadder than when she had first seen Bella's neglected gravestone. Then she wiped away the tears that had welled up in her eyes and determined to come back with flowers once she had picked up her purse from the hotel. Deep in thought, she didn't notice the woman watching her from behind another plot as she walked away.

Back at the hotel, Lara's hangover had eased enough to face a piece of toast, so she went straight to the breakfast room. Sitting alone at a table, the landlady's daughter, Flora, was nursing a glass of orange juice. Her face lit up when she saw Lara.

'Oh, thank goodness you're here. I was thinking all sorts of terrible things.'

'Why wouldn't I be here and what terrible things were you thinking? Is anything wrong?'

'A woman died last night, and I was worried it might be you. It wouldn't have been a good look for us,' she said, with a smile.

Lara looked confused. 'This woman you're talking about, how did she die?'

'They're still not sure but it looks like suicide.'

'Oh, dear! And you thought it was me.'

'Well. Yes, because, when you didn't come down to breakfast, I knocked on your room and there was no answer. So, I thought it could have been you because you were in that pub around the same time.'

'The Royal Oak?'

'Yes. She was actually three miles from here on the way to Copston. I knew it was the wrong place, but I thought you might have lost your way. Were there many women in the pub, last night?'

Lara doubted she would walk three miles without realizing it was in the wrong direction, however, she was too polite to say. 'Quite a few. There were four of us, a gang of bikers, and I think, some school staff. How did she do it?'

'Jumped off the pedestrian bridge that goes over the by-pass just outside of Copston.'

'That's terrible. I remember that bypass and it was miles away. Do they know who the woman was?'

'The police haven't said yet. I'm sure they know who it is though.'

With that, the doorbell rang, and she disappeared, returning a few moments later with two police officers.

'Er, these police officers are here to talk to you. I'll leave you to it.'

Lara looked up at the two police officers with a sense of dread. She wondered why they had come to see her.'

'Hello. Are you Lara Campbell?' asked the police officer nearest to Lara.

'Yes. Is it about that poor woman who died yesterday?'

'Yes, I'm afraid so. Can I ask what you have heard about the incident?'

'I'd just been told about it before you arrived. Some woman killed herself by jumping off a bridge. I didn't see anything though.'

'The woman was Hanna Evans. It seems you spent several hours with her last night, along with two other women.'

Lara was dumbstruck. Several thoughts began to race around her mind. The most unsettling one was: would the other women blame her for the tragedy?

'Can you answer some questions about last night, Miss Campbell?'

'Why? I mean, of course. I'm sorry but I didn't really know her. We were only together for a couple of hours.'

'Yes. We heard she left earlier than planned. Do you know why that was?'

'She said she felt unwell. A headache, I think she said.' Lara believed that it was something that Hanna saw in the photograph that upset her, but as she didn't want to risk losing the photograph, she chose not to mention it.

'You left just after Miss Evans. Did you see her outside The Royal Oak?'

'No, but I didn't really look. She certainly wasn't walking the same way as me because I would have seen her. It's a straight road from the pub to this hotel.'

'Yet, that is precisely the way she would have walked. Are you certain that you didn't see her walking in front of you?'

'Yes, I'm certain. She must have had a lift from someone for part of the way.'

'Perhaps she caught the bus,' said Flora, who had returned to the breakfast room.

'I doubt that as there wasn't a bus at that time. What time did you get back here, Miss Campbell?'

'I don't know exactly. I think it was about ten o'clock, maybe ten-thirty.'

'Did you speak to anyone here after you got back?'

'No. There was nobody about, so I just went straight to bed.'

'At ten o'clock! That's a bit early to go to bed, isn't it?'

'Well, there was nothing else to do. The TV in my room doesn't work' she said, avoiding Flora's eyes.

'Don't you have a smartphone or something?'

'There's no Wi-Fi here and I didn't want to use my data.'

One police officer was looking at Lara in a way that made her feel uncomfortable. He clearly thought she was hiding something.

'The other women said that you were asking a lot of questions about your late sister.'

'Yes. I'm writing a book and I want to include her.'

'What are your plans for the rest of your stay?'

'I'm hoping to speak to anyone else who knew her. I don't suppose you knew her, did you? Her name was Bella Young.'

'No, but I've heard about her case. It was tragic. Be careful, though, as not everyone around here will be happy to talk to you.'

'I don't see why they would feel like that. Bella's killer was caught so there is nothing to hide.' Lara was getting irritated by the small-town attitude of the police officer.

At the sound of Bella's name, the other police officer turned to look at Lara and spoke for the first time. 'I didn't know Bella Young had a sister.'

'I was adopted at five so can't really remember much about her. She was fostered by a local family.'

'Have you spoken to the foster parents?' asked the older police officer.

Lara shook her head. 'No. They emigrated to Canada a few years ago, and to be honest, I would rather speak to her friends first.'

'But surely the foster parents would have photographs for your book,' he continued. 'Why don't you write to them?'

'I'd have to ask the council for their address and it's the weekend now.'

'You haven't come prepared, have you?'

Lara's cheeks coloured and she wondered if the police could tell that she was lying. Then she told herself that it wouldn't matter anyway. It was her business who she wanted to speak to. And the photograph might not be important. If she was breaking the law, it was a stupid one. No. She would concentrate on Bella's friends for now. Something told her that they had the answer.

The two police officers left the hotel in silence. Neither spoke until they were back in their car.

'A very unbelievable story,' the older one remarked, as he turned the ignition and pulled the car onto the road.

'Not necessarily. She wants to find out about her past. That's what adopted kids do when they are old enough.'

'But why now? She's had years to trace her roots, but it takes her until now to do it.'

'She said she wanted to talk to her sister's friends first. Perhaps they would be able to give her the foster parents' new address.'

'I just don't buy it. It would have been far easier to go through the official route.'

'Perhaps she's impulsive. If she had given it more thought, she might not have bothered coming at all.'

'Maybe. Maybe not. She might have been acting like we were an inconvenience to her, but I think she's hiding something. It was in her eyes, just like her sister.'

Making their way to their third interview of the morning, the police officers were nearly bowled over as a man charged past them on the garden path. The man did not stop to apologize nor take any notice of their attempts to call him back. The police officers shrugged and then turned back to face the door. It wasn't him they wanted to see.

'Nice area,' one commented, as he gave the door a solid knock. It took three more attempts before there was any sign of movement behind the patterned glass, then a couple of minutes more until it opened. A woman wiped her hand over her familiar-looking face then pulled the belt of her dressing gown tighter around her when she looked at the visitors.

'Not you again. What do you want now? Dave's not here and you can't come in without a warrant.'

'There's no need for us to speak to Dave, Tanya. It's you we need to ask a few questions.'

'Me? Why do you want to ask me questions? You can't pin anything on me.'

'It's not what you think, Tanya. We could talk out here, but I really think it would be better for you and your neighbours if we went inside. It's about Hanna Evans.'

Tanya stepped back pulling the door with her allowing them to enter the hallway. Then she led them into a small lounge. Although it was mid-morning, the curtains were still shut and there was a potent smell of fish and chips and cigarettes in the room. The younger officer visibly winced as he was forced to breathe in the stale air, while the older one stood poker-faced.

'What about Hanna?' Tanya asked, as she opened the window, then waved a cushion around to clear the air. 'Is she all right?'

'I'm afraid not. She was killed after falling from a footbridge last night.'

Tanya lowered her arm and gathered the cushion towards her. She looked at the two men one by one as if she was trying to work something out in her head. Finally, she spoke. 'Are you kidding? What happened? Was it an accident or … suicide?'

'At this point in time, we are not sure, therefore, we are gathering as much information about her last known movements as possible. You were seen with her in The Royal Oak last night, so we'll need you to answer some questions.'

Tanya told the police officers that she had bumped into an old friend, Jenny, who'd recently moved back from London, so they arranged a reunion drink with Hanna, a mutual friend. Bella Young's sister, Lara, joined them. They each made their way there separately and arrived at the pub at eight o'clock, give or take five minutes. Each had two glasses of wine before Hanna left at approximately ten o'clock.

'Why did Miss Evans leave before you?'

'She got upset about the conversation we were having,'

'And what was that conversation about?'

'It was about Bella Young.'

'Were you reminiscing about the old days?'

Tanya looked a bit confused but merely nodded.

'So, what was it about the conversation that upset Miss Evans?' he asked Tanya.

Tanya's expression changed as though she had remembered something. 'Come to think of it, it wasn't the conversation. It was seeing the photograph.'

'What photograph?'

'The one Lara brought with her. I expect it brought it all back to Hanna. She disappeared for a few minutes then came back and said she wanted to go home. We offered to go with her, but she said she would get one of the taxis outside the pub.'

'Did you see her get into a taxi?'

'No, but there were a couple outside when we arrived. I'm sure she got in one of them unless they'd gone by then. I don't understand what she was doing on the footbridge. She must have tried to walk home but it's miles.'

'And what time did you leave the pub yourself?'

'About thirty minutes later. Jenny was tired.'

'Did you get the same taxi as Jenny?'

'No, because we were going in opposite directions.'

'What about Lara Campbell? Presumably, you shared a taxi as far as her hotel.'

'No. She left not long after Hanna.'

'Why?'

'I can't remember. Perhaps you should ask her.'

'We already have.'

'Then you'll know she's up to something.'

Chapter Four

Lara snapped off the stems of the flowers so they would fit into the faded metal vase, then stood back for a few minutes. She knew it would probably be the last ones that were placed there for a good while as her time in Weston was going to be short. Maybe there was a fund she could contribute to that would take care of it. In the gloom of the neglected stones, there was something beautiful about the silence and serenity of the grounds.

Bella's gravestone was crowned with a line of yellow leaves which must have blown over from outside of the churchyard, annual visitors of the forgotten souls. Once more, she thought bitterly of how nobody had cared for the grave of a murdered girl. She thought about each of the three former friends that she had met and knew that only Jenny had shown any sadness about Bella's death. With friends like Tanya and Hanna, who needed enemies, she thought, before reprimanding herself for speaking ill of the dead.

Suddenly, a robin perched itself on the gravestone, its beautiful life juxtaposing the depressing surroundings. Lara had heard some people believe that robins were the spirits of their dead loved ones.

A lump rose in her throat. She tried to stand as still as the stone statues, frightened of scaring the bird off, but then a large crow swooped down, and the robin was gone. It was time for her to go too as she could feel specks of rain in the air. She whispered a farewell to the grave before turning her back on it once again.

As Lara walked out of the church grounds, she noticed a man hanging around outside. He looked out of place. There was no dog with him nor was he carrying flowers. Wearing a black leather jacket and ripped jeans that definitely weren't designer, he was either a biker or a mugger, Lara thought. As she walked closer to him, he looked up and she recognized him immediately. It was the man from the Spar, and he was staring at her again. How could brown eyes look so cold?

'Why have you come here?' he asked sharply.

'Why do you want to know?' she replied, with a confidence she did not feel. 'I could ask you the same question. I take it you are not here to lay flowers.'

The man shuffled his feet and turned around as if to check no one was coming. Was he going to attack her? No. He looked angry for some reason, but she didn't feel in danger.

'A friend of mine has just killed herself after being with you. There was nothing wrong with her so it must have been something you said.'

'You were friends with Hanna?' she said, quite surprised. It was difficult to imagine the scruffily dressed man being in the same circle as frumpy Hanna. From first impressions, she was surprised that he had any friends at all. 'How do you know I was with her? Have you been following me?'

'Don't flatter yourself. I was in the pub last night, too. So just what did you say to upset her?'

'I don't remember saying anything that could have upset her. I just asked her some questions about her memories of my sister.'

'Yes, and I bet I know what sort of questions they were; the same sort of questions your sister used to ask, no doubt.'

'What do you mean? You are making no sense. Who are you anyway?'

The man continued to stare at Lara and his face hardened even more.

'I knew Bella. We used to hang around together though none of us liked her much. She wasn't a nice girl.'

Lara recalled that Hanna had said the same thing before getting upset but she felt the need to stand up for her sister.

'That's not true. Jenny liked her. Tanya said she liked her too, so Bella couldn't have been that bad.'

'Jenny used your sister to make herself look like a saint. But she was going away to university so would have ditched her, just like she ditched the rest of her friends. Tanya was glad that next to Bella she looked classy. Bella had no real friends so what are you doing here?'

'I'm writing a book -'

The man scoffed before she could finish her sentence. 'Yeah right. And I'm Pablo Picasso.'

Lara's eyes were welling up and the man seemed to mellow slightly. 'A word of warning. There are people around here who will be very unhappy about you digging up the past. You can't trust people you don't know. You should leave now before anyone else gets hurt.'

He walked away leaving Lara with mixed emotions. She was scared by the hostile words of the stranger, yet angry by what she had inferred to be veiled threats. Most of all she felt vindicated. There was no doubt that something was amiss about her sister's death. Coming to Weston had been the correct decision and she was not leaving until she had all the answers.

Back at the hotel, Lara was pleased but surprised to find the landlady up and about. It was, after all, only eleven o'clock.

'I wonder if I could speak to you for a few minutes, Mrs Parsons.' she asked the startled woman.

'Is there a problem with your room, dear?' she replied.

'Oh no. My room is lovely. I just wanted to ask if you knew the woman who died yesterday. I was out with her you see, but I know virtually nothing about her. Her name was Hanna Evans.'

'Yes, I heard. I can't tell you much as she doesn't live in this village anymore, not that she lives anywhere now."

'Was she married?'

'No. She lived with her mother who is disabled. They moved into a converted bungalow in Copston a few years ago. I haven't seen them since.'

'Yesterday, you told me that you remembered my sister, Bella. Can I ask what you remember about her? You must know that she was murdered twenty years ago.'

'Yes, I know. Everyone here knows.'

Mrs Parsons gestured for Lara to follow her into the breakfast room, and they both sat down.

'Bella was a very pretty girl, but I always knew she would get herself into trouble. Not that I thought she would die, mind you. I just thought she would get pregnant or end up on the wrong side of the law.'

'Why did you think that? Did she steal or hang around with boys a lot?'

'Yes, she did both. And one time in particular she got herself into quite a lot of trouble.'

'What happened?'

'She was arrested for stealing a car. As if that wasn't bad enough, after she stole the car, she drove it around the area until it rolled over. The silly girl was very lucky to survive … I mean, survive that crash.'

'Yes, I know what you mean. Did she go to court for that?'

'No. They let her off due to her age. She was only fifteen. There was a hit-and-run not long after and a lot of us thought it might have been her. There was no proof, though.'

'Oh, dear. I didn't know that. It doesn't sound like she was doing very well.'

'But she was doing very well, thanks to my John. He got her through all her exams and, if she'd wanted to, she could have gone to university. She was a bright girl with a lot of talent, but she used it the wrong way.'

'What do you mean by that?'

'It was just the way she looked at you. It wasn't a friendly look. She made you feel like she was trying to work out how to hurt you. It was as if she hated everyone. I tried my best to be kind to her, what with the circumstances, but then she threw it back in my face.'

'I still don't really know what you mean,' Lara said, slightly frustrated at what she thought were riddles. 'Please tell me what she did.'

'My son was a couple of years older than Bella but always helped her with her studies. It paid off and, as it turned out, she did very well in her exams. John also taught her how to play the guitar. He told her that she was talented and encouraged her to write her own songs. Then she came here while John was at university asking me for a loan of two hundred pounds. I was surprised and asked her what she wanted it for. She didn't tell me but just said John would be glad.'

'Was that the night of the ball?' Lara asked.

'I can't remember when it was exactly. Why?'

'Sorry, Mrs Parson. I don't know why I asked that,' Lara lied while thinking of Bella's last diary entry. 'Did you tell her to wait until you'd spoken to your son?'

'Yes, of course, I did, but she just looked at me with those eyes of hers and told me she'd be back soon.'

'What happened then? Did she come back?'

'No. She died not long after. I never told John about it.'

'Why not? Surely, he might have explained what it was about.'

'Oh, I knew full well what it was about?'

Lara felt as though everyone was running rings around her, giving her little snippets of information but nothing substantial enough for her to feel that she was making progress. Laying back against the feather pillow, she went over what had happened the last couple of days.

She had rushed to Weston without doing any research, thinking that all she had to do was turn up. Everyone would be willing to share what they would about their recollections of the terrible event, she'd assumed. However, it was quite the opposite. Not even Jenny had really told her much that was useful.

Was she telling the truth about being too drunk to remember much about that night? Why was she so much drunker than the others? It was hard to imagine Jenny being in such a helpless situation, even if she was only a teenager at the time.

Lara remembered what the man had said about Jenny using Bella. What reason would he have to lie? Yes, maybe Jenny was no more helpful than Tanya or Hanna had been. It was strange that she had lost all contact with her friends immediately after moving away. Lara sat up and reached for her notebook. However, little it might seem, it was important not to forget a single piece of information. She picked up her pen and began adding to her earlier observations:

• Jenny said she was too drunk to remember much about that night. This was confirmed by Tanya and Hanna. Tom Bailey tried to attack her, but the others scared him off.

• Hanna saw Bailey's car leaving the coast shortly after midnight – as did the others. She admitted that she did not like Bella. She killed herself after running out of the pub. Something in the photograph upset her. Could she be the killer?

• Tanya was very hostile towards me and said I had no business being here.

• Mrs Parsons said Bella asked her for two hundred pounds. This was probably the money Bella was referring to. She implied that it was blackmail. I need to find out about her son.

- The vicar said that Bella was in the church choir but stopped going.
- The mystery man said that no one liked Bella. He asked me what I was doing here then warned me away.

She had already spoken to six people who had known Bella. Now written down, the information gathered was more than she first thought. There must have been others, including the foster parents, of course, and she would write to them eventually. She'd lied about not having their new address but doubted they would know any more than they'd told the police twenty years ago. At the time, they'd had other foster children to keep them busy. Instead, she thought of other people who might have information.

First, there was Mrs Parsons' son, John. He clearly knew Bella well. Then, there were Bella's teachers, whoever they were. Finally, there were the police officers at the time of the murder. And that was it. She could not think of anyone else who might have useful information.

She tore out the page and placed it in the wastepaper basket. The idea of visiting Bella's teachers was not realistic. For a start, she had no idea who any of them were. Moreover, they probably lived miles away. It was also far-fetched to think that the police would be willing to give her any information. As far as they were concerned, the right person was charged and convicted of the crime. No. The police would not be willing to talk to her, of that, she was sure. And where was John? He was probably settled down with a young family. She had the feeling that Mrs Parsons would not be happy for Lara to bother him.

Lara reached out to her bag and took out the tiny object she did her best not to look at. Clutching the passport-size photograph to her chest as if the person in it could feel her, she began to cry. Lara did this at least once a week, usually when at her lowest. Lying on her side, she tried to imagine that he was still with her, loving her as much as she had loved him, and loved him still.

She and Frank had dated since high school. He had made her feel like a whole person again after she had struggled to cope with her family situation. Of course, she had always known she was adopted and had only ever experienced a happy family life with her parents. Blood and biology were merely words until science classes had taught her about black-and-white facts, facts that left no room for any alternatives.

Then, Frank taught her that true love knew no boundaries and that her home could not be more special, just like their relationship. It had been just like that Mamas and Papas song. It had got better every day - friendship first, then lovers, then marriage. At least, it should have been marriage because it was all arranged, all paid for. But then

Frank left her. There had been no warning signs. One morning, two weeks before the wedding, she woke up and he was no longer there. An aneurism they said. It could happen to anyone they said. Yet, it did not happen to anyone. It happened to the man she had loved for over ten years of her young life.

Afterwards, she fell into an abyss and would still be there if it hadn't been for the sanctuary she found back at her parents' house. And that was where she still lived, eighteen months later. But she was recovering. She had a teaching job at a local high school which would start after Christmas. Even though it was still a few months away, she was excited to be entering a new phase of her life. But first, she had to deal with the distant past.

'I just can't believe Hanna would do such a thing. How could she do that to her poor mother? She's left that old woman all alone. Who is this Lara woman, anyway? She could be crazy for all we know. Could she have pushed Hanna off the bridge?'

'Don't be ridiculous, Simone. Lara is a sweet girl.'

'You've only known her five minutes, Jenny. She could be as evil as her sister.'

'Oh, come off it, Simone. You were as mean to Bella as she was to you. Bella was not evil, and she certainly didn't deserve what happened to her.'

There was silence and Jenny thought that Simone had hung up until the latter apologized.

'I'm sorry, Jenny. It's been a bad morning all around. Chris came home this morning still drunk, and when I asked him about it, he just ignored me. I can see us heading for divorce.'

Jenny did not want to comment on Simone's marriage but did defend the husband she still counted as her close friend. 'Don't be so harsh on him, Simone. He's got a stressful job and should be allowed to have a blowout now and again.'

'And I let him. He spends every Friday night with his precious friend who he thinks more of than me. He and Ben should grow up. They're not teenagers anymore. Chris is a married man with two children.'

'I didn't know they still bothered with each other. Anyway, I thought I saw Ben outside the pub last night.'

'No, he was at his house with Chris. I asked Chris this morning. They were together all evening.'

'It must have been someone else then. Those bikers all look the same,' Jenny laughed, eager to keep things light.

There was silence before Simone brought them back to the initial topic of conversation. 'Aren't you wondering why this woman's turned up here after all this time, Jenny? She could be dangerous.'

'Calm down, Simone. She's writing a book about her life as an adopted child so it's natural that she'd want to mention her sister. We're the only people who can tell her about Bella.'

'I hope you're not saying too much, Lara. You didn't tell her anything about that night, did you? I don't want to relive that time, especially with Bella's sister.'

'No, of course, I didn't,' Jenny replied nervously. 'But what could she possibly find out that could do us any harm, Simone?'

But Simone didn't answer. She knew full well the harm it would do.

Chapter Five

It was evening and Jenny was sitting on the stairs in the hall, a laptop balanced on her knees. With her immaculately painted nails, she plugged and unplugged various leads connecting the telephone, the router, and her computer.

In all the time she was living in London, she never had a problem with using Wi-Fi. She wondered if London was closer to the satellites or whatever it was that made the internet work. Now, after spending several hours trying to get rid of the "no internet connection" icon in the bottom right-hand side of the screen, she gave up and dug out a still polythene-wrapped ethernet cable.

Connected at last, she began searching for jobs in publishing: literary agent; editor; publicist, copywriter. Reading through the various job specifications brought a degree of uncertainty to Jenny as she saw the number of applicants each job already had. A year ago she wouldn't have hesitated for a minute before applying for any of these positions. She knew every part of the industry as well as anyone else. Yet, after only a short time out of the circle, her confidence was already plummeting.

Hearing a knock at the door, she put down the laptop and answered it. An old friend was standing on the doorstep.

'She's thrown me out, Jen. I've got nowhere to go.'

'Why? What's happened, Chris?' she asked, while the man walked inside and sat down without being asked. She wasn't as surprised as she made out.

'She thinks I'm seeing Tanya,' he replied, laughing to himself.

'Tanya!' she shouted. 'And are you?'

'What! Are you kidding me? I can't believe you are even asking me that, Jenny.'

'Well Chris, I've been away for almost twenty years. The last time I was with you and Tanya was when we were eighteen. So much has changed since then. I was amazed to hear that you and Simone were married, to be honest. You never used to ...'

'Never used to what?'

Jenny found herself blushing as she remembered the constant attention Chris had paid to her when they were in school. How was she going to articulate what she was thinking? She tried. 'You never paid her attention while we were in school, Chris. When did you start seeing each other? And why wasn't I invited to the wedding?'

'Does it matter when we started dating? And the reason you weren't invited to the wedding was that you disappeared without a trace once you went to university. Why didn't you keep in touch with anyone? I suppose you thought Weston was no longer good enough for you.'

Jenny looked embarrassed at Chris's accusation. After Bella's death, she was desperate to put everything behind her, even if that meant forgetting her school friends too. But she was able to hit back.

'You are a fine one to talk to, Chris. I've heard that you disappeared for years once you started playing football professionally. Poor Hanna wasn't good enough for you then, was she?'

'That's not fair, Jenny. Hanna and I were never serious enough to have a long-distance relationship.'

'I think you're speaking for yourself, Chris. Hanna was crazy about you. In fact, I don't think she ever got over you. She was never in your league, though, if you'll pardon the pun.'

Chris did not laugh. 'Don't make me feel guilty because I didn't love her'.

'I wasn't, Chris. Look, we were both career-driven and didn't care who we left behind so let's call it a draw. Anyway, why does Simone think that you're having an affair?'

'Because she's a paranoid bitch,' he said bitterly.

And she's also your wife, Jenny thought, shocked at the vitriol in his voice. 'I think you need to talk to her. Can you go back tonight?' she asked, with concern. 'I mean, it's your house too, isn't it?'

'I'd rather not tonight, Jen. Give her a chance to cool down. I couldn't stay here just for one night, could I?'

'Just tonight, Chris,' she replied. Then they hugged.

Lara had given in and was scanning the internet for anything about Bella. She decided that she was spending enough money on staying at the hotel so a few more pounds a day for internet charges wouldn't make much difference. Searching through old newspapers on a tiny screen was fiddly and frustrating, but she eventually found some information.

There was a short report in a mainstream newspaper about the murder, but it hardly gave justice to the horror of that night twenty years ago. The tiny article merely mentioned the names and ages of the victim and perpetrator. There wasn't even a picture of Bella. Lara kept searching for a report on the trial of Tom Bailey but without success. The national media's interest had moved onto other murders around Britain which remained unsolved for longer than a couple of days. Bella's murder wouldn't make any television show.

She began to imagine possible names of more local newspapers that would have covered the crime. Weston was too small a village to have its own newspaper, but it must come under the umbrella of a larger local press. Knowing the name of the town where the ball was held, she put in Copston Herald. There was no result. Copston Press. Nothing. Copston News. At last. There it was.

"Tom Bailey, twenty-three, has been sentenced to life in prison for the murder of eighteen-year-old Bella Young. Bailey, who denied the charge, was convicted after the jury reached a unanimous verdict.".

That was it. Two sentences which told her nothing that she didn't already know. Then, as she scrolled down to the bottom of the page, Lara saw several more news items under related news.

A hit and run and a burglary. There was one more link to an article called: "Another sexual assault in Weston". She clicked on the link, but the page was blank. Not only murder but sexual assaults, hit and runs, and burglaries too. Suddenly, Weston didn't seem so quaint. Beneath the façade, there was danger in the pretty, seaside village.

Detective Inspector Paul Croft had been middle-aged since he joined the police force straight from university. The black bootleg jeans, white t-shirt and long mousy hair had been replaced by a suit and short back and sides. He rarely smiled or showed any emotion, but his mouth was open wide after hearing the coroner's words.

'You can't be serious. Hanna Evans fell forty feet, landed on her head and was run over by a ten-ton truck, so how on earth can you say that she was already dead before falling?'

'A little thing called medical knowledge. If she'd been alive when she hit the ground, the blood splatter would have been significantly worse.'

'It's hardly clear cut though, is it?' remarked the detective. He hated the way the medical staff talked down to the police officers.

'It is clear cut in my profession, Croft. Hanna Evans was dead when her body left the footbridge. Unfortunately, due to the state of her remains, it is unlikely I will complete my job of finding the cause of death. However, I do know that it was not suicide. She could not have lifted herself over the railing; someone else did. It is your job to find out who that someone was.'

Jenny worried that she would have trouble finding it, but the bungalow wore its number like a medal. It was number thirteen, and the superstition came to mind as she walked up the path. She rang the doorbell and waited, knowing it might be a while. After five minutes, the door was finally opened, and she held out the flowers she was carrying.

'Hello, Mrs Evans. I'm so sorry about Hanna.'

'Oh, it's you. Come in dear.'

Jenny walked slowly behind as Mrs Evans shuffled awkwardly into the sitting room, her Zimmer frame battling against the thick pile carpet. The older woman sat back in an armchair, probably where she spent most of her time. Still holding the flowers, Jenny looked around for a vase. There were two on the hearth, but they were already occupied with dusty plastic flowers. Not wanting to offend Mrs Evans, she sat down on the leather sofa and laid the bunch down next to her.

She scanned the rest of the room for signs of a younger life but there were none. Displayed on the mantlepiece was an array of cheap-looking ornaments, one framed photograph, and, in the centre, a grandmother clock, the clunking of which added to the depressing atmosphere.

'It's good of you to visit, Jenny. No one else has bothered.'

'That's terrible, Mrs Evans. Can I do anything for you -shopping, cooking, cleaning?' she asked, staring at the dust underneath her.'

'If you would do a bit of dusting for me, dear. Hanna always did it you see. Not that she was any good at it. She thought that I couldn't see it because I'm an old woman. Well, I might be nearly eighty but I'm not blind.'

Jenny found a yellow duster and a tin of Sparkle under the sink and began the one task she hated above all others. She picked up each ornament to dust around, aware that the older woman was watching her every move. The framed photograph was an old wedding shot of a young couple, their expressions anything but joyful.

'This is a beautiful photograph of you and Mr Evans.' Jenny remarked tactfully. 'I don't remember him much. He died quite young, didn't he?'

'Yes, that's Arthur. He was fonder of the fags than he was of me. Useless man.'

'You must be devastated by what's happened, Mrs Evans. Hanna was such a lovely woman.'

'She didn't care about leaving me alone. I told her not to go out and that I shouldn't be left on my own, but she still went out. Look at me now. I have no one to look after me.'

Jenny had forgotten how mean Mrs Evans was to her daughter but was determined to force one unselfish remark out of her, nonetheless.

'I have so many special memories of Hanna at school. She was a shy girl. I don't think she ever got into any trouble.'

Mrs Evans did not appear to agree. 'Oh, she got herself into enough trouble all right. I don't know where she got her ways from.'

The comments baffled Jenny. What trouble? Hanna never got as much as a telling-off in school. Her mother must be confused.

'I can't imagine what you mean, Mrs Evans. She certainly didn't get into any trouble when she was with us.'

'Well, it wasn't when she was with you, but I don't want to talk about it.'

Jenny shrugged. 'Mrs Evans, did Hanna get much post of her own?'

'I doubt it. Why do you ask?'

'Oh, nothing important. It's just that an old friend of ours sent me a wedding invitation so I just wondered if Hanna got one too. I could let the friend know. You haven't noticed a handwritten letter coming with the rest of the post, have you?'

'A wedding invitation won't be much use to her now. And I don't notice anything like that because Hanna always dealt with the bills. That's another thing for me to worry about.'

Jenny had had enough and decided it was time to go. She replaced the duster and polish, made a cup of tea for Mrs Evans, and then politely said her goodbyes. She was certain the woman had been wrong about Hanna being in trouble, but she would ask Tanya when she got back. Tanya would know.

On the way out, she noticed a pile of letters on the hall table. As to be expected, the letters were mostly junk mail but hidden between two catalogues was a small envelope. It was the same writing. Jenny slipped it into her bag and then walked out of the door for the last time.

Lara was startled to receive the second visit from the police in less than twenty-four hours. This time, however, the police officers were in plain clothes, suggesting that the purpose of the visit was more serious than suicide.

'Lara Campbell, we'd like to ask you some questions about your relationship with Hanna Evans,' said the man who introduced himself as Detective Croft.

Lara stared at the two detectives open-mouthed. 'Relationship! I didn't have any relationship with her. I only met her for a couple of hours.' She wondered if the detective was being deliberately provocative, and his next question confirmed her suspicion.

'I heard that she was a friend of your sister's. Is that correct?'

'Yes, although she didn't seem to like Bella very much.'

'And did that make you angry?' Brooks, the other detective, had joined the questioning. His voice betrayed a slight London accent, suggesting he wasn't local to Weston either.

'No, it didn't. Well, I was a little upset, to be honest. I thought she was being a bit tactless considering she knew I was sitting right next to her.'

Detective Croft took hold of the questioning once again. 'Can you tell us why you came to Weston, Miss Campbell, I mean, why you really came here?'

Lara could feel the blood rising in her neck and she struggled to find an answer, so she remained silent. Detective Brooks joined the questioning once again.

'We've heard about your so-called book, Miss, but don't really believe it.' His manner was deliberately mocking.

Lara's shoulders slumped but she wasn't ready to tell them about the revelation at Tom Bailey's parole hearing. Instead, she stood her ground.

'Why do you think I'm lying? My sister was murdered, and I want to know the circumstances around that. That's why I'm here – to talk to Bella's friends.'

Croft stared at Lara in the same way that other people in the village had done - as if she had two heads. 'You could read about it on the Internet. I'm sure it's there somewhere.'

'There's hardly anything about it, actually. I think I read four sentences altogether.' Lara took out the photograph of the girls at the school ball and passed it to Croft. 'I intend to speak again to these women before I leave Weston, at least, the ones that are still alive.'

It was impossible to read the impression on Croft's face as he examined the images in the photograph. When he spoke, his voice was equally flat. 'Hanna Evan's death is now being treated as murder; therefore, we will need you to accompany us down the station to write a statement.'

'You don't think I had anything to do with it, do you?' Lara asked.

'We just need to get everybody's account of the night written down before they start to forget some of the details.'

'Okay, if it helps. I'll just get my jacket,' Lara said.

After she had left the room, Brooks moved closer to Croft and whispered, 'Was it just me or did she seem a little unsurprised about the murder?'

73

After finishing at the police station, Lara asked to be dropped off at the beach. Her statement was short as there had been little to say beyond what the police already knew - Hanna getting upset and leaving the pub alone, followed shortly by herself. She couldn't prove that she had not seen Hanna outside the pub, but she did mention the bikers who would have witnessed her walking away in the same direction, but slowly. They'd certainly watched her arriving. Now she needed to speak to Jenny to allay her fears that she wasn't the only one who had been asked to make a statement.

As she approached the small terrace of shops which housed the café, she noticed a man leaving the café. He was tall, blond, and very good-looking. And she'd seen him before. He was the man who Hanna was talking to at the bar.

Jenny did not appear surprised to see Lara when she answered the door.

'Hello, Lara. I was just about to ring you. Has Paul spoken to you?'

'Who?'

'Paul Croft. He's investigating Hanna's suicide, or murder as they are now saying.'

'Yes. He was one of the detectives who just interviewed me.'

'Interviewed you! That makes you sound like a suspect Lara,' Jenny said laughingly.

Now, Lara was confused at the other woman's seeming lack of concern about the situation. Perhaps years of living in the city had numbed her to murders in her neighbourhood. 'To be quite honest, Jenny, I think I am a suspect. It sounds crazy but I thought I was going to be arrested.'

Jenny laughed again. 'It sounds ridiculous because it is ridiculous. There's no need to worry. That's just Paul's way. He's always had a serious manner, even when we were in school. Paul's probably in shock at having such a serious crime to investigate.'

'Jenny, you are talking as if I know him as 'Paul'. I only met him an hour ago, and that was as Detective Inspector Croft.'

'Oh yes, silly me. Of course, you don't know him.'

'Did he know Bella?'

'Yes, of course, he did. Didn't he tell you that?'

'No, he didn't. He just said that Bella was a friend of Hanna's.'

For the first time, Jenny looked serious. 'Oh, I see. But surely, they're not suggesting you killed Hanna for some sort of revenge. I mean, that's ridiculous.'

'Jenny, stop saying it's ridiculous. I know it sounds ridiculous, but somebody murdered Hanna and I do have a motive, however unlikely.'

'What motive - that she didn't like your sister? You'll turn into a serial killer if that's enough to make you murder people.'

Jenny's reference to Bella's huge unpopularity in the village made Lara delve deeper.

'Jenny, why did so many people hate Bella?'

The other woman merely shrugged her shoulders before saying, 'I don't know. They were probably jealous of Bella's popularity with the boys.'

'So, the boys liked her?'

'Well, yes. She was an eye-turner, but I doubt any of them were looking for a friend.'

'Are you saying she slept around?'

'No, absolutely not. She didn't sleep with anyone, not that I know of anyway. But she was a tease. She enjoyed the attention she got from the boys -and the girls for that matter.'

'I find it difficult to believe that so many people would hate her for that reason.'

Jenny's face changed and Lara knew that there was something that she wasn't telling her.

'Do you think she was blackmailing people?' Lara asked.

'Blackmailing! Of course not. Why on earth would you think that?'

Lara told her about the conversation she'd had with the landlady; how Bella had asked for money and how the landlady had construed it as an attempt to blackmail her. As she was speaking Jenny was shaking her head and looking increasingly angry.

'That woman is a crazy alcoholic. She hated it that her son didn't charge Bella for tuition so she could buy even more wine.'

'So, Bella didn't ask her for a lend of two hundred pounds?'

Jenny went quiet again but this time she appeared to be searching her memory before nodding. 'Yes, I do remember something about two hundred pounds. Bella told me that she was in touch with a man from a record company. Apparently, he'd asked her to come to the studio, but she couldn't afford the train fare and accommodation. I remember her saying that John Parsons had offered to lend her the money. Bella didn't have her own bank account, so he told her to ask his mother to give it to her. He'd intended to reimburse his mother when he got home from university. I don't remember what happened after that though.'

'Bella died, that's what happened, Jenny.'

'Oh. I wonder why Mrs Parsons still thinks it was blackmail after all this time. Surely her son told her the truth.'

'If he did tell her, she didn't believe him either. But you believed Bella.'

'Yes. I always believed her. We were best friends.'

Lara's eyes filled with tears at the kind words. 'Have you got any more photos of Bella?' she asked. 'I've only got this one.'

Jenny left the room for a few minutes and then returned with a photograph album. Together they looked through the various class photos from which it was impossible to see the personalities of those pictured in identical poses. Next came the sleepovers, school trips, and birthday parties. In these less formal settings, it was clear that Bella was closest to Jenny, and also that there was always a distance between Bella and the other girls. Jenny was clearly her only friend. When they reached the last page of the album, Jenny shut it without showing the final photographs. Surprised, Lara asked,

'Weren't there more photos to see?'

'Oh, Bella's not in those ones,' Jenny replied quickly.

But Lara could tell she was lying. 'Why don't you want me to see them, Jenny?'

Jenny looked at her sadly. 'They were taken at the end of the night. It was so close to ... you know.'

'But I'd still like to see them, Jenny.'

Reluctantly, Jenny opened the album once more to reveal the last few photographs from the school ball. There was one taken of the five young women as they were leaving the ball, each one holding up an empty glass.

'Can I keep this one?' Lara asked, looking at the joy in her sister's face.

'Of course, you can, Lara.'

In another one, obviously taken earlier on, the blond man was standing with his arms wrapped around a laughing Jenny.

'That's the man I saw at the bar,' Lara remarked, wondering if that could be the reason behind Jenny's reluctance to show all the photographs.

'The one talking to Hanna. Are you sure?' Jenny asked. 'I don't think he was supposed to be there.'

'Positive,' Lara said, before turning back to the photograph. The other people pictured were mere bystanders. Hanna looked miserable while Tanya and Simone were clearly bored. There were two other young men and Lara recognised both of them.

'Is that the detective?'

'Yes, that's Paul. See what I told you. He's always looked serious, though that picture of him was taken shortly before he finished with me.'

'I'm surprised at that. You don't seem suited, somehow. I mean, you are always so cheerful while he seems like a real misery. I think you had a lucky escape there.'

Jenny laughed. 'It was nothing serious, but my pride was dented. How dare anyone finish with me!'

Lara laughed too. 'And this one here,' she asked, pointing to a sullen face, 'who is he?'

'That's Ben but you haven't met him yet?'

'Oh, but I have,' Lara replied, looking at the image of the man outside the church.

Chapter Six

Lara was convinced that Jenny still hadn't told her half of what she knew. She'd only mentioned dating Paul Croft as an aside. Didn't she think it might be important? Then Lara remembered the lie she'd told Jenny about the imaginary book. Why would Jenny give information about herself when the book wasn't supposed to be about her? Maybe it was time to tell her the truth.

While trying to unravel and sort the information into bullet points, she was shocked to hear loud banging on the door of the hotel. Not sure how many people, if any, were in the hotel, she crept out of her room and walked over to the top of the stairs, waiting to see if the landlady would appear. The banging continued until the landlady finally walked precariously across the hallway and, after looking through a peephole, opened the front door. Lara could hear a woman's voice coming from outside. It was a familiar voice.

'Where is she? I want to see her now.'

Lara watched on from behind the bannister as a furious-looking Tanya marched inside and waved a piece of paper in the landlady's face. Mrs Parsons did not answer.

'There is something seriously wrong with that woman you have staying here, Mrs Parsons, and I would advise you to throw her out.'

Lara rushed down the stairs before the confused landlady could respond to Tanya's second outburst. 'What's wrong? What have I done now?' She was in no mood for Tanya's insults.

Tanya turned to look at Lara. 'Do you think you can get away with sending me an anonymous letter? You do know sending threatening letters is against the law, don't you?'

'Tanya, I have no idea what you are talking about. Is that the letter?'

'As if you don't know. First Hanna, now this. I'll be going straight to the police station tomorrow morning, and I'll tell them they should look no further than you. You've come here to cause trouble and I wouldn't be surprised if you killed Hanna.'

'I didn't send you that letter and I'll remind you that slander is also against the law.'

Lara's tone was such that Tanya's expression turned from one of fury, to fear.

'I don't believe you. You're bluffing.'

'I'm really not, Tanya. Just let me read the letter, please.'

Tanya warily held out the letter which Lara took and read. It was a note, rather than a letter, with only three short sentences printed in the middle of the paper.

"Bella cannot rest. She knew your secret. It's time to tell the truth."

Lara stared at the words before the paper was snatched away from her.

'Don't even think about ripping it up,' Tanya said. Then, after only a few minutes inside, she left the hotel.

The following morning Lara looked carefully at the photograph she'd slipped under her cardigan while Jenny was making more tea. It was a wide-shot photograph of everyone in the hall so she was sure that Jenny wouldn't notice it had gone. Everyone in the photograph was focussed on other things, not the camera. It probably wasn't important, but she wanted a photograph of everyone who had been in her sister's short life.

When she looked more carefully, she spotted Bella, almost hidden behind a group of boys. It wasn't the best picture, but it would do. At least she had the other photograph.

With Hanna's murder and Tanya's visit, Lara felt that things were accelerating. She decided to extend her search for answers. There had to be somebody who would tell her more about the circumstances surrounding Bella's murder, someone who knew all the details. Although she had intended to see Jenny early that morning, she would put it off until later. There were more important people to talk to. She knew the name of the detective who had overseen the case, so she asked Flora about him.

'He lives in the next village along the coast,' she replied. 'It's only about a mile as the crow flies but it'll take you a good thirty minutes by car as it's all winding lanes. You'll need to drive back out of Weston then look out for the turning to Easton. It'll be somewhere on the left.'

'I'm sure I'll find it. Do you know which house he lives in?' Lara asked.

'The biggest one. That's about all I know. Easton is even less exciting than this village, so I've never bothered to go there.

'Is he still working?' Lara asked. 'Perhaps I could find him at the police station.'

'No. He retired a few years ago and I don't think he's been back here since. Of course, you could ask about the case at the police station. I don't think they'd give you his address though. It's sure to be confidential.'

'What's he like, Flora?'

'I don't know because I've never met him.'

'So, how do you know so much about him if you don't mind me asking?'

'My mother knew him quite well. She is always calling the police about something. I'm sure she'll be able to give you his address once she gets up. You do know he's that detective's father, don't you? Why don't you ask him what you want to know instead?'

But Lara had no intention of talking to Paul Croft because for some reason she didn't trust him. She thanked Flora for the information and left the hotel.

Lara got in her car and set Google Maps towards Easton, hoping that, once she got there, the biggest house would be obvious. Unfortunately, it was the turning to Easton that was not so obvious, and, as Lara found, almost impossible to distinguish from the large number of farm tracks and lanes. Finding herself lost, she kept driving in, what she hoped, was the direction of the coast. As the road continued to drop, she felt she was on the right track, and at last, she pulled into a small fishing cove. Parking the car against a rock wall she stepped out into the salty sea air and the almost deafening sound of seagulls.

It was a tiny harbour with about five boats moored to the sea wall. Apart from her and the seagulls, there was no sign of life and Lara's heart sank. It seemed that she would have to get back into her car and keep looking for her destination. Suddenly, there was movement and she walked towards a man who was leaning over a boat, either oblivious to or uninterested in the car that had just parked up.

'Excuse me,' she called out. But he did not seem to hear her so she walked up to his side. As she got closer, she could see his profile and her heart began to beat faster. She looked around and saw no sign of any other person so she considered creeping away.

He didn't appear to know she was there anyway. But then he turned towards her, and his eyes flickered with recognition. He dropped the rope he was holding and stood up straight.

'I see you haven't taken my advice,' he said bluntly. His dark brown eyes showed even more disdain for her than at the churchyard.

Lara was nervous but, determined not to show it, she walked even closer to the man before speaking.

'You're Ben, aren't you?' she asked while staring into his eyes.

'Yes. What if I am?' He looked uncomfortable.

'I was just being polite before I ask you for information.'

He turned his back on her again. 'Don't tell me. You want to ask me about Bella. Well, don't bother.'

'It's not you that I want to talk to actually. I'm looking for the biggest house here.'

He laughed and pointed to a small concrete shed. 'That's the biggest house here. Are you interested in buying it?'

Lara's heart sank once more as she realised that she was, without a doubt, in the wrong place. It had taken her an hour already and she was unsure if she had enough petrol to continue driving blindly. With a sigh, she turned around and walked back to her car. She turned the ignition and was in the process of doing an awkward three-point-turn, when she saw Ben approaching the car. She wound down the window just enough to hear what he wanted to say.

'What are you looking for?' he said, through the small gap.

'Gerald Croft's house. I was told it was the biggest house in Easton, but this obviously isn't Easton so I'll have to keep looking.'

'That's Easton, over there,' he said, pointing to a small cluster of houses that were tantalisingly close.

'Oh. How long will it take to get there by car?' she asked.

'Forever if you have no sense of direction. Do you get seasick?'

Lara looked confused before answering, 'No, why?'

'I can pop you across in the boat for a tenner. It would only take half an hour.'

Surprised at his change of mood, Lara turned off the engine and sat in silence. She looked across at the water which was calm. Knowing that she shouldn't get into a boat with a man who had displayed such a dislike of her, her instinct was to decline the offer. However, he now seemed different, more amiable, and his offer was tempting. Was it something she said that had changed his mind about her? Or was he faking it just to get her into the boat?

As if reading her mind, he said, 'Well? If you don't want to risk it, just say. I haven't got all day.' The annoyed tone had returned to his voice.

'How would I get back?' she asked, with a hint of suspicion in her voice.

Ben pulled a face as if she was being ridiculous, then said, 'I won't leave you there.'

'Okay,' she said quickly, and gathering her bag and jacket locked the car and followed him to the boat.

Once they were seaborne the air got colder, and Lara wrapped her jacket more tightly around her shivering body. Ben paid her little attention as he focused on the horizon. Lara wondered if it was entirely necessary for him to concentrate so much on the water when he had a passenger.

Without the engine on, the boat was travelling away from their destination, but she knew enough about sailing to know that the tide wouldn't allow them to head straight there. She was wondering, however, why he didn't just use the engine that was beside him. Perhaps he was showing off.

After a while, he walked over towards her and pulled the sail across to the other side, changing the direction of travel. At that point, Lara breathed a sigh of relief. Although she had tried not to worry, she knew it was a risk to let a virtual stranger take her out to sea. Especially if that stranger had shown only contempt for her. But a gut feeling convinced her she would be fine and there was something dependable about his demeanour. He was totally in control. Sure enough, Ben delivered Lara safely across the water and helped her jump out of the boat onto dry land.

'I'll wait here,' he said, without looking at her.

'Thanks. I don't suppose you know which house it is?' she asked timidly.

'It's right behind you,' he said, before walking away.

Gerald Croft's house was only large in relation to the surrounding cottages which barely looked habitable. Lara's knuckles stung as they hit the heavy wooden front door of the house that would not have looked out of place on Grand Designs. The owners hadn't worried about blending in with the other houses, she thought. The door opened slightly to reveal an oldish female face.

'Yes,' came the voice through the gap. 'What do you want?'

'Hello. I wonder if you can help me. I'm looking for Gerald Croft. Does he live here?'

'What do you want him for?' the woman asked suspiciously.

'It's about my sister. He was in charge of her case, and I'd like to talk to him about it.'

The door opened wider, and the woman looked at Lara curiously. 'Who's your sister?'

'Bella Young. She was murdered.'

'Oh, dear. Yes, I know. But why do you want to speak to him now?'

'I just want to meet him as he saw my sister at the end. Please. It'll only be for a few minutes.'

The older woman looked uncomfortable. 'He doesn't like talking about his old cases.'

Lara knew she had to lie if she was going to get past the woman. 'I've spoken to the police, and they suggested that I should come here.'

After a few seconds, the woman stood back. 'I'll see if my husband is happy to talk to you. He's been unwell, you see.'

A few minutes later, the woman returned and opened the door wider for Lara to step inside the house. She showed Lara into a large living room where a man was sitting in an armchair.

'Gerald, this is the young lady who would like to speak to you. Sit down, dear. I'll make us all some tea,' she said, before disappearing out of the room.

The man looked up at Lara but did not speak, making the atmosphere even more uncomfortable. She decided to speak first.

'It's good of you to see me, Mr Croft,' she said. 'I'd like to ask you about my sister's case. I don't know if your wife has already told you, but her name was Bella Young, and she was murdered twenty years ago. You were the investigating officer.'

Still, Croft was silent and appeared to be thinking about something. He looked about seventy-five years old, much older than his wife, and what Lara was expecting him to be. His hair was white and his face red and bloated, while the way he sat on an armchair suggested that he was a man in pain. It was a stressful profession and it had clearly taken its toll. Flora had said he was in his sixties.

She waited for his wife to come back into the room before speaking again. 'Anything you could tell me about the case would be really helpful.'

'I take it you want to ask me about your sister,' he said as if he hadn't heard her last comment.

'Yes,' she replied. 'I feel that I owe it to her to know what she went through.' She took the cup of tea offered to her.

Surprisingly, it was Mrs Croft who spoke next. 'She was attacked while walking home late on her own. Young women don't realise how many predators there are out there waiting for an opportunity to strike.'

'She was strangled. Is that right?' Lara asked, looking at Mr Croft.

'Yes,' he said.

'But she wasn't raped, was she?'

'No.'

'Isn't that strange? I mean, what was the point of attacking her?'

'He must have been scared off by something before he had the chance. There was a mark around one of her wrists which suggested he'd attempted to bind them, perhaps with the same thing he used to strangle her. Why are you asking me about this now, Bella?'

Lara took a deep breath before correcting him. 'Lara. My name is Lara. So why kill her?'

'So she wouldn't go to the police of course,' Mrs Croft answered.

'Maybe he didn't intend to rape her. Maybe he had another reason to kill her.' Then she remembered the attack on Jenny. 'Do you think he was responsible for the sexual assaults at that time too? Jenny Masters said he assaulted her just before Bella died.'

'I don't know anything about that. She didn't come to us about it. But he probably was responsible because they stopped after he was jailed,' Croft said.

'Why didn't you pursue it, Mr Croft? Surely he should have been tried for that as well.'

Gerald Croft shrugged his shoulders. 'What was the point? We had no proof it was him, and we already had him for murder anyway.

Lara couldn't help but feel the sexual assault allegations were irrelevant, so she got back to her original point. 'I think there may have been another reason for my sister's murder.'

The man sitting opposite her narrowed his eyes. 'What other reason could there be?'

'I think Bella was blackmailing somebody, at least, that's what the landlady of my hotel implied. That would have been a reason to kill her, surely.'

'So, you think she was blackmailing Tom Bailey, and that's why he killed her?' Mrs Croft said.

'Maybe. Maybe not. What evidence was there against him?'

'I can't remember. It was a long time ago,' he said.

Mrs Croft did remember. 'Her blood was in his car, and he had form. He was guilty. Look, why are

92

you asking all these questions? You said this was a brief visit.'

Lara took a deep breath. 'I have reason to believe that he didn't do it. I can't tell you what it is until I check something first.'

Suddenly, Gerald Croft stood up, his face now paler, before saying,

'What happened to Bella will stay with me until the day I die, but it is in the past, and I don't know what good would come of reliving it.'

Lara knew it was probably her last visit to the Croft's house, so she was determined to ask one more question. 'Did you find the murder weapon?'

He shook his head before turning his back on her. Then he was gone.

'That's all we can tell you, dear. I'm sorry about your sister but I'd be grateful if you wouldn't call around again. It upsets my husband a great deal.'

Lara thanked the woman and left the house.

Mrs Croft went into the kitchen where her husband was making a sandwich. 'Don't worry. She won't come back,' she told him.

But he still looked angry. 'Why did she have to ask about the murder weapon?'

As Lara walked back down the cobbled path leading to the tiny harbour, she considered what little information Gerald Croft had told her. His wife had said more but it felt as if she was guarding her husband. Although she'd been invited in, Lara knew she was not welcome in that house. She hadn't known about the evidence found near Bella's body. Nor had she heard much about the convicted man, Tom Bailey, before the parole hearing. Mrs Croft said that he had form but what kind of form? Assault? Rape? Murder? She wondered where she would find out about Bailey's past crimes. Was he really the sex attacker back then?

She looked ahead and saw Ben leaning against the side of his boat. He was watching her too.

'Was he any help to you?' he asked.

'Oh, he wasn't that helpful, to be honest. It was a long time ago, so he's probably forgotten many of the details.'

'Only if he's got Alzheimer's. It's not every day there's a murder in this place.'

They glanced at each other at the irony of his words, and he quickly changed the subject.

'Come on. We need to get back before the tide goes out.'

Lara stepped into the boat and noticed the temperature had fallen since she had left it only thirty minutes earlier. She looked longingly at the cabin as, to her relief, Ben started the motor and the boat moved back out to sea. Then, just as she thought she would freeze to death, he motioned for her to move into the shelter. Was that a smirk on his face she noticed as she wasted no time in complying. Shielded from the sea breeze, Lara untensed her body and looked around the small space. It was empty except for some pencils, a few mugs, and a square tin, the type used to house tobacco and cigarette papers.

She looked up at Ben who seemed to be deep in thought. She tried to picture him as he was twenty years earlier when he had mixed in the same circles as Bella. What did he look like as an eighteen-year-old? He would have had the same thick, dark wavy locks as he had now, but his face would have been softer, less weary. Perhaps he wouldn't have been as tall as he was now, but it was difficult to imagine him any thinner.

Had he really hated Bella, or did she make his eyes turn, too? Suddenly, he shifted his focus, noticing she was looking at him. To her confusion, Lara found herself blushing and hoped that he hadn't noticed.

They had reached the harbour and she fumbled in her bag for the fare. As she handed him the ten-pound note he nodded, probably to avoid saying thanks, she thought.

'If you get lost again, just head for Copston. It's the nearest town for miles and it will put you back on the road to Weston.'

'Thanks. Do you want a lift anywhere?' she asked. 'No charge.'

'I've got my bike,' he said, with no reaction to the jibe about money. Then he reached into his back pocket and pulled out a familiar-looking envelope. 'Are you sure you don't want any money?'

Chapter Seven

Ben didn't appear to know anything about Tanya's letter despite his own letter being almost identical to hers bar a slight variation of the same handwriting. Lara thought it was better not to enlighten him about the other letter as she knew that she would be the main suspect. By now, Tanya might have gone to the police but that didn't worry her. They couldn't prove who sent the letters. Lara had considered going to the police station herself, but it would have to wait until the following morning as it was already getting dark. But as it turned out, Lara didn't have to go to the police station because they had come to her, at least one of them had.

Mrs Parsons rolled her eyes when she saw Paul Croft standing outside the front door. 'At least you're not wearing a uniform,' she said, under her breath, while leading him into the breakfast room where Lara was drinking a hot chocolate.'

'Is it about this afternoon?' Lara asked, surprised at how quickly news seemed to have spread.

Paul ignored the question and asked one of his own. 'Have you been sending anonymous letters to some residents of Weston, Miss Campbell?'

'Oh, I guess Tanya has been in touch. The answer to your question is no. It wasn't me. Why would I do something so obvious?'

'Why did you think Tanya had been in touch?' he asked.

'Well, she thought it was me too and said she was going to the police about it.'

'Has Tanya also had a letter?'

Lara stared at him in confusion. Did he even know that she had just got back from his parents' house?

'Yes, she has. And Ben has had one too,' she replied slowly.

'Ben who?'

'I don't know his surname, but he was a friend of yours once.'

'Ben Sutton! Did Tanya tell you that Ben has also received a letter?'

'No. He told me. I was with him earlier,' she explained, wondering about the confused expression on Paul's face. 'Have you had one too?'

Once again, he ignored her question. 'How did you come to be with him? Was he in the village?'

'No. I met him at the harbour.'

'Which harbour?'

'To be quite honest, I don't know where it was because I was lost. He knew that I was Bella's sister and showed me the letter. He thought I'd sent it too.'

Paul looked doubtful. 'I don't know who sent those letters. It could just be a prank. 'Did Ben threaten you in any way, Miss Campbell?'

'No. Actually, he was quite helpful as he gave me a lift to Easton. That was where I was trying to get to. I did have to give him a tenner, though. I don't suppose I should have told you that, what with you being a policeman.'

But Paul wasn't interested in any cash-in-hand fares that Ben was doing. He continued with his line of questioning. 'Why did you want to go to Easton?'

Lara swallowed before she replied. 'I went to see your father, Gerald Croft. I assumed that was the reason for this visit.'

Paul's face turned ashen. Lara now wondered if the person sitting opposite her was Detective Inspector Croft or Bella's old school friend. She wasn't sure what had shaken him most - the mention of Ben or the visit to his parents' house. His silence was making her nervous, and she found herself reaching for her notebook. Her actions appeared to snap him out of his thoughts.

'What's that?' he asked when he saw her placing the notebook on the table in front of her,

'It's my notebook. I need to jot everything down for when I finally get to write my book. By the time I get home, I might forget things that have been said about my sister.' Even as she said it, she knew that she was pushing the lie.

Paul didn't mention the supposed book that she was going to write. Instead, he asked Lara if he could read the notes she had made up to that point. Both knew that he couldn't demand to see it, so the tone of his request was almost pleading. Lara refused to show it to him mainly because she couldn't remember everything that she had written. Had she been rude about anyone? Had she been rude about the police? But she wanted to be as helpful as possible so decided on a compromise.

'I'll read out what I've written so far,' she said, turning to the first page of writing. She saw that Paul had also taken out a notebook.

Lara related all the conversations she'd had since arriving in the village three days earlier. She began with her thoughts on the tiny hotel, the details of which Paul didn't record in his notebook. He only began writing when she talked about her visit to Jenny's café.

'So, Jenny told you that she gave the photos to her friends after Bella's death.'

'Yes, that's right. Her mother sent one to my sister's foster parents who eventually forwarded it to me.'

'Then, you, Jenny, Tanya and Hanna met at The Royal Oak. What was the atmosphere like that night?'

'It was short and far from sweet. Tanya was very nasty to me.'

'What did you find out from them?' he asked coldly, not interested in what he regarded as women's bitching.

'They said that Simone and Bella argued on the way to the ball but not much happened once they got there. After the ball, they all hitched a lift with a young couple most of the way home. Before that, they'd refused a lift with Tom Bailey, and he turned up again once they got back to Weston. They walked the rest of the way home separately but heard Jenny screaming. Bailey had tried to attack her. I'm sure you already know this,' Lara said.

Paul glanced up. 'Why would I know that?'

'Well, you were there too, weren't you? Jenny said you were part of their gang. She also said you were dating so she must have told you about it the next day. You must have noticed Bella there too.'

'It was hardly a gang and Jenny was just a fling. And by the way, I did not see Bella at all that night. I'm happy for you to write that down too,' he said, with sarcasm.

'What did you think of Bella?'

'Will you continue reading your notes?' Paul said, still not willing to be the one answering questions.

'Yes, of course,' she said, but she paused after returning her attention to the notebook. It had been a most curious comment that the landlady had made regarding the friends. She had written the words verbatim in her book. "Be careful. You don't know those women. Not all friends can be trusted." She didn't know whether to mention it to the detective. Perhaps he was included amongst "the friends".

'What was Hanna upset about?' Paul asked.

'I don't know. They were laughing at the photograph and Hanna picked it up to take a closer look. That was when she said she felt unwell. It surprised everyone when she left.'

'Did she leave straight after seeing the photograph?'

'No. She said she needed to talk to someone, but they must have gone. It might have been the man I saw her talking to earlier. His name is Chris. I think you know him too.'

'Can I see the photograph again?' he asked, refusing to bite at the mention of his school friend.

Lara took the photograph from the sleeve of the notebook and pushed it across the table. Paul's eyes moved across the image as if he was examining each girl. Then he took a photograph of it with his phone. It appeared to Lara that he had not seen the photograph before.

'Carry on,' he said.

'The next morning I visited Bella's grave and met the vicar. He told me that Bella had been in the church choir when younger. He said she had a voice like an angel. The grave was neglected, and I made a note to buy some flowers. When I got back to the hotel, Flora told me that a woman had been killed during the night. Then the police came. They said it was suicide.'

Lara continued until she reached the end of her notes. 'I haven't had a chance to write about today, but it was quite eventful, what with meeting Ben again and then speaking to your father.'

'What did my father tell you?'

'He told me about Tom Bailey, how he had left evidence at the scene, and that he had form. He isn't in any doubt about Bailey's guilt.' She didn't mention that it was the wife who did most of the talking.

'Of course, he isn't because Bailey is guilty. If I were you, I would forget everything and go back home. No good will come of you bothering people about the past. A woman's already been murdered.'

'But isn't that a reason to reopen the investigation?'

Paul gasped before answering. 'Reopen the investigation! What for? Bailey has already served his sentence. Like I just said, no good will come of raking over a crime that was solved twenty years ago.'

After Paul had left the hotel, Lara mulled over their conversation. She had a feeling that he was just as unsettled by recent events as her, even if he didn't say as much. He would not even say if he'd received a letter or not. However, he had asked her questions that weren't related to Hanna's murder. Jenny and the others had just given her snippets of information about Bella, which were as vague as they were incomplete. For the first time, she felt a glimmer of hope. Paul might not have given her any information, but the questions he'd asked had told her something. Paul was interested in more than Hanna's murder.

Jenny knocked at the green, fibreglass door and hoped it was the right one. Had new houses always looked identical? It wasn't long before she heard movement from inside the door and, when it opened, she saw Simone's surprised face looking back at her.

'Oh, Jenny. I wasn't expecting you. Come in.'

'Chris told me what happened, but I didn't tell him that I was coming around. To be honest, I hope I'm not making things worse between you two by interfering.' She didn't go as far as mentioning that Chris was staying with her.

'It's okay,' Simone replied, as she slumped onto a stool in the kitchen. 'It's not your fault that you've walked into a warzone. We've been arguing for months; ever since that one was born,' she said, gazing at the ceiling.

'Have you tried marriage guidance? I'm sure the two of you can fix things.'

'Chris won't talk about anything,' Simone said. 'I know he's really unhappy, but he won't let me help him. Every time I try to touch him, he freezes. It's like I disgust him. Do you think he could be having an affair?'

'I really don't know, Simone. Surely, if he was, he would be trying to cover it up by being extra nice to you. Guilty husbands buy flowers, you know. He told me that you thought he was having an affair with Tanya. I really don't think that's true.'

'Why not?' Simone asked. She was unconvinced by her friend's assurances.

'Because when we were out the night of Hanna's death, Chris was at the bar and Tanya wasn't even aware that he was there. When I mentioned it to her afterwards, she said she wished she'd known as she hadn't seen him for years.'

'Well, that's a lie for a start.'

'What do you mean, Simone?'

'Chris wasn't at the bar that night. As I told you before, he was at Ben's house.'

Jenny realised that Chris had clearly lied to Simone about his whereabouts that night. Lara had confirmed it when she'd seen the photograph of Chris. Unless Lara was lying, Chris was not at Ben's house. And Jenny was certain that Lara would not lie about what would be a trivial matter to her. However, Jenny kept quiet as she didn't want to mention Lara's name again.

'And it's not true that they haven't seen each other for years. My mother saw Tanya walking behind him about a month ago. She followed him into the park. They were obviously meeting.'

'Maybe it wasn't them.'

'She knows her own son-in-law Jenny, and Tanya's black mop stands out like a belisha beacon.'

They both smiled at the oxymoron then Jenny looked at Simone's tired face and, for the first time, felt sympathy for the young wife and mother. Had she really got what she wanted by marrying Chris? Chris clearly didn't love Simone anymore and probably never did. You can never make anyone love you were seven words of wisdom her mother had told her when her heart had been broken by a fellow student at university. It was the first man she had loved, and she'd gotten over it.

'What did Chris say about the park?'

'He lied about some mad woman following him around. As if I'd believe that.'

'It could be true, though. What about that woman who's always hanging around the village? She's a bit strange.'

'So is that woman you've befriended. What colour is her hair?'

'Black but she's only just got here, Simone.'

'That's what she told you. Perhaps she's only been staying here for a few days but there are hotels in Copston too.'

Jenny hadn't considered that Lara might be lying to her about the hotel. She didn't seem the type. But what if Lara was telling lies? Jenny decided that she would need to be more careful about what she said to her new friend.

'When are you going back to London? I don't believe you'll hang around here for long, Jenny.'

'It's not that bad, Simone, though I am missing London. I'd need to get another job before going back. It's impossible to get accommodation without one. Saying that, it's almost as impossible to get a job without anywhere to live.'

'You should hurry up before you get caught up in this world.'

'What do you mean by that, Simone?'

'Don't you remember what it was like before? Everyone talking about everyone else, making up stories and accusations, sharing tittle-tattle. So many people act like big fish when you live in a tiny place like Weston. If I could go back, I would have left twenty years ago too.'

'Don't be daft, Simone. Everything works out for the best. You have two lovely children and a nice house. I don't have anything to call my own.'

'You are luckier than you realise, Jenny. You don't have to live in the past, and we know what that was like.' Her expression turned serious. 'Look, Jenny, I know we said we'd never speak of it again, but I think you are playing with fire talking to this girl. One slip and everything could come out. For heaven's sake, go back to London before all our lives are ruined.'

Too aware of what Simone meant by her last comment, Jenny decided it was time to leave. She'd always liked Simone and hadn't wanted to lose touch with her when she went to university. However, staying in touch with her would have meant staying in touch with the others too. And she didn't really like the others much. But it was too late to rekindle her friendship with Simone who, Jenny was sure, felt the same way. Both women said goodbye without promising to meet up again.

Chris and Tanya were sitting next to each other on Jenny's tiny settee while laughing at the old images of themselves in Jenny's photo album. Neither visitor was aware of Jenny's trip to see Simone earlier that day. Jenny didn't believe for one minute that Chris and Tanya were having an affair, but she would observe them anyway.

'Look at my hair,' Jenny moaned, 'My mother used to tie it back in plaits so tight I looked like I had a facelift.'

'Well, mine's the opposite,' Chris laughed. 'It certainly doesn't look as if I'd combed it that morning. My mother never bothered getting up to check the state of me.'

'That's because she was always working nights,' Tanya said. 'Your father should have made more of an effort. Men are all the same. I always wanted to tie my hair back, but my mum insisted on me wearing it long.'

'You and Bella could be sisters in this photo,' Jenny remarked. 'The teachers were always getting you two mixed up, weren't they?'

'Only the ones who couldn't be bothered to do their job properly,' Tanya replied curtly. 'We both had dark bobs. If Chris had worn a dark wig, they'd have mixed him up with us too.'

All three laughed as they continued to share memories of their childhood. Then they moved on to the last pictures of them together. There were several photographs of the school ball that showed the friends in various parts of the dance hall.

'Look at Paul chatting to the teachers. He always acted like he was too mature for us,' Tanya said. 'And look at poor Hanna. I can't believe you went out with her, Chris.'

Jenny quickly changed the subject. 'Let's not forget why we are really here. Someone is threatening us, and we need to share what we know to be able to work out who it is.'

'You two don't have to share anything with me because I already know who that person is,' said Tanya.

'Would you care to share?' Chris asked. He was beginning to get agitated by Tanya who he'd always found unpleasant.

'It's Lara, of course. She's stirring up trouble for some reason, trying to frighten us.'

'No, she isn't. She just wants to know about that night. I wonder why Hanna got so upset after seeing that photograph. What do you think, Chris?'

'How would I know? I haven't seen Hanna for years.'

The women exchanged glances before Tanya challenged him. 'Chris! You talked to Hanna that night in the pub. Were you too drunk to even remember? Hey! Have the police spoken to you because they've talked to us? If they haven't, you should talk to Paul. He's in charge of the investigation.'

'How do you know I was …what's with all these questions and demands? Who do you think you are, anyway? You're nothing but a nasty piece of work.' He was glaring at Tanya who was shifting nervously in her seat. Neither woman had seen him that angry before.

'Come on, Chris. Tanya didn't mean anything,' Jenny said, trying to salvage the evening.

But Chris grabbed his car keys and stormed out of the lounge. A few seconds, later Jenny and Tanya heard the front door slam.

'What is wrong with that man?' Tanya asked. 'He's obviously hiding something. It must have been Chris that Hanna wanted to speak to in the pub.'

'We already know she spoke to him despite what he said.'

'How dare he speak to me like that? I think he's hiding something. Perhaps Hanna met him later and they argued. Perhaps the police need to know about this.'

Chris knew he was over the limit, but he had to get away from that situation. To think he'd been accused of having an affair with that awful woman. He didn't mind looking at the photographs. He'd seen most of them before so there were no surprises. But once Jenny and Tanya started digging for information, he couldn't take the risk. However bad it looked, he had to leave.

There was only one person he could trust so he drove the miles of winding road until he arrived at the harbour. He leaned against the car and stared out to sea. In the distance, a tiny mark gradually increased in size until the various parts identified themselves as a sailing boat. Chris raised his hand to the still anonymous vessel, knowing that Ben was the only sailor who used the tiny harbour. It was a wonder his boat hadn't been stolen or vandalised, such was the lack of security. Perhaps no one else knew it was there. The salt sea air was a change from the smell of family life and for a moment he envied Ben's solitary existence. As the boat approached the jetty, he walked over to meet his childhood friend. Ben jumped onto solid ground and greeted Chris by nodding briefly. If he'd known what would happen next, he might have remained at sea.

'Ben, I need your help.'

Chapter Eight

There'd been a breakthrough in the Hanna Evans case. A witness saw two women on the footbridge about an hour after Hanna left The Royal Oak. They appeared to be fighting. It was a long shot as the sighting was fleeting, but the driver was able to describe one woman as having very dark hair, perhaps black. The description didn't match Hanna whose hair was light brown. The detectives on the case put their heads together but no one obvious came to mind. Of all the local women known to have violent tendencies, not one of them had dark brown, or black hair. So they had to look outside of the mugshot gallery.

Two women immediately came to mind – Tanya Price and Lara Campbell. Sergeant Brooks was adamant that Lara should be the prime suspect, but Inspector Croft did not agree with his colleague. Although the death had happened just after Lara's arrival in the village, it could just be a coincidence. Nothing was known about Lara Campbell so that had to be put right. In the meantime, they focussed on the other woman whose background they knew only too well. Had the two friends somehow come across each other later that night? Tanya Price was known to have a temper and had been thrown out of several pubs. It was only down to luck that Tanya's face wasn't included among the mugshots. It was time to pay her a second visit.

It was getting late, and Lara realised that she hadn't eaten since breakfast. Grabbing her keys, she slipped out of the hotel with the intention of finally trying out the local fish and chip shop, which she would eat in her car when she got back not to upset the landlady. Just as she started the ignition, a car pulled into the driveway and blocked her in. Despite putting on her headlights to alert the other driver that she was about to leave, a man got out and rushed into the hotel. An irritated Lara followed the man back into the hotel where, seeing no sign of him, she tapped on one of the doors off the hallway. There was no response at first and, as Lara stared at the private sign on the door, she hoped the landlady wouldn't be cross, or drunk. Finally, the door was opened, not by the landlady but by the man who had blocked her in.

'Do you mind moving your car? I can't get out,' she said.

For a moment, the man looked confused before saying 'Who are you?'

'I'm staying here. Who are you?'

Lara could see that the man was clearly stressed about something and, glancing over his shoulder, she was shocked to see Mrs Parsons sitting on a chair with her face bloodied and her arm hanging limply.

Lara's eyes shot back to the man in front of her and she stepped backwards away from the door.

'Wait,' he called after her. 'She's okay but I'll have to drive her to A & E so they can check her out and set her arm. We'll be gone in a few minutes. I'm her son, by the way.'

As she pulled up outside the chip shop, Lara noticed a small gang loitering outside. There were about seven or eight youths, all wearing hoodies, taunting a woman with a carrier bag. At first, Lara assumed the woman was a customer who had just left the chip shop, but then the woman turned towards the car and looked back at Lara. It was the woman who had been causing a nuisance in the grocery store. Lara hesitated. What if she became the youths' next target? Then, feeling ashamed of her cowardice, she got out of the car and marched past them into the shop.

After ordering haddock and chips, she plucked up the courage to complain about the intimidating youths outside but the man behind the counter merely shrugged his shoulders before saying,

'You're not from round here are you, love? She's always pestering them. She's the menace.'

'Who is she?' Lara asked, realising that the woman probably lived there when she was a child.

But the man behind the counter was not in the mood for casual gossip. 'You don't need to know, and I haven't got time to tell you,' he said, before ringing the till.

After paying, Lara drove back to the hotel where she ate the food in her car even though any odour would probably dissipate before Mrs Parsons got back from the hospital. She thought about the woman outside the chip and wondered if she had always been that way. Maybe she'd fallen under the curse of alcohol after a difficult period of her life.

Then she thought about the landlady and hoped things were okay. Lara assumed that she had fallen over, probably drunk, and telephoned her son to come over. How many sons were there? She'd only mentioned one but there could be more. Was it the son who might have been blackmailed by Bella?

Tanya had only been at work for a few minutes when she was called into the staff room where Paul and his colleague, Sergeant Brooks were waiting for her. As she opened the door, she gave them both a confused look before saying,

'Hi, Paul. Look at you in plain clothes. You are looking more like your dad every day.'

'Can you confirm the time that you left The Royal Oak pub on the night of Hanna Evan's death?' Paul ignored Tanya's belittling observation.

Tanya was aware of the seriousness of the visit so answered the question without hesitation. 'It was about half past ten, I think. It could have been a bit later. I was with Jenny so I'm sure she will confirm the time. She's much better at that sort of thing than I am.'

'Did you wear a coat that night?' Brooks asked, taking over the questioning.

'A jacket, yes. It was chilly. What's that got to do with anything? Why are you asking me such a stupid question?'

'What colour was your jacket?'

'Grey. I don't understand.'

'Does it have a hood?'

'No. Look, what is all this about?'

'We believe that her death was not self-inflicted. A woman of your description was seen following her in the vicinity of the bridge she fell from.'

'What! I don't believe it. Why would anyone want to kill Hanna? Hang on. Why are you questioning me about it? You are joking, aren't you? I was Hanna's best friend.'

'Just answer the question,' said Brooks.

'Okay! It was too early to go home so I went clubbing after I left the bar.'

'Keeping an eye on your kids, were you?' Brooks asked mockingly.

'Get lost,' Tanya hissed.

'What time did you get to the club?' Paul took over the questioning once more. He didn't like his partner's manner any more than Tanya did.

'I don't know. Just after the taxi dropped me off there?'

'The thing is we've checked with the taxi firm, and you were not dropped off at the club. You asked the driver to stop at the cashpoint to allow you to withdraw money. However, after a few minutes, you informed him that you were unable to pay the fare, and he left you there.'

Tanya fell silent and looked down at her feet. Then her tone became less confrontational and more sheepish. 'Okay, okay. Look, I was so embarrassed that I pretended that I went to the club, but really I just walked the rest of the way home.'

'Yes, and the journey home would have taken you across the bridge that Hanna Evans was on when she died. You would also have been walking over at roughly the same time. Did you see her, by any chance?'

'No, of course not. I would have said if I'd seen her, and I didn't walk over the bridge because I'm scared of heights. I used the underpass instead.'

'At that time of night? It's a dangerous place for a young woman walking alone.'

'Evidently not as dangerous as the bridge,' she replied.

'They even suggested I was the other woman on the bridge. Can you believe it? I'm a flipping suspect for Hanna's murder.'

Tanya's voice was so loud that Jenny was able to hold the receiver six inches away from her ear and still feel her ear drums shuddering.

'Listen, Tan, they asked me a load of questions about that night with Hanna, too. Paul acted as though he'd never seen me before in his life.'

'But did they accuse you of killing her?'

'No, but I'm not a brunette like the woman seen on the footbridge with Hanna. I could have worn a wig, I suppose. Anyway, you should have told me that you didn't have cash for the taxi. You know I'd have lent you the money to get home. Were you seriously going clubbing? You told me that you were going straight home.'

'Of course, I didn't go clubbing. I told the taxi driver that so he would let me get in. They're like that on a Friday night, you know. Not interested in other fares.'

'We should have picked a quieter night to go out. Friday nights are for the youngsters.'

'Oh behave, Jenny. You sound like my grandmother. We're not that old. And I bet you were a regular in those famous London nightclubs.'

'Only when work required me to go. I always hated it though and much preferred a quiet wine bar.'

'Well, I hate to break it to you but there aren't any wine bars in Weston.'

Jenny did not bother to reply to Tanya's sarcasm. Instead, she told her about her trip to see Hanna's mother. Tanya said that she was surprised to hear what had been said about Hanna. Like Jenny, she insisted that their quiet friend had been the best-behaved of them by far.

'She told me everything,' Tanya insisted. 'I would know if she'd got up to no good.'

'Unless she kept it secret,' Jenny replied.

119

After the call, Jenny wondered if Tanya knew more about Hanna than she'd claimed on the phone. She was Hanna's best friend so it wouldn't be so strange if she did know more about the recently deceased woman. Then she thought about Tanya's so-called journey home from the pub. Perhaps she really had intended going to the club, not for a dance but making some quick money. It wouldn't surprise Jenny. She had always been wary about hanging around with someone whose boyfriend sold drugs. Now the same drug dealing boyfriend was her husband. And to think people thought Bella was trouble.

Paul Croft walked wearily up the layered steps that led to the front door. It had been the most difficult day of his seventeen-year career. All he wanted to do was shut the door and forget like he did every evening; lose himself in one Netflix series after another. But tonight, he knew that was not going to be possible. This was his first murder case, and his colleagues would be watching him closely. He knew they didn't think that he was up to the job and that he'd only made inspector through his father's reputation, the man who had solved the last murder in Weston after only a few days.

Paul had a lot to live up to. His colleagues would be watching his every move, watching every dig he carried out and he was frightened of what those digs might uncover. If only that woman hadn't shown up after all this time. He knew she was lying about writing a book because her notes were mostly about other people in the village. There was virtually nothing about her sister. Now she was pestering his father for details and who knew where it would lead.

Inside the house, his wife was where she always was at seven o'clock in the evening - at the dining table surrounded by paper. It would be another hour at least before she put down her pen and switched her attention to her husband, so he went upstairs, laid down on the bed and closed his eyes.

So far, his life had been good, far better than he could have hoped for. He'd started in the police force straight from university and quickly moved out of uniform and into the glamourous world of criminal investigation. After seventeen years he was ready to move on to something bigger and was applying for transfers to any big city that would take him. It had taken some time to persuade his wife to leave her headship but now she agreed to take a career break. It was about time they had children before it was too late.

He'd been confident about their future until Hanna Evans's murder, but now he could feel the foundations slipping away.

Chapter Nine

There was no fresh milk or bread in the breakfast room the following morning and Lara began to assume the worst, but then Flora appeared wearing jeans and a t-shirt rather than her usual black skirt and top.

'Sorry. It's a bit chaotic this morning. I'll replace the milk now.'

As she left the room again, Lara called after her,

'How is Mrs Parsons?'

'She's fine but she had to stay overnight in hospital. My brother will be around though. Ah, here he comes now. Morning John. This is Lara. She's staying here for a few more days.'

The man from the night before walked into the room carrying a mug in one hand and a piece of toast in the other. Lara looked at him properly for the first time. He was about forty and handsome in a distinguished way, his ruffled black hair displaying early signs of grey at the temples. There was something of the old Hollywood movie star about him. He sat down at the table next to Lara and apologized for any inconvenience she had suffered as a result of the landlady's accident.

'Oh no. Everything is fine and I'm glad she's okay.'

'Yes. She tripped over the cat and banged her head on the coffee table. It actually broke her fall as her arm was only sprained, not broken. When she gets home she won't be up and about for a couple of days, so I'll stick around till she's fit enough to work.'

Lara felt embarrassed to be in the middle of their family misfortune, particularly as she appeared to be the only guest at that time. In light of this, she made the obligatory offer. 'Would it be easier if I found somewhere else to stay?'

He smiled. 'Only if you don't mind staying in a completely different area. This is the only guest house around for many miles.'

Of course, Lara already knew that. She had considered staying in the nearest town to be less conspicuous, but that would have involved an hour round trip.

'Well, if you're sure. Weston is the place I would prefer to be. I could keep an eye on your mother if you want to go home sooner.'

He smiled again. 'That's kind of you Mara, but you are a paying guest, therefore, I will be at your service.'

'Lara.'

'What?'

'My name is Lara.'

'Right. Isn't that what I said?'

'No. You said, Mara. Not that it matters.'

'I'm sorry. I have a slight speech impediment which means my vocal mechanism has a mind of its own.'

Lara laughed, even though she was not sure if he was joking or not. 'I really hadn't noticed. People always get my name wrong even though it was popular a few years ago.'

'Ah yes. Lara Croft. I must confess to having had a major crush on Angelina Jolie when she was covered in mud. And that long black plait.'

Lara blushed and instinctively reached for some strands of her own long dark hair which she sometimes plaited. Then, as if he had read her mind, it was his turn to blush.

'Whoops. Please excuse my foot-in-mouth disease too. I'd better leave you to eat your breakfast in peace now. If you need anything just come looking.'

Chris Farmer was at a crossroads in his life, but he didn't know what was at the end of each direction. He tossed one pebble after another into the crashing waves as he attempted to sort out his life. The late autumn sea looked as unwelcoming as the choices he faced.

Perhaps he should get back in the car, turn around, and go back home. However, he didn't know if that was still an option. Lately, his wife's mood had changed from concern about his unhappiness to irritation, and now anger. She was unlikely to put up with him being like this for much longer. For so many years he'd ridden the wave of a lie because it suited his dream, but now that dream didn't matter to him at all. It was time to move on, wherever that place was.

He could stay with Ben for a while until he got his head together. When he needed his help, Ben had always been there for him. He was a true mate. But even Ben wouldn't want him hanging around for long. Chris thought about their teenage years when they were joined at the hip. But that was before Tom Bailey came along.

The two men hardly spoke after the trial. There was no celebratory lads drink when Chris was taken on professionally, or when Ben got accepted into the Navy. Simone refused to invite Ben to the wedding, but Chris knew he wouldn't have gone anyway.

When Ben left the Navy and returned to Weston, there was no friends reunion. Gradually, however, the acknowledgements began. The unplanned meetings were awkward at first, but time and maturity diminished the anger and upset. They even had the odd drink together now and again. They were friends once more.

However, Chris could tell that Ben was reluctant to get mixed up in his messy marital situation. He was at sea when Chris and Simone began dating so wasn't there to stop his friend going down the wrong track. Now, the weary ex-sailor did not care about the mess Chris had got himself into. Ben was a lone wolf whose life was his own and he wouldn't let anyone get in the way of his lifestyle. How Chris envied him. So, that particular route was also a dead end, but Chris didn't want to turn back. He would stay with Jenny as long as she'd let him. Yes. Jenny would help him through this period, and he would help her too. She couldn't hide the turmoil behind her lovely smile. Despite appearances, Jenny was torn up inside too.

After breakfast, Lara found herself walking back to the church hoping for inspiration. She was dismayed and confused to find that only stalks remained of the flowers she had recently put on Bella's grave. But then she saw a rabbit chomping on the flowers of another grave. Trying to feel better about the sight in front of her, she wondered if Bella knew about the visitors to her grave. But it would be small comfort because that would mean she was still down there, in the cold, wet earth, six feet away from the living.

For a few minutes, Lara stood in silence listening to the sound of the wind whispering through the trees, with an irrational hope that she would hear her sister's voice telling her she was happy. Suddenly, there was a voice, but it did not belong to her dead sister. Whoever the voice belonged to was not near enough for Lara to hear the words being spoken. Curious to see who else was in the graveyard, she followed the narrow path between a line of headstones and vases to the other side of the church where she saw a young woman standing over a gravestone. The woman was crying but they sounded like tears of anger rather than grief. Was the woman angry at the deceased for leaving her?

Lara was scared to move in case she made a noise. She didn't want the woman to see that Lara had been watching her. But the woman did turn around. Lara knew that she had seen her before but could not remember where. For another few seconds, they stared at each other until the other woman began walking towards Lara. As she got closer, Lara could see the woman's white face and long black hair and she remembered where she had seen her before; it was the woman who had been begging outside the food store.

Lara watched as the woman approached her, then stood aside to allow her to pass. But the woman did not pass. Suddenly, Lara felt a blow to her cheek, causing her to tumble against a gravestone. Terrified, she looked up, but the woman had gone. After wiping her hand across her face, she saw blood on her palm, and reached over to her bag, expecting it to be minus a purse. But her purse was still inside, along with cash and bank cards. It was not a mugging so it must have been a random attack by a drug or drink-crazed woman. Yet, something told her it was personal, not random.

She walked over to the gravestone in front of which the woman had been standing. It was situated at a place farthest from Bella's plot and was surrounded by sunken graves and crumbling headstones. It was nearly as old and neglected as

Bella's grave. There were no flowers, and the vase was mottled with rust. A trickle of blood ran down her cheek and landed on the plot as she read the inscription:

Thomas Bailey 1955-2001

'She must be related to Tom Bailey somehow, and that's why she hit me. She knows who I am and blames me for his imprisonment.'

'Why would she blame you, Lara? You weren't even here at the time of the court case. I can see why they'd blame me and the others, but not you.'

'I know. It doesn't really make sense, but the woman didn't look capable of rational thoughts. Did Tom Bailey have a daughter?'

'The Baileys are a huge family. She could have been a daughter, sister, or aunt. I've never met any of them, except for him, of course.'

Jenny was dabbing TCP on Lara's cut cheek which was beginning to come out in a bruise. Lara winced as the antiseptic seeped through her grazed skin but was grateful for Jenny's assistance. She had been shocked to see a dazed Lara walking into her café but, luckily for Lara, the café was empty of customers. Jenny wanted to call the police, but Lara was reluctant. If she saw her again, could she summon up the courage to approach her? Something told Lara that the woman had answers.

'Could it have been his grave?' Jenny asked. 'Maybe he died in prison, and they buried him in secret.'

'No,' Lara said firmly. 'He is still in prison but will be released soon.'

Jenny looked at Lara in astonishment. 'How do you know that? You've acted as if you'd never even heard of him before you came here. What exactly do you know about Tom Bailey?'

Jenny appeared to be shaking and Lara wondered if she was cold. She finally told Jenny about her encounter with the man convicted of her sister's murder, and how he had been granted parole. However, Lara didn't reveal everything about the meeting; how she had worked out that he couldn't have killed Bella.

'Oh, you poor thing. That must have been horrific for you. How can they let him out? He's only about forty-three so he's still dangerous.' Jenny was no longer shaking.

'He's been in prison a long time for one murder, Jenny. Do you know of any other crimes he committed?'

'I don't think he was in prison for anything before he killed Bella, but he probably would have ended up there anyway. He was a real creep.'

'In what way?'

Jenny shivered. 'A real peeping Tom. That was his nickname as a matter of fact.'

Lara thought she might be sick when she thought of herself sitting so close to Bailey. She quickly changed the subject and told Jenny about her encounter with Ben and how he had taken her over to Gerald Croft's house. Jenny was surprised to hear how helpful Ben had been until she heard that he had charged Lara ten pounds for the boat trip.

'That man is such a scrounger. He really should get a proper job while he is still young enough.'

'What does he do for a living, at the moment?' Lara asked.

'He charges men, and it's always men, to go out with him in his boat to fish. Of course, it's cash in hand because he thinks that he's above paying tax.'

'But where does he live? Surely not on his fishing boat?'

'He probably still lives with his parents. I'm sure he wouldn't dream of paying a mortgage or rent.'

'That's mad. Why would he want to live at home all his life?'

'Because it's a lovely house. And no, he hasn't always lived at home. He joined the Navy straight after school and only came back a few years ago. I suppose I was a bit harsh on him as he's been to far more places in the world than I have.'

'He's certainly an interesting person,' Lara said. 'You can't blame him for wanting to live without rules after so many years in the Navy.' Then she changed the subject once again. 'Have you spoken to Tanya about the letter?'

Jenny pursed her lips before replying. 'Yes. In fact, she came here yesterday to discuss it. To be honest, she wanted to go to the police, but we persuaded her not to.'

'We?'

'Chris and me. He had a row with Simone, so he is staying here for a few days, but I'm sure they'll work things out.'

'Who do you think sent the letter to Tanya?'

Jenny gave Lara a confused look before saying, 'The same person who sent them to me and Hanna. And Chris got one too. But we don't think it was you, Lara. At least, I don't.'

'Oh, dear. I suppose it makes sense that all of Bella's friends were sent one. Thanks for trusting me, Jenny. It means a lot.'

Chapter Ten

The print on the box was tiny so she hadn't bothered to read it but now, standing with her finger on the start button, Lara realised her mistake. It was an oven-only meal and she had no access to an oven. She took out the chilli con carne and stared at it. What would happen if she microwaved it anyway? She was sure it wouldn't kill her, particularly as it was vegetarian, but the foil dish might damage the microwave. One thing for certain was that she could not face walking back to the store and she was in no fit state to drive.

On the way back she had called into the shop to get something to eat, knowing that Tanya didn't work mornings. By the time she reached the hotel, her eye had started to throb, so she took two paracetamol and went back to bed. On waking up, she discovered the eye was swollen and she could barely see out of it, but now the pain had eased, and she was very hungry.

There had been no sign of anyone else in the hotel, so she assumed that John had gone back to the hospital to pick up his mother. She couldn't remember seeing his car in the drive when she got back to the hotel a couple of hours earlier. It would only take a few minutes to nip into the kitchen and grab a microwaveable dish. She might even have time to wash it.

The door with the private sign creaked as though it knew she was an intruder and she paused, listening for any sounds of movement. But there were none, so she crept into the kitchen. It was no more than a family-sized kitchen which was clearly too small to cook several breakfasts at once. John had called it a guest house rather than a hotel, but it was really just someone's house.

As it was small, the cookware was crammed into one cupboard and Lara had to stretch to the back in order to reach a Pyrex bowl. After nearly dropping the bowl when a large spider ran out from its hiding place, she closed the cupboard door and stood back up. Suddenly, a voice came from behind her, and the bowl jumped out of her hand, landing on the ceramic tile with an ugly smashing sound. John was standing at the door aghast.

Lara looked down at the broken glass feeling like a criminal. 'I'm so sorry. I bought an oven-only meal by mistake, but I thought if I could borrow a Pyrex dish, it would be okay. I didn't want to risk damaging your mother's microwave.'

'What on earth's happened to your eye?' John seemed to be unaware of the broken dish on the floor.

'Er, somebody hit me but I'm okay, really I am.'

'You don't look okay.'

She knelt back down to pick up the glass but in doing so managed to cut her hand.

'Leave that and sit down over here,' he ordered, pointing to a chair next to him.

'You look as though you've been in a boxing match with someone well over your weight. Let me see your hand.'

Before she knew it, he was holding her hand upright and squeezing her palm in several places, looking for any splinters of glass.

'So, you are telling me that you have been living on microwave meals since you got here,' he said while stretching her hand up to his eyes.

'Well, not exactly. I had fish and chips last night. It's been a few days since I ate anything healthy, I suppose.'

He shook his head as if he was annoyed and Lara worried that she'd been rude about his mother's hotel.

'I'm sorry. I wasn't being critical,' she said quickly. 'I love it here.'

'No. I was thinking how unsuitable this house is for paying guests. It's okay for workers who just need a bed for the night and then disappear, but not for tourists. There are no restaurants in the village so any hotel should provide evening meals. This house is too small.'

'I'm not really a tourist though.'

He lowered her hand and looked at her. 'Yes, my mother told me. You're writing a book about your sister. I knew Bella quite well.'

'I know. Your mother told me.'

'Maybe you should just interview my mother. She seems to know everything,' he said, grinning.

'How is she?' Lara asked.

'She's miserable because she couldn't come home today. It seems that she had quite a bang, so they want to monitor her for twenty-four hours. And I'm not fetching her at midnight!'

'Oh, dear. Are you sure that you don't want me to go? I don't want to be a nuisance.'

'Stay here as long as you like. My mother wouldn't speak to me again if I threw out her only guest. Anyway, it'll give Flora something to do. In fact, it will give me something to do while I'm here. Now, one thing which should be thrown out is that cheap and nasty ready meal because tonight, Lara, I shall cook you an evening meal. It's on the house of course.'

Lara blushed at the thought of being waited on by John. She hated dining alone in public. It was bad enough wolfing down a ready meal by herself in an empty room. But she knew she couldn't refuse his kind offer.

'If you're sure. I don't want to be even more trouble.'

'You have no choice in the matter. I've already started cooking,' he said, holding up a kitchen knife.

'Is that all?' the shop assistant said to the elderly woman as she handed her a new carrier bag. But the woman wasn't listening. She was staring at one man in the queue, but he didn't notice her, unlike several other impatient customers standing behind him. He was called to the next counter.

'Hi Ben,' Tanya said, while instinctively reaching for a packet of tobacco. 'I hear you were at the pub the other night. You should have said hello.'

'I wasn't there,' he replied. 'I was just hanging around outside.'

'You bikers are a nuisance, you know. While I'm on the subject, did you notice Chris Farmer there? We thought he was at the bar but when we asked him about it, he denied it.'

'Well, maybe you should mind your own business. You and your other friends should concentrate on your own lives,' he replied.

'All right! There's no need to be rude, Ben. I do have my reasons for asking. He was talking to Hanna the night she was murdered, and I wondered what they talked about.'

'I wouldn't know what they were talking about because I wasn't anywhere near them.'

'Okay. I get the message. Anything else?' she asked, while glancing over to the growing queue.

'A packet of rizla papers,' he said, handing over what seemed like a lot of cash.

'Here's your change.' She rolled her eyes as he walked away, pledging not to bother with the small talk anymore.

As Ben left the store, he tossed the twenty-pence piece onto the lap of the woman sitting outside. She looked up and thanked him, then watched as he got on his motorbike and drove away. Seconds later, the woman with the new carrier bag came out of the shop and smiled at the young woman. They walked away together.

At seven-thirty Lara entered the breakfast room and sat down at the only table with cutlery. The first thing she noticed was that the table wasn't set for one. As she looked at the placings, uncertainty set in. Had she misunderstood John? Was he intending to dine with her? Of course, that was natural as he was a guest too and it would be silly to sit at different tables. She calmed down.

The smell of garlic was drifting from the direction of the kitchen and her appetite overcame any nervousness about the next couple of hours. If only she had a glass of wine. As if reading her mind, John entered the room carrying a bottle and two glasses.

'I bought red and white just in case you have a preference. Or would you prefer a soft drink?'

'Red for me, thanks,' she replied. It was now clear it was a table for two. 'The food smells delicious.'

'It's nothing too gourmet, I'm afraid. There wasn't a wonderful choice of vegetables in the local store so your dose of Vitamin C will have to come from the salad side dish.'

Lara laughed as she took a sip from the glass of wine just handed to her. 'It sounds like you have gone to a great deal of trouble. I must contribute something.'

'You already are,' he replied.'

Although she blushed at the comment, Lara felt warm inside. She barely knew John but after only a sip of wine, she felt completely at ease in his company. Over the next few hours, she learnt that he was twice divorced with a seventeen-year-old daughter. He and his first wife were on fairly good terms and still exchanged birthday presents.

'That's nice for your daughter. I suppose it must have been difficult for her when you split up.'

'She was still a baby so didn't know any different. Kath and I moved in together while at university to save on rent. It wasn't supposed to be a milestone in our lives. Then she got pregnant. Of course, we married because it seemed the right thing to do but, unfortunately, it wasn't. The dynamics of our relationship had changed for the worse. We realized that we had been friends more than anything else and neither of us wanted to spend the rest of our lives married to one another. It seemed sensible to split while Tammy was too young to notice.'

'But you married again,' Lara said.

'Yes, but that time I waited until I was much older. Charlotte and I met through mutual friends, and it was love at first sight … that is it was love at first sight for me,' he added. His tone was bitter.

'She must have loved you to marry you.'

He smirked. 'She loved my job, not me.'

'Your job?'

'Nothing glamorous unless you're into wigs.' The tone of his voice had become humorous once more, but his face was sad.

'John, what are you talking about? What do you do?'

'I'm a judge.'

Lara burst into laughter.

'So, you are not impressed.'

'I was wondering if you were a drag queen, but I must admit that a judge sounds almost as bizarre.'

'Bizarre is not what I was expecting you to say.'

'I don't mean being a judge is bizarre. I thought judges were old. You can't be much into your forties.'

'I'm forty actually but I'll try not to be offended.'

'Getting back to Charlene -'

'Charlotte.'

'Getting back to Charlotte, what caused you to split up, if you don't mind me asking?'

'She got frustrated with my lack of ambition. I didn't go into law for the thrill of holding a gavel. I wanted to be someone who sought justice for everyone, not just the people who could afford the best lawyers. Anyway, that's enough about me. Who is waiting for you at home?'

Lara wasn't ready to bear her soul, even after John had done so, and her hesitation was enough for him to quickly change the question.

'Do you get on well with your parents?'

A relieved Lara talked about her happy upbringing and how much she loved her parents, especially her mother, who still worried about her as if she were still a child.

'I have never wanted for anything. My friends envied my large bedroom which I didn't have to share with anyone being an only child, well, *their* only child anyway.'

'Are they both well?'

'Yes. They are nearly seventy and haven't had a night in hospital between them. It's a pity I don't have their genes.'

'What did you do when you left school?' he asked.

'When I finished school, I went into teaching, but I've taken a break from it for a year. I've got a job at a high school which starts after Christmas so I'm hoping that works out well for me.'

'It sounds to me like you're considering a career change?'

'I don't know to be honest. The last year has been difficult, and I haven't felt able to give the pupils the attention they deserve. Hopefully, things will get better soon.'

'Sometimes you have to care about yourself,' he replied. 'Is there anyone special in your life?'

Willing herself not to well up, Lara merely shook her head and raised an empty glass to her lips. This prompted John to jump up.

'I'll get us another bottle.'

Lara shook her head again. 'No, it's okay. I've had quite enough already. I'm not used to drinking. In fact, I think I'll go up to my room now. Thank you for a lovely meal, John.'

Before John had a chance to suggest a coffee, Lara had disappeared. He picked up the dishes and returned to the kitchen.

It was a clear night and Tanya shivered as she turned off the high street towards the towpath. Evening temperatures were falling each day regardless of how warm the afternoons had been, and she made a mental note to dig out her warmer clothes once she got home. The towpath was deserted but she wasn't scared as she had walked it thousands of times, although it wasn't quite the same without a dog. Hopefully, she wouldn't have to wait long. She didn't want to give any passing man the wrong impression. For now, there was no sign of any men and she relaxed. The water glistened as it reflected the night sky and she remembered how beautiful the disused canal could be. Perhaps it was time to get another dog to give herself a legitimate reason to be lurking about on a dark evening.

She heard footsteps coming from behind her and reached into the bag she was carrying. As she pulled out the small parcel, she spoke to the approaching figure. 'Didn't we say ten thirty? I've been here ages.'

Suddenly she was coughing up the water which had flowed through her wide-open mouth. There was no chance to work out why she was in the canal. She just had to get out as quickly as she could. Looking up through her watery eyes she saw a figure bending down as though to reach her. Thank goodness, she thought, as she felt the hand grasping for her shoulder, wait no, her hair. Then she was under the water again but this time she was unable to lift her head out. Someone was holding her head down. In a last desperate attempt to escape, she pushed her feet against the canal wall and sprang back with as much force as she could manage. The hands lost their grip, and she was free. She raised her head above the water, gasping to refill her lungs with air. The figure was still there. Tanya glimpsed the black locks of hair coming from the hood just before the rock smashed down on her face and she was below the water once again.

Chapter Eleven

It was only seven o'clock, but Lara could hear movement coming from downstairs. John had given Flora the day off, so it had to be him down there. Lara felt nervous even though she told herself there was absolutely no reason to. John was merely looking after the hotel while his mother was in hospital and that was all there was to it. He was already twice divorced so it was almost certain that he was in another relationship, even if he hadn't mentioned one.

A flash of horror ran through her mind as she remembered that there was only one bathroom in the tiny hotel. She'd noticed Mrs Parsons using the same one as the guests so there obviously wasn't a family bathroom somewhere. What if she bumped into John while she was on the landing? What if he wanted to use the bathroom at the same time? Then she heard footsteps on the gravel outside and the sound of a car engine starting.

She rushed to the window in time to see John's car reversing out of the driveway. He could be going back to the hospital or just nipping to the shop. Determined not to make the same mistake again, she rushed out to the bathroom and had the quickest shower possible before putting her pyjamas back on and running back to her room. A few minutes later, she heard the car pulling into the drive. He was back.

When she got downstairs Lara saw that the table was set for one and she wondered if she'd offended John the night before. If she had offended him, he covered it well as he entered the room whistling and carrying a cafetiere of coffee and a jug of cream.

'Would you like the full English – sausage, bacon, egg, beans, mushrooms and toast?' he asked, holding an imaginary notepad.

Lara smiled before ordering poached egg on toast. She laughed when he said it might be a while as he had never attempted to poach an egg before.

'I shall try to the best of my ability, but I only bought a dozen eggs. Therefore, if I get as far as the tenth egg without success, you will have to make do with scrambled.'

'Now you mention it, I meant to say scrambled not poached,' she said.

But he returned ten minutes later with two perfect poached eggs on hot buttered toast, provoking a gasp of approval from Lara.

'I think you were lying about the eggs. Have you already eaten?' she asked.

'Yes. I had a bowl of Shredded Wheat earlier, and, in case you're wondering, I only had two.'

'I hope you didn't buy all that stuff just for me,' she said. 'I would have been happy with Shredded Wheat too.'

'To tell you the truth there are some burly builders checking in later so I thought I might as well offer them a decent breakfast.'

'Will your mother mind you doing that?' she asked.

'Not as long as she doesn't find out. I rang the hospital earlier and they are operating on her arm to reset a bone. You might not see her again.'

'Oh, dear. Poor Mrs Parsons. Maybe I'll visit her tomorrow.'

John sat down at the table and poured himself a coffee. 'How long are you going to stay here, Lara? You are spending a lot of money to hang around such a miserable place, and that's just this house.'

They both laughed before he continued in a serious tone. 'I wouldn't charge you but it's my mother's business and she's a wizard at accounting.'

He remained silent while waiting for Lara to speak. She was still eating so it had not been the best moment to ask her such a question. But she was thinking too. Finally, she opened her mouth.

'John. If you had been the judge in Tom Bailey's trial, would you have found him guilty of Bella's murder?'

'Wow! That's a sixty-four-thousand-dollar question. I suppose I should have seen that one coming. Look Lara it's not my role to find anyone guilty or not guilty. I merely advise the jury on the evidence they have to consider then it is up to them.'

'What happens if you think they have come to the wrong verdict? That must happen sometimes. Surely you can't let an innocent person go to jail.'

'I know what you are suggesting but it is too late now. Tom Bailey was convicted of Bella's murder and has already served a long sentence.'

'And he's just been granted parole,' Lara said. 'He'll be back here any time soon.'

'I don't think you should be here then. He's a dangerous man who's killed before and is more than capable of doing so again.'

'How would I go about getting the police reports on Bella's case, John?'

'Is there any reason for doing that?'

'I don't think he did it. In fact, I know he didn't, and I need to know why he was convicted.'

John's expression was one of astonishment after hearing Lara's declaration. 'What makes you think he isn't guilty? It can't be anything that's in the public domain.'

'Well, it's in my domain and I intend to tell the police once I have all the facts.'

'Will you at least tell me first?'

'I will tell you, John. Just give me more time. So, how can I get the police reports?'

He appeared to think carefully before replying. 'You can send for the court proceedings records. They'll tell you what the evidence was against him plus witness statements, and defence arguments. I'm sure that after reading them you'll change your mind.'

'Thanks, but I doubt it. Now, as for these court records, I don't know where to start looking. Will you help me?'

'No, I won't.'

This time there was no doubt. It was murder. Tanya's bloodied face was a sign that the attack was personal, rather than a robbery gone wrong. Besides, the assailant had left behind any likely target, including her handbag. It now seemed certain that Tanya Price did not murder Hanna Evans.

'At this rate, you will be our number one suspect,' Brooks told his colleague, as the body was removed from the canal path.

Paul didn't appreciate the humorous comment and, snapping his notebook shut, he walked back to the car.

His colleague, however, was all too aware of the implications of this second murder. 'Seriously, Paul, I'm worried about these two deaths. This is a tiny town. No, it's not even a town, it's a village. There hasn't been a murder here for twenty years and now we have two that are clearly related. It's about time we brought in Lara Campbell for questioning. She's the only woman left that matches the witness's description.'

'There is the Bailey woman,' Paul said. 'Perhaps something has pushed her over the edge. She must have heard that Bella Young's sister has shown up here. I'm sure that would upset her.'

'That's unlikely though, isn't it? People don't suddenly become serial killers. We know all there is to know about Connie Bailey, whereas, for all we know, Lara Campbell might just have stepped out of a psychiatric hospital. No, these killings have only happened since Lara Campbell came here and my money is on her.'

'That's not enough though. We don't know that there is a connection between both deaths. I'm still not convinced that Hanna Evans was murdered and this one could be a domestic. What on earth was she doing down here so late at night? Check her husband's whereabouts for last night. Did he report her missing?'

'No, but he might not have noticed her gone. He has been known to travel out of the area. Selling his wares, no doubt.'

'Just like his wife,' Paul said, looking at the drugs in Tanya's handbag.

Initially, Lara was shocked and upset by John's refusal to help her trace the court records. When he explained his reasons, however, she accepted them while vowing to press on with her mission, nonetheless. He'd insisted that she could be getting herself into danger by looking into the police investigation, especially when those same police officers were locals. As a peace offering, he insisted on taking her out for coffee and cake and, finding it hard to stay cross with him, she accepted.

Thirty minutes later they were sipping cappuccinos in Jenny's café and discussing the spectacular view. John had suggested driving out of the area, but Lara secretly wanted to see Jenny's reaction when they walked in together. Jenny smiled at them as she took their order before making a call on her mobile.

'Did you find Bella attractive, John?' It was the question Lara had wanted to know the answer to since meeting John Parsons.

'Did I find Bella attractive? That's a bit personal, isn't it? Well, she was attractive. Of course, she was attractive, but I wasn't attracted to her. That's a special feeling, isn't it? Bella wasn't my type.' His eyes shifted momentarily towards Jenny.

Lara followed her companion's gaze. 'Do you know Jenny well?'

'Not really. She was Bella's best friend, so I only knew what Bella told me about her.'

'And what was that?'

'That Jenny was kind, beautiful, and generous. Some thought that Jenny was using her, but Bella always defended her. She even wrote a song about her, well the lyrics anyway. I helped her with the music.'

'You are a very talented man,' Lara said.

'And you are teasing me. Bella became a far better musician than I ever was. I merely helped her with the chords.'

'I wish I could have heard her sing,' Lara said quietly. 'There's nothing left of her. It's as if she never even existed.'

'Of course, it's not,' John said softly. 'Bella is alive and kicking in both our memories. I'm sure Jenny misses her too.'

'Maybe she loved Jenny. She never had a boyfriend, did she?'

'It was probably a schoolgirl crush. Please don't take offence at this but socially, Bella was out of Jenny's league. I'm sure she looked up to Jenny.'

'They were hardly schoolgirls. I know Bella wasn't exactly prom queen material, but Jenny said she had a lot of male admirers. Tanya suspected Bella was seeing someone. If it wasn't you, who could it have been?' Lara watched for any agitation or anger from John after her comment but there was none.

'A bad type, no doubt. When she was fifteen she was involved in a car crash. The car was stolen from a car park. Witnesses saw a man in the car, but he got away. Bella took the rap for it. He could have been the one who Jenny is talking about.'

'Yes, I know.' The number of times John had said Jenny's name had not gone unnoticed by Lara, but she made no comment on it. 'Your mother mentioned it to me. Didn't Bella ever tell you who the man was?'

'No, but it was definitely one of her friends – Chris, Paul, or Ben. It's hard to imagine it now. They all have or had respectable careers.'

As have you, she thought.

Suddenly the café door was flung open, and a woman rushed over to Jenny. She was hysterical. Lara and John watched on as the woman yelled at Jenny while pointing over to them. Then the police walked in.

'She's crazy. She's going to kill all of us. You have to arrest her, Paul.'

Lara looked on in shock as the woman pointed at her accusingly while Jenny attempted to calm her. Detective Paul Croft was also looking at her with suspicion.

Jenny did her best to calm the hysterical woman. 'What's brought this on, Simone? You need to calm down.'

'Tanya's dead now. She's been murdered, just like Hanna. It's obvious she did it,' Simone cried while looking at Lara.

Paul Croft told Simone to sit down before walking over to John and Lara's table.

'Where were you between ten o'clock and twelve last night, Miss Campbell?'

'She was with me. We were having dinner at my mother's hotel. We were together from seven o'clock,' John replied before Lara had a chance to gather her thoughts.

Tanya had been murdered, and Lara sensed that everyone in the café suspected her, everyone except John.

'And this dinner lasted for the entire period?' The question from the other detective was suggestive and Lara blushed.

'No. We went to bed separately at about half past ten.'

'Is this correct, Miss Campbell?'

'Yes. I'd had a long day and the meal tired me out.'

'Can you be certain that Miss Campbell didn't leave the hotel later last night, Mr Parsons?' Paul's tone was respectful towards the off-duty judge.

'Yes, because she wouldn't have been able to get back in. Guests are not given keys.'

'Do you usually have such an early night, too?' asked Detective Brooks, addressing John with less respect than his colleague.

'I had work to do. You can check my computer records.'

'They must be in it together. He had a thing for Bella.'

'Be quiet, Simone. John wasn't even here when Hanna was killed.' Jenny had resumed her role as mediator.

'Everyone here will need to come to the station to make a statement. Simone, can you tell your husband to accompany you?'

'I don't know where he is.'

'I'm here.' Chris walked over to his wife and held open his arms. Everyone gasped when Simone turned towards Jenny and slapped her across the face.

It was Lara's second statement. She had resisted John's attempts to coach her while they made the journey to the police station together. Their statements were sure to match, and she still had faith in the police despite the miscarriage of justice regarding her sister. Surely the two murders should convince people that Tom Bailey had not murdered Bella. She would use the police interview to persuade them to reopen the case.

However, the police did not give Lara the opportunity to speak beyond answering their questions. Her alibi for Hanna's murder was non-existent as no one had seen her once she'd left the Royal Oak. John accounted for her movements the night before, but did they believe him?

They'd gone to the police station together and given their statements to different officers. Paul interviewed her. Perhaps he couldn't bring himself to question John whom he clearly respected. However, Paul had no such qualms when it came to Lara. He said he would be keeping an eye on her from then on.

While driving back, John insisted on knowing everything Lara had written in her statement. 'The police can feel under pressure to solve a serial killer case, and that's what leads to so many false arrests.'

'What about false convictions?' she asked.

'It would be extremely unusual nowadays, what with so many advances in forensic science. But being arrested is bad enough. It can sully a reputation forever. "There's no smoke without fire" is a common phrase in the Law Courts.'

'As you're a judge, an arrest would be far worse for you.'

'Why did you miss out the all-important adjective?'

'False arrest,' she replied.

'You might have told me Chris was staying here, Jenny.' Simone had calmed down and all three were sitting around one table in the now closed café. Jenny's hand nursed her stinging cheek but any anger she felt was towards Chris. He had persuaded her to betray her friend.

'To be fair to Jenny, she was reluctant to let me stay. She insisted it was just for one night,' Chris said. But his defence of Jenny seemed to irritate his wife.

'I don't see your bags packed, Chris.'

'Give me a chance. I have to find somewhere else to stay.'

Simone looked defeated. 'You can come home tonight. The children won't want you wandering around while there's a serial killer on the loose.' She left the café before her husband had a chance to respond.

Simone fought back tears as she got back into her car. She had been married to Chris for ten years and had known him for twenty. Despite this, however, she wondered how much she really did know him.

When injury forced him to retire from football, he was a broken man, both physically and emotionally. He needed someone to move him forward and she had been quick to take on that role.

Her father was the owner of a semi-professional football club and she'd persuaded him to give Chris a chance as coach. It worked. Chris was back in the game he loved thanks to her. They married soon after. It was a traditional church wedding which made the local paper. Suddenly, Simone was the envy of dozens of women as Chris excelled at his new career. They were the perfect couple from the outside – young, successful, and glamorous. But he didn't love her. Not that she cared anymore. He had given her the two children she craved, and she no longer cared about the late nights, mystery messages, or suspicious odours on his clothes.

She could imagine Tanya sinking so low as to have an affair with her friend's husband, but not Jenny. Now Tanya was dead, as was poor Hanna, and there had to be a connection between the murders and the anonymous notes. The appearance of Bella's sister made the connection even more likely. Were the two murders connected to the trial? Her initial impression was that Lara was the culprit, but on seeing her slight frame and innocent face, she was no longer sure. Whoever killed Tanya and Hanna, would probably come after her too. Suddenly she turned the car around and headed in the opposite direction towards her parents' house.

'You know you have to go back Chris, not just for yourself but for the kids too. They'll be devastated to lose their dad.' Jenny was shocked to hear Chris expressing his wish to stay with her another night even though Simone was allowing him to go home. They'd spent the last couple of hours trying to get hold of Tanya's family members without success. Much to her shame, Jenny was secretly relieved as she'd never had time for Tanya's husband or parents. Finally, their attention returned to Chris's marital problems.

'I can't face it right now. I can't face her, and I can't face her family. For the past ten years, I have been indebted to them. Every decision I make, every word I say, I have to consider how they will react. One word from Simone and I'll be out of a job.'

'But that's ridiculous, Chris. You are excellent at your job. Simone's father would be crazy to sack you and Simone wouldn't do it to the children. I'm sure they'd be devastated if you left.'

'It doesn't matter now. I've had an offer from another club, a bigger club. I need to get away from here and that's my ticket.'

'But Chris your whole life is here. Don't throw away everything without trying to put things right first.'

Chris put his head in his hands. When he looked up Jenny could see tears in his eyes. 'Jenny, I need to tell you something. I should have told you years ago.'

Jenny grabbed his hands in hers before saying, 'It's okay, Chris. I know. I've always known.

Chapter Twelve

Mrs Parsons hobbled across the hallway with the help of her daughter. Flora was struggling with two holdalls in her free hand, so Lara rushed across to help her.

'It's good to see you looking well, Mrs Parsons. Your son has been taking good care of me.'

'Huh! He's done his bit for the next five years,' Flora snapped. 'Now I have to take care of this place, as well as studying.'

'Oh, do stop, Flora,' Mrs Parsons said. 'I don't know what I would have done without John coming down. His work can't wait for my recovery, unlike your studies.'

'The prodigal son returns, then goes away the next day,' Flora whispered to Lara.

Lara followed the two women into the kitchen, laid the bags on the floor then exited before witnessing any further family business. So, Flora was taking over the role of carer from John which meant that he would be leaving soon. Disappointment swept over her as she made her way back upstairs. It was comforting to talk to someone who cared about Bella, who tried to help her and had genuinely liked Bella. She wondered if John liked her too, though she doubted it would be in a romantic way. She was not ready for that anyway. But there was a connection between them that made her look forward to being with him. Suddenly, he was right in front of her causing her to jump.

'Sorry! I should have looked where I was going, Lara. Are you okay?'

'Yes, thanks. You surprised me, the second surprise I might add. John I've heard you're -'

Lara, I have to go back to Cambridge this afternoon. I'm sorry to leave you, especially with all that's been happening. Here's my card. Ring me if you need to talk.'

Lara did her best to hide her feelings. 'Thanks, John. Because of you, I feel like I know Bella now, at least more than I did before.'

John hugged Lara and kissed her on the cheek. 'I'll try to get back here in the next few days. Please take care.'

Lara was startled and confused by the show of affection and didn't notice he'd gone until Flora called out to her.

'Would you like some dinner?'

'What?' Lara realised the female voice wasn't John's then saw that Flora was waiting for an answer to her question.

If she'd seen her brother's actions, Flora made no comment. 'I'm making a pasta dish if you'd like some. You shouldn't go out alone with a killer on the loose.'

Well, at least Flora didn't suspect her of the murders. 'Thanks. I love pasta.'

'It's a veggie sauce.'

'Even better.'

Flora began to walk away then stopped and turned around. 'Was my brother able to help you?'

'What do you mean?'

'Was he able to help you find out about your sister? My mother told me about her. She and John knew each other well, according to her.'

'Yes, he did help. He told me about her musical aspirations. She was very talented, it seems.'

'I was too young to remember her. There's quite a gap between my brother and me.'

'Yes, I'd gathered that. You must have been very young when John went away to university.'

'I don't even remember him going, just coming back for holidays. He was always with some woman or other.' She paused as though remembering something. 'Did he give you a photograph of her? He was always taking photos.'

'Oh. He didn't mention anything about photographs. He couldn't have taken any of my sister.'

'I'd be surprised if he didn't. He's got a box full of them in the attic. Wait here!'

Lara heard Flora's footsteps running up an unseen flight of stairs. After several minutes, she returned carrying a battered cardboard box.

'Don't worry. I've had a flick through them and can't see anything X-rated. My brother had a lot of girlfriends, so I can't tell if she is in here or not.'

There were images of many different women amongst the photographs in the box, all of them young and pretty. Of course, that meant nothing as John was also young at that time and was probably just as charming as he was now. Lara carefully sifted through the contents of the box, amazed at how many faces she saw. Then she saw Bella. With a guitar resting on her knee, hair curled, and eyes made up, she looked like an eighties pop star. Did John really not find her attractive? Perhaps he wouldn't admit it if he had.

Lara stared at the photograph of Bella. If only voices could be stored in boxes, she thought. Then, as if by magic, a cassette slipped out from under the piles of photos. It was the kind of cassette that teenagers used to record the pop charts on, but John didn't seem the type to do that. The tape was labelled *B*. After taking it out of its case, she placed the battered tape in the cassette holder. She hesitated. What if it snaps? Or worse, what if it gets tangled up in the cassette player? But John must have forgotten that it existed, or he would have mentioned it to her.

Ben was angry and uncooperative when the detectives asked him to make a statement.

'Why should I? It's got nothing to do with me?'

'But you knew Tanya Price. Anything you remember about any contact you've had with her could be crucial,' Paul said, trying his best to placate Ben.

'I knew her twenty years ago as you know full well. I take it you're talking to all her customers.'

Paul lowered his voice. 'Listen Ben we are trying to piece together everything we can about Lara Campbell. You spent some time with her yesterday. You need to tell us about that meeting.'

Ben grinned before saying, 'You can't seriously think she's a killer. She's as jumpy as a box of frogs. At no point did I feel like I was in danger.'

'Stop being an arse.' The other detective couldn't understand why his superior officer was letting Ben wrap rings around him with jibes and sarcasm. 'Where were you the night Hanna Evans died?'

Ben grinned again. 'Why didn't you just ask me that? I was with Chris Farmer. We went out on the boat. He'd had an argument with Simone and wanted to clear his head.'

'What time was that?' asked Brooks.

'No idea. I don't have a watch. The sun was setting if that helps.'

'And how long did you spend out on the boat? Sunset is before eight o'clock right now. That doesn't give you an alibi, Ben.'

'An hour or so. Then we had a drink in the house.'

'Oh! So now we have a different story. Were you inside or outside with your friend Chris?' demanded Brooks.

Ignoring Brooks, Ben looked at his old school friend. 'What about you, Paul? Have you got an alibi?' Then he walked away without another word.

'What is his problem?' asked Brooks angrily. 'No wonder he has no friends. He's a layabout without a purpose.'

Paul watched his former friend climb onto his motorbike and ride out of sight. 'Don't be so critical. I had a drink with him when he first left the Navy. All he ever talked about at school was joining the Navy, seeing the world, and protecting our shores. When ISIS took hold in Iraq, he blamed himself for being part of the forces that allowed it to happen. That's why he left the Navy and cut himself off from the world.'

'Huh! He should count himself lucky he wasn't in the army like my brother. I bet he didn't even set foot in Iraq.'

The voice was pitch-perfect, reflecting the years spent in the church choir. Listening to the tape, Lara was transported to a time in her late sister's life that was filled with hope and ambition. Bella had a talent, no, a gift. If only she'd had the chance to share it with the world. As she listened to the lyrics along with the painfully beautiful melody, Lara wept. The whole song was near the end of the tape, the earlier recordings being outtakes filled with errors. John's voice could be heard in the background, giving various instructions, his tone ranging from gentle to irritated. As the song ended, he clapped and whooped. The recording continued:

Perfect. That was perfect. You are perfect.

Thanks. Can I have the tape?

Okay, after I make a copy.

Silence.

What's wrong?

Nothing.

Yes, there is. I can tell you are keeping something from me.'

I wrote to a record producer, and he wants to meet me.

Which record producer? Stock, Aitken, or Waterman?

Don't laugh. He's independent. I sent a photograph.

For goodness's sake, Bella. He's clearly not interested in your voice.

Will you lend me money for the fare and one night in a hotel? It comes to two hundred pounds.

No.

Why not? I thought you wanted to help me.

I'm not giving you money to meet some dodgy guy who likes your picture. And I'm sure he intends making use of that hotel room.

You're jealous!

How can I be jealous of a man I don't know? I told you I'd help you find gigs and track down scouts, but I want to be there to keep an eye on things.

167

So that's it. You hate it that I might make something of myself without you. All you want is to feel good about yourself. You don't care about me at all. I bet as soon as you finish university, you'll forget all about me. You just don't care. If you did, you'd lend me the money.

Lend you the money! Why don't you go into comedy instead?

I will give you the money back. He said he'd reimburse me.

Don't be so sure he'll give you two hundred pounds for the little rendezvous. Perhaps you'll need to book another night at the hotel.

You basta -

Get out! I never want to see you again.

Lara kept listening, hoping to hear her sister's voice again. But there was silence until the play button jumped up to signal the end of the tape.

Simone watched the soapy hands of her mother splashing around in the sink, occasionally lifting a piece of cutlery or crockery to examine. What was it about mothers that made them refuse to use a dishwasher, Simone thought? This irritation helped detract from her mother's other irritating habit which was to tell her daughter "I told you so" about her marriage to Chris. She was right, of course, but Simone was never going to accept that her marriage should not have happened when she had two children from it.

'He's probably got another family somewhere. I've always said that, haven't I?'

'Not to me, you haven't, and I think I would have noticed by now, Mum. He doesn't earn that much.'

'I've told you that he's been seen sneaking around in places he shouldn't be. This is a small town, Simone, and nothing goes unnoticed. And where is he now? Shacked up with your other friend. He certainly didn't waste any time.'

'Jenny's not interested in him in that way. They're just friends.'

'Now that I can believe. If she were interested, he would have married her, I'm sure. He was always like a sick puppy around her.'

'Thanks, Mum. Thanks a lot.'

Once again the two detectives were looking through CCTV footage but this time it didn't take long to find what they were looking for. Tanya could be seen walking down the slope leading to the canal at about ten thirty pm. Over the next half hour, other than a few habitual dog walkers, only one person could be seen walking the same way. That person was Ben. Minutes later, he came back down the ramp and walked off towards the high street. There was no obvious explanation for his being there innocently, and he hadn't mentioned it during the ad hoc interview. One thing was certain. Ben had been all over the place regarding his alibi. The timings were out. He could not have been with Chris on the boat, or in his house while also caught on camera in Weston. It was either a mistake or a lie. The Chief Inspector ordered the arrest of Ben Sutton.

'Why didn't you tell me about the cassette?' Lara was giving John the opportunity to tell her about the argument with Bella because she wanted to give him the benefit of the doubt.

'What tape? I don't remember any tape?'

'This tape,' she said, holding the tape in front of the video camera.

'Oh. If it's mine I can't believe it still plays. And I don't remember recording Bella singing, but I obviously did. I must be getting old. I'm sorry about that, Lara. Of course, I would have given it to you if I'd remembered.'

'It's not just Bella singing, though. You are both arguing on the recording.'

'Were we? That doesn't sound unusual. Bella was a feisty young lady.'

'She didn't sound feisty. You were really mean to her. It sounded like she slapped you.'

The half-smile on John's face faded and he no longer looked amused at Lara's interrogation. His eyes moved away from the camera, seemingly a reaction to the reference to Bella's slap. He remained silent.

'Did Bella slap you?'

'That must have been the time she asked me to lend her the fare to London.'

'John, did she slap you?'

'Yes, she did. And I deserved it. I was frustrated when she wouldn't listen to the danger of meeting a stranger. Ironic, I suppose.'

'Did you make up after that argument?'

'No. At least I don't remember seeing her after that, but she did write to me afterwards. She wanted to lend money but this time for a guitar. She was probably lying about the guitar and just wanted it to try her luck with that so-called agent again. This time I gave in and told her to ask my mother for it, but I don't think she did. I'm sorry, Lara, but I'd forgotten about that argument.'

'How could you forget when her life ended so violently?'

'Unfortunately, in my job, I am all too familiar with violent ends.'

'But you said you cared about her. How can you compare her to dead people that you never even knew? I don't believe you forgot.' Lara threw the phone onto the bed in anger. Then she stared at it, waiting for it to ring. But John didn't ring back.

'I wish you'd buy a bloody phone,' Chris shouted, as he slammed his car door shut.'

'I have a phone,' Ben replied, knowing full well what his friend meant.

'What is the point of a landline when you are never on land? You could at least have an answering service.'

'What's so urgent?' Ben asked. This was the fourth time in as many days that someone had visited him at the harbour. It was not the solitary life he was used to.

'You need to listen. I've heard through the grapevine that you're about to be arrested for Tanya's murder.'

Ben did not respond immediately. Instead, he stared out to sea which made his friend nervous.

'Ben! They could come for you any minute.'

Finally, Ben turned around. 'What am I supposed to do? My boat will only go out so far.'

'This is serious, Ben.'

'I believe you.'

The two friends stood silently, digesting their predicaments, until Ben spoke.

'It looks like we've got ourselves caught in a lie. Fancy a ride?'

There was no time to worry about rolling up his tracksuit bottoms. Chris waded out to the tiny rowing boat in which Ben was returning to land. Then Ben changed direction to row back out to the sailing boat he'd just tied to a buoy. It seemed a pointless exercise given that they could have talked on the shore, but Chris was used to his friend's odd ways. Once they were settled on the sailing boat, Ben was the first to talk.

'So, what were we doing while Tanya was being murdered?'

'We were out on this boat, of course. Nobody can prove otherwise, Ben.'

'That didn't cover us for the time she died so I said we went inside and got drunk.'

'Okay. I'll say I forgot about leaving the boat to go inside. It'll still work.'

'Unless one of us was seen somewhere else. I think they are on to me. They might have found my image on CCTV somewhere else. If I am, then your alibi is scuppered too, Chris.'

Now it was Chris who stared out to sea. Both men remained silent for a few minutes. Once again, it was Ben who broke the silence.

'You shouldn't hitch your wagon to my alibi, Chris. There's no need for you to be involved in this. If they have me on camera somewhere I shouldn't be, I'll deal with it. But I can't deal with your problem too. I'm not taking the rap to cover your backside.'

'It's too late. I've already said I was with you, Ben. You can't turn your back on me now.'

'It's too late for you Chris, not me.'

Chapter Thirteen

Lara replaced the remains of the stalks with fresh roses. Were roses suitable for a sister? She wasn't sure, but no one would judge except Bella ... if she were able to see her own grave. The roses were expensive and would probably be eaten by the rabbits within hours, but it didn't matter. It gave Lara the chance to buy something special for her sister, her only blood relative. Of course, she would tell her parents about her feelings, and they would understand. They had always intended to contact Bella when their daughter had grown up. And they did try but Bella's rejection was too raw. Why didn't they take her too?

Lara had grown up in a respectable family who taught her the values of education, law, and order, and kindness to others. Most importantly, they gave her a stable family life. She had benefited from the upbringing they had given her after the terrible start she'd had with her blood mother and father. Not once had Lara felt any connection to the man and woman who had failed her. They had not cared about her or Bella as much as their drugs and alcohol. It was their fault that she and her sister were thrown into the last chance saloon of social services.

It had not been an easy decision for her parents to refuse any sort of contact between their adopted daughter and her sibling. There was a significant age gap. Bella was eight years older than Lara as their father had spent six years in prison between the two births. The two sisters were not close. The elder sister had no time for little Lara who contributed nothing to her hard existence. There was that one chance of a reunion, of course, but Bella rejected it. Lara could understand why Bella might feel angry about Lara coming to visit her just because the disadvantaged sister had done well at school. Bella's formative years were spent among drugs, alcohol, and violence.

Lara would probably never know what Bella endured during those years before each parent's death rescued her. Was Bella rescued though? No one protected or guided her. If only she knew that Lara was here with her now even if it was too late. Suddenly, a robin jumped onto the top of the gravestone. Lara reached out her hand, but it flew up onto a nearby branch. Time to go. After one last look at the flowers, she walked out of the church grounds noticing the robin was following her. She wondered if it was Bella.

Outside the grounds, she began walking in the direction of the sea.

'What's your game?'

She spun around to find a man's angry face leering into hers. It was a face she didn't recognise, patterned with tiny scars and pockmarks. Terror filled her. Although shorter than her, he was stocky, and she knew he could overpower her with one hand tied behind his back. He grabbed her shoulders and began shaking her. Too afraid to speak, she looked around for help but only traffic was passing. Was he going to hit her? He didn't hit her, but he did slam her against the stone wall of the church grounds and continued to shout, his words spitting in her face.

'You killed her, but you will not kill anyone else.'

'Get off her!'

A second male voice entered the melee. Ben hurled the other man away from Lara and the men began arguing. Finally, the unknown man walked away.

'Are you okay?' Ben asked her. 'Did he hurt you?'

Lara was shaking but she wasn't injured. 'Thanks. Who was that man?'

'Dave is Tanya's husband. He's got a temper which gets him into trouble a lot. Are you sure he didn't hurt you?'

'Yes, but he did scare me. I don't know what he would have done if you hadn't stopped him. Where did you come from? I didn't see you.'

'I was passing when I saw him grab you.' He glanced over to his motorbike which was parked a few feet away. 'Where are you going?'

'To see Jenny. Do you think he's gone?'

'Yes. He ran back towards town. What are you doing here?'

'I was putting flowers on my sister's grave. That is allowed, isn't it?'

'Of course, it is,' Ben said defensively. 'I forgot she was buried here.'

'I'm sorry. I had a row earlier and took it out on you. Thanks again for helping me.'

'What happened to your face? Dave didn't do that.'

Lara instinctively touched the cut on her face. It was already healing so clearly not fresh. 'A woman hit me while I was here the other day. I think she may have been on drugs.'

'Did you report it to the police?'

'No. I've seen her before. She looks troubled enough, so I didn't want to make things worse for her.'

Ben's eyes narrowed. 'What did she look like?'

'Mid to late twenties. Wears dark jeans, I think. And a hoody. Longish black hair, unbrushed. I've seen her begging outside the local shop.'

'Connie Bailey, no doubt. Troubled is not a strong enough word for her.'

'Bailey? You mean from that family.'

Suddenly, Lara felt an affinity towards the young woman who'd assaulted her. That could have been her if she hadn't been adopted.

'Do you want a lift?'

Lara glanced over at the motorbike. Was he kidding? 'I've never been on a motorbike before.

And what about a helmet?' Why didn't she just politely refuse?

'You don't want to run into Dave again already. Come on. I'll go slow.'

Jenny was bemused to see Ben parking up outside her café then helping Lara off his motorbike. She stepped outside to greet them, but Ben had already ridden off without a glance at his old school friend. A spark of resentment hit her as she watched Lara waving off her secret school crush - moody Ben who had never shown her the attention the other boys and girls had. The only girl he'd bothered with was Bella, but they were only wayward friends, at least that's what Bella always said. Maybe he was gay.

'How much did he charge you this time?' she asked.

Lara was still upset by her encounter with Dave and didn't respond immediately.

'What's the matter, Lara? You look shaken up. Was it the ride?'

Over a cup of tea, Lara told Jenny about her encounter with Dave, and how Ben had saved her from a possible physical assault. She didn't mention that her back was stinging from the contact with the stone wall. That was a type of assault but the last thing she wanted was to get Dave arrested.

'Dave is a scoundrel of the worst kind. He always was. It's his fault that Tanya got involved in drug dealing.'

Lara was shocked. 'Tanya was a drug dealer?'

'No. Tanya was the runner. She was a good girl until she went out with him. I told her to ditch him, but she was smitten. When Dave was kicked out of school, Tanya continued to sell drugs for him.'

'Did Bella know?'

'None of us knew until she confessed to the police. They interviewed all of us after Bella's murder. Tom Bailey had claimed that he met Tanya to buy drugs that night.'

'But I thought she was with you when he gave you a lift.'

'She was. Tom said that he met her during the ball. She admitted selling him drugs earlier that week, but not that day.'

'Did that come out in court?'

'No, because it wasn't relevant to the time of the murder. Bailey was just being vindictive when he said that about Tanya, even if she did sell drugs.'

'But why would Bailey lie about that? Perhaps that was the truth.'

'Lara, Bailey was too busy committing murder. Why won't you accept that?'

Jenny was right about one thing. Lara didn't accept that Tom Bailey had killed her sister. Undeterred, she veered the subject back to Tanya.

'And you really didn't know about her selling drugs until then?'

'No. My parents would have freaked if they'd known about her.'

'Why didn't they arrest Dave for drug dealing?'

'Because she never said where she got the drugs. She said that she was scared of being punished. They let her off because of her age but everyone thought Paul's father had a hand in that, her being his son's friend.'

'She was lucky.'

Jenny shook her head. 'Perhaps in one way, she was lucky. But it was a lesson she never learnt.'

'Could she have been murdered by a rival gang?' Lara asked. 'It's said that some coastal towns have a drugs problem. The young people don't know what to do with themselves.'

'Every day is like Sunday,' Jenny laughed. 'It's not that bad though. Where else would you get these views?'

Not getting the Morrisey reference, Lara moved on to the other murder. 'I suppose that wouldn't explain Hanna's death. She didn't look the type to break the law.'

'Absolutely not. Poor little Hanna. She didn't have much joy in her life. But I'm not sure that Hanna was murdered. I think the police have got it wrong and she really did kill herself. Poor thing.'

'Tanya said that you all had boyfriends around the time of the school ball.'

'They weren't proper boyfriends. We just hung around together. I had a brief encounter with Paul but that came to nothing. And there was Hanna and Chris, of course, but that didn't last long either.'

'Hanna went out with Chris?' Lara exclaimed. That was not mentioned before.

'Yes. She was crackers on him. I think that's why she didn't date much afterwards … because she was still holding a candle for him.'

'Why did they break up?' Lara asked. She wasn't impressed with the local heartthrob's taste in women.

'I suppose she was no longer good enough. She wasn't exactly the WAG type.'

'I could tell that when I met her.' Lara realised how catty she was sounding so moved the conversation away from Chris. 'Have you still got the selfie from the night at the pub?'

'Yes, I'm sure I have. Why?'

'Will you send it to me?'

Jenny looked confused. 'You're not in it.'

'I know but Bella's friends are.'

Jenny grinned. 'For your book, I suppose.'

In the police interview room, Ben was sitting opposite Croft and Brooks. There were no informalities this time, no whispering between old friends. Paul Croft resumed the role of detective while, this time, Ben was a person of interest.

'Where were you at approximately ten forty-five last Tuesday?'

'At home.'

'Can anyone vouch for you?'

'I live alone.'

'That's unfortunate.'

'I like it.'

'Earlier, you told us you were with Chris Farmer. Was that a lie?'

'I got the days muddled.'

Paul Croft, clearly irritated by Ben's elusive answers, got to the point. 'We have CCTV footage showing you near the canal at precisely that time.'

'Then I suppose that is where I was.'

'So, you just lied.' Brooks said.

'No, I was mistaken. I don't have a timetable that tells me when and where I need to be throughout the day.'

'Okay,' Paul said, 'Let's get to the reason you're here. What were you doing there at that time?'

Ben raised his one hand before saying, 'Okay. I admit it. I wanted to buy some cannabis from Tanya, but she didn't show.'

'But she did show, didn't she? We have footage of her on the canal bank waiting for someone.'

The colour drained from Ben's face. Up until that point he had been surly and his tone mocking, but Croft's last comment appeared to throw him. He looked worried. 'Where did she die?' he asked.

'We're asking the questions, Sutton, not you,' Brooks snapped.

'On the towpath,' Paul replied, ignoring his colleague's unhelpful remark. 'Her body was pulled from the canal the next morning. That's why we need to know your precise movements, Ben. So far you had the motive and opportunity.'

'What motive?' Ben shouted. 'Why would I want to kill her? She doesn't mean anything to me.'

'Drugs. You knew that she would be carrying drugs. Maybe you didn't fancy paying for them,' Brooks said. He saw no need to mention that the drugs were still in Tanya's handbag.

'But I didn't buy any. She wasn't there.' His voice was getting louder, and he was becoming flustered.

Suddenly, the door opened, and a suited woman entered the dingy room. She turned towards Ben. 'Don't say another word, Mr Sutton,' Then looking back at the two detectives, she shook her head as if disgusted. 'I hope you informed my client of his right to a solicitor.'

'We were just about to,' Paul replied.

After twenty minutes of "no comment", Ben was released without charge. He learnt that his parents had hired the solicitor immediately on hearing of their son's arrest. Despite himself, he was grateful to them.

As soon as Lara got back to the hotel, she began jotting down the morning's events. So, Tanya was a drug runner. What if Bella knew that and was blackmailing her friend? However, it couldn't have been that much of a secret if Jenny knew too. The encounter with Tanya's husband was as frightening as it had been unpleasant, yet somehow, she didn't think it was significant. He was angry about his wife's murder, and it was natural to blame it on Lara. She was, after all, the one digging up the long-buried past. And Tanya certainly had things to hide. But did she kill Bella? It seemed so unlikely that Lara refused to consider it. It had to be someone else, most definitely a man.

Her thoughts turned to John. His mother had implied that Bella had tried blackmailing John just before she died, but she didn't say what it was over. He sounded angry on the tape and could have hit Bella. Although he didn't seem the type, Lara didn't really know him at all. The police should have checked his alibi for the night of Bella's death, but they had firmly set their minds on Tom Bailey.

She thought about the men who were in the photograph that Jenny had shown her – Ben, Chris, and Paul. Maybe Ben was being blackmailed? He didn't hide his dislike of Bella. But what was his secret? He bought soft drugs, hardly the most serious offence for an eighteen-year-old to commit. Then there was Paul. He had a respectable career, one which would not allow any criminal record. When he visited Lara at the hotel on his own, she believed it wasn't in a professional capacity. Rather, he was there as a former acquaintance of Bella, Hanna, and Tanya. He seemed worried.

Last of all was Chris. All she knew about him was that he was married, had two small children, and was some sort of football coach. He had shown no interest in Lara, so it looked like her presence in the village did not bother him. Any of those three men, four including John, could have killed Bella. But so could a lot of people.

She took out the photograph of the five young women. Three of them were now dead, all of them murdered. Her phone pinged to reveal that Jenny had sent the selfie. Lara opened the image and looked at the three women. They were all smiling but their eyes told a different story – boredom. None of them really wanted to be there. Lara enlarged the picture to look at the woman she had met only fleetingly. Hanna was plain with mousy hair. Jenny was right. She looked more like a librarian than the girlfriend of a glamorous footballer. Even with her old friends, she looked nervous with the fingers of her one hand gripping the silver and onyx bangle on her arm. The bangle! Lara had seen it before. She picked up the torn photograph and looked closely at Bella. She was wearing that same bangle. Then she took out the photograph Jenny had given her. It was too difficult to see the detail, but Bella was wearing a bangle as they left the ball.

What are you going to do?' Paul's wife was gazing at the books in front of her even though it was obvious her attention was elsewhere.

Paul remained silent. His eyes were also fixed on the pile of books on the table as if he had an interest in them.

'You can't do anything. If you do, it's all over,' she said, answering the question for him.

'It's not quite as simple as that Rachel. There's talk of the case being re-opened to see if Tom had a particular grudge against any of us. If that happens, I'll have to explain where I was that night.

'Why? Just keep saying you were too drunk to remember. They believed it before.'

'Yes, but that was because they had no reason to care if it was the truth or not. The case was a slam dunk.'

'I hate those Americanisms. Haven't you got your own expressions? Anyway, nothing's changed as far as Tom Bailey is concerned, so just leave things be Paul.'

But Paul knew he couldn't leave things as they were. He had never been officially questioned about Bella's death, one of the dubious advantages of being the investigating officer's son. He only had to answer his father's occasional questions and even that was "off the record". Up until now, no one had commented on his absence from the trial, and it certainly wasn't in his interest to do so. But now he might have to.

Chapter Fourteen

For the first time, Lara considered the possibility that her sister's killer was female. Is it possible to tell the sex of an assailant from the marks left on a body? Hanna must have got the bangle from Bella one way or another. Would she kill her for it though? It was hard to believe. Lara thought of the friends' accounts of the night. They said that they were together which should rule out any of them committing such a crime alone. Surely the others wouldn't lie to protect a killer amongst them. They had all stated that Tom Bailey threatened them shortly before Bella was murdered so that had to be true. The friends claimed that they walked together until separating to go to their individual homes. Then Jenny was heard screaming and her friends chased off Bailey. He was trying to rape her. Jenny then stayed with Tanya which should rule both of them out. But what about Simone and Hanna? Neither of them had an alibi once they separated.

Lara snapped her notebook shut. She had to find out where both girls lived at the time. Could either of them have possibly returned to kill Bella? It might not have taken long if they lived close to the coast. After so many possibilities raced around her head, Lara decided to phone Jenny once again. Despite feeling that Jenny hadn't been completely open with her, she still trusted her.

An hour later, Lara was sipping a cappuccino. She took out both photographs of the five girls and then opened the selfie that Jenny had sent her. 'Jenny, look at the bangles. They're identical.'

A clearly nervous Jenny picked up the three images. Her eyes flicked from one photo to the other before she shook her head in confusion. 'Yes, it does look like the same bangle. Hanna must have lent it to Bella for the ball. Wait! That's not likely. Hanna wouldn't have done that for Bella.'

'She must have taken it from her,' Lara said.

Jenny's hand dropped from her mouth then she shook her head. 'Chris gave Hanna that bangle a few days after the ball.'

'Why? Why did Chris give Hanna a bangle?'

'I told you, they dated for a while,' Jenny explained. 'At the ball, they had a huge row and finished but Chris bought her the bangle as an apology. I suppose she kept it.'

Once again, Lara tried to imagine dowdy Hanna as the girlfriend of a glamorous footballer. 'What did they row about?'

'What?' Jenny looked lost.

'You said they had a huge row at the ball. What was it over?'

Jenny thought for a while before saying, 'Chris wanted to go clubbing with the boys instead of taking her home. She was insecure about their relationship and was always worried that he'd leave her for someone prettier.'

'How sad,' Lara said.

'Yes. Poor Hanna. He left her anyway when he joined a football club.'

'Did he go on to the nightclub?' Lara asked.

'I don't think he did, to be honest. Maybe he felt guilty about lying and that's why he bought the bangle for her. Fancy her keeping it all these years. She must have still carried a candle for him.'

'Jenny, Chris didn't buy the bangle. It was Bella's. No jewellery was recovered from Bella's body, or it would have been returned to me as her next of kin. Someone had to have taken it from her. And that's what Hanna realised when she looked at the photograph. She saw Bella wearing it and came to only one conclusion – Chris killed Bella.'

Lara knocked on Paul Croft's door. She needed to tell him about the bangle and how it could prove that Chris killed Bella, whatever Jenny said. As soon as she realised Chris was in the frame, Jenny had insisted the two bangles were not the same. She was obviously fonder of him than she was of Hanna.

The house was a three-storey Victorian terrace which seemed too large for a young couple without children. Standing on the porch, she could movement and braced herself for the upcoming encounter. Of course, she knew that it was wrong to go to his house, but she couldn't wait. If she went to the police station, they would palm her off with some constable. Or maybe not even that.

The door opened and Paul's wife looked at the visitor with curiosity, and then suspicion.

'I need to speak to Paul,' Lara said, without introducing herself.

'Who are you?' His wife now sounded suspicious too.

Lara apologised for the intrusion, realising how it might seem to the woman watching her, a strange young woman, looking for her husband. 'Are you Mrs Croft? My name is Lara Campbell. Your husband has interviewed me about the recent murders in the village. I have some important information to give him.'

'If that's the case, you need to go to the station. He won't see you here. This is our home.'

'But it's urgent. What I have to say will help his investigation. Is he here?' Lara raised her voice in the hope that, if Paul Croft was home, he would hear her. It worked.

'Who is it, Rachel?' he said, from the top of the stairs.

'It's Lara Campbell, Detective Croft,' Lara shouted before the other woman had a chance to reply. 'I need to speak to you urgently. It's about Hanna's murder. I think I know who did it.'

Paul walked slowly down the stairs and gestured for Lara to follow him into the kitchen. He closed the door behind them.

'What about your wife? Will she mind?' Lara asked, remembering the suspicion coming from Mrs Croft's eyes. She wondered if their marriage lacked trust. Did Paul play around? No. He didn't look the type.

'You really should have gone to the police station. Someone there would have taken your statement.'

But you let me in any way, Lara thought. 'I didn't want to waste any time. I've found out that Chris Farmer must have killed my sister. You have to question him about the night she was killed. Ask him about the bangle he gave to Hanna. It belonged to my sister.'

Paul rolled his eyes before opening the kitchen door again. 'You said it was information regarding Hanna Evan's murder, not a twenty-year-old solved case.'

'Don't you think they're linked?' she said angrily. 'What about the anonymous letters? How did you ever get to be an inspector?'

Paul's way of responding to the insult was to grab Lara by the arm and pull her back to the front door. 'If you think there was a miscarriage of justice regarding your sister's murder, maybe you should put it in your book. For now, I'm busy solving current murders.'

Lara stared at him with incredulity. 'Well, if you won't do anything, I'll ask Chris Farmer myself. I know where he lives.' A second later, the door was slammed in her face.

Ben hadn't seen his parents in over a year. It wasn't that he didn't get on with them, just that there never seemed to be the time. After all, it had been their decision to move over a hundred miles away. But now the time had come to show his appreciation for them stepping in to help him. He hadn't even considered asking for a solicitor but on reflection, he should have done so immediately. After nearly three hours, he finally reached his destination. Before he'd even got off his bike his mother had opened the front door. She looked unimpressed with his mode of transport.

'This is a nice surprise,' she said, as she stepped onto the drive. 'I do wish you'd buy a car, my dear. Those things are dangerous.'

'So are cars, Mum,' Ben replied, kissing her on the cheek. 'Is Dad in?'

''Yes. And you'd better prepare yourself because he's in a terrible mood.'

Ben walked straight into the kitchen, opened the fridge, and poured himself a large glass of orange juice. It was one of those things that he never got around to buying.

'You need a wife to look after you, Ben. I bet you haven't had a decent meal since you were last here.'

Ben knew that his parents were disappointed with him. His younger sisters had provided them with more grandchildren than they could remember the names of. It was beyond him why they would want any more. He assumed it was to carry on the family name.

'Hello, Son.' His father had joined them in the kitchen, too impatient to delay his lecture any longer. After a nod, Ben's mother left the room.

'Hi, Dad. Thanks for sorting out that solicitor for me. I'll pay you back, of course.'

'Don't be ridiculous. I don't care about the money. Just tell me what on earth is going on back there.'

'All I know is that two women are dead, and the police think they were both murdered. I'm not so sure.'

'They weren't just two women, Ben. They were your school friends. I'm surprised that you are not more upset. Why did the police arrest you?'

'Because they haven't got the slightest clue who the killer is and I'm a sitting duck without an alibi.'

'What do you mean you haven't got an alibi? Not for either of the murders?'

'Yes, Dad. That's what I mean. I was out on my bike the night Hanna died. I was parked up outside with some other bikers and saw her leaving the pub. After that, I forgot all about it.'.

'What about Tanya? Where were you then?'

At his father's questions, Ben was growing more and more nervous. Mr Sutton was a retired solicitor and Ben knew he would comb through his son's movements until no stone was left unturned. He knew he couldn't keep to the story about being with Chris, not now he was a suspect and the police had him on camera near the scene.

'I was there at the canal where she was killed. I'd gone there to meet her, but she wasn't there. I swear Dad, she wasn't there. She must have already been dead. The thing is they've got me on CCTV. They know I was there.'

'Why were you meeting her? Drugs I suppose. You need to pull yourself together, lad. Get yourself a proper job and you won't need that shit.'

Ben was shocked. He'd never heard his father swear before. 'I hate to tell you Dad, but that's not my biggest worry right now.'

His father looked strangely calm. 'Did you notice anyone else hanging around the canal?'

'It was dark and difficult to see but I thought I noticed someone's shadow further down the path. But if anyone else was there, they would have been caught on CCTV too. Unless there's another way to get up there. I'll check it out first thing tomorrow. If there is no other way out of the canal path, I'm in big trouble.'

'Don't worry about the CCTV. They need more than opportunity. They need evidence and they won't find any if you're innocent. Relax. If that's all they've got, they are wasting their time on you. I hope you're staying for dinner?'

On cue, Mrs Sutton returned to the kitchen. 'Of course, he's staying for dinner. Now sit there and tell me about more pleasant things that have been happening in Weston. I've heard Jenny's moved back. Now why don't you ask her out.'

Pretending to know Chris's address had been a bluff that hadn't worked. Lara had hoped that Paul would call her back which of course he didn't so he obviously wasn't concerned about her visiting a murderer.

She had no more luck when she phoned Jenny for the address. It wasn't clear if Jenny was being loyal to Chris or protective of her. "Leave it for now. I'm sure the police will know what's what." That's what Jenny had advised her to do, and Lara wondered if she should listen to her.

Ben told her to mind her own business, in so many words, though he seemed to have softened towards her. John was the only person who'd been willing to help her. However, since discovering the tape, she no longer trusted him. She would have to be careful what she said about him though, when talking to Flora and Mrs Parsons.

At the hotel, Mrs Parsons was back on her feet and bossing her daughter about. To Lara's surprise, the landlady was close to tears when she saw her paying guest was still there.

'Hello, my dear. I hope you've been looked after well. Please accept my apologies for not being here.'

Lara nodded. She was also pleased to see that John's mother had seemingly recovered. As Flora had slipped away, Lara took her chance. 'Mrs Parsons, could I speak to you for ten minutes? Maybe after Flora's gone home.'

'Flora's not going anywhere tonight, not with this murderer around. He could get her, me, or you. We're better off in here where it's safe and sound.'

Lara wondered if the bang on the head had affected Mrs Parsons' memory. Should she remind her that she only had one daughter present, not two? However, touched by the concern, Lara nodded and took out her notebook. 'Mrs Parsons, what do you know about Chris Farmer?' He is the same age as my sister, Bella. Well, what she would be now.'

Mrs Parsons shook her head.

'Oh, you know, Mum. Chris Farmer the football player. Bit of an Adonis – tall, blond, gorgeous.' Flora had reappeared with a mug of tea.

'Ah yes, I know the one. He's still about, isn't he? Hangs around with that miserable bloke on the motorbike.'

'Ben? Oh, he's not so bad,' Lara said. 'He gave me a lift on his bike. I was going to see Jenny.'

This didn't impress Mrs Parsons. She shook her head once again and decided that Lara needed a talking to. 'Listen to me, young lady. Don't speak to him again. Despite coming from a good home, he was trouble when he was younger. Once I saw him driving around in a car that he'd obviously stolen. He couldn't have been more than fifteen years old. I told his aunt, but she wouldn't listen. She was always sticking up for him too, saying he was shy when instead he was just plain antisocial. He didn't want a proper job and that's why he joined the Navy. Fancied sailing around the world instead of working for a living. She even left him her house so he can still saunter around doing nothing.'

'That's lucky for him but she must have loved him a great deal. I'm sure he didn't force her to do it.' Lara's general comment was to hide the shock she felt on hearing Ben had stolen cars.

'Well, his sisters weren't happy about it. They used to spend their holidays in that cottage.' Mrs Parsons said, returning the conversation to Ben's misdemeanours.

'Where is the cottage?' Lara asked.

'It's in Easton. On the cliff top.' Mrs Parson looked at Lara suspiciously. 'Why do you want to know where it is? Don't you dare go there, my girl. Now I think it's time you went home to your family. You need looking after.'

'I only want to ask him about Chris.'

'Now he's a fine young man. A good job and a happy marriage. The perfect husband.'

Chapter Fifteen

It was late and it was dark, but Lara didn't care, not even when the rain began to get heavy. She was furious at what she'd learned from Mrs Parsons. Ben was so aloof when he talked about Bella, yet he'd been the one that got her into trouble with the police. Of course, he couldn't possibly have been allowed to get a police record, not coming from a "good family" as Mrs Parsons had described them.

After waiting for the landlady's wine time, she slipped out of the hotel and started the journey to Easton. While driving, she planned what she would say to Ben when she reached his house. Should she come straight to the point and accuse him of enticing her sister into stealing a car? Or maybe she would ask him if he knew anything about Bella's brush with the law and see how he reacts. The worst thing he could do is ask her to leave.

Suddenly, a car was right up behind her, so she veered into the side of the road to allow it more space. But the car didn't overtake, perhaps because its wing mirror was broken. Lara moved back into the middle of the lane, assuming the car would be turning off soon, but the two cars remained almost bumper to bumper for another mile passing several turn-offs. Talk about joyriders, she thought. To her relief, the turn-off to Easton was coming up so she signalled left hoping the car behind was paying attention as she needed to slow right down. Thankfully, the car backed off to give her space and she waved her hand as a sarcastic acknowledgement.

There was only one row of cottages overlooking the sea so Ben must live in one of them, Lara thought as she parked her car. The wind had picked up and the rain was stinging as she walked into it. She counted the cottages. There were twelve. Only a few lights were visible suggesting that several cottages were empty. They were probably holiday lets.

She slowly made her way up the path leading to the row of cottages intending to look out for a motorbike parked outside. Surely, his would be the only one. But there was no motorbike, and her heart sank. She hadn't considered the possibility that he might not be home. That had been stupid of her. What made her think a single man would be home alone on a Friday night? It was no use. She'd have to come back early the next morning when he'd probably be sleeping off a hangover.

As she began to make her way back to the car, she noticed a vehicle coming down towards her. Its wing mirror was broken. The car lights were not on and suddenly she felt scared. She walked quickly towards her car while scrambling for keys, but they weren't in her bag. She must have dropped them. The other car pulled up but too far for her to see the driver. Was that what the driver wanted? Then the car drove away and disappeared back up the lane.

'What are you doing here?'

After nearly jumping out of her skin, she turned around to find Ben standing about thirty feet away. He was walking down from the row of cottages.

'I didn't think you were in,' Lara replied. She knew that wasn't answering his question, but her nerve had gone. The subject of the stolen car was put to one side.

'Are you here to see Gerald Croft again?' he asked.

'No. I'm not here to see him. Actually, I came here to see you.'

'Why?'

'I want to ask you something. It's about your friend, Chris.'

He looked surprised. 'What do you want to know about him? And why are you asking me?'

'Because I don't know who else to ask.'

'You'd better come in then.'

When she heard someone knocking on the door, Jenny assumed that Chris had already lost the spare key she'd given him earlier. However, it was Paul standing on the pavement, shivering in the cold sea air. It was obvious he was not there in a professional capacity. She asked him in.

Sitting around the kitchen table the policeman looked through a pile of old photographs while Jenny watched on. He wouldn't say what he was looking for, but Jenny had a pretty good idea what it was. She had listened patiently to Lara's ridiculous accusations. First, Hanna killed Bella, and then Chris did. She'd advised Lara against doing anything rash, but the other woman clearly had not listened to her. Only a couple of hours after Lara had rushed off, Paul had turned up. Jenny was glad that Chris had gone out somewhere and wasn't expected back until much later because Paul was also asking questions about him. How long had he been staying with her? Had they talked about the murders? Did he seem angry or depressed? It sounded as if Chris was a suspect.

'So, this is the bangle,' Paul said, peering through a magnifying glass. 'It looks expensive for a girl like Bella to have.'

'I never noticed her wearing anything expensive. She must have borrowed it from someone.'

'But who? No one liked her except you, Jenny.'

'Yes, I suppose that's true. Surely she couldn't have bought it herself. I know she spent time with John Parsons. Perhaps he gave it to her.'

'I'm surprised you didn't notice her wearing it being that you were such close friends.'

Jenny looked embarrassed. 'I guess we weren't as close as all that.'

But that wasn't the only mystery regarding the bangle and Jenny waited patiently for Paul to mention the other one.

'Do you think this could be the same bangle Hanna was wearing the night she died?' Paul asked bluntly.

'No. Of course, it isn't. What are you suggesting, Paul? That Chris is a thief?'

'Or worse,' he replied.

Jenny shook her head in disbelief. 'I can't believe you would even think that of Chris. You were good friends once, Paul.

'But we're not friends now, Jenny, and haven't been for years. How much did you feel you had in common with Hanna and Tanya that night in The Oak? I bet that the only thing you talked about was the past. You can't judge people by how they were twenty years ago.'

'But that's just it, Paul. We're not talking about Chris Farmer, the man who has left his wife and children. The man you are suggesting might be a murderer is the eighteen-year-old Chris, the Chris who was your friend.'

'Perhaps I'm talking about both men.'

Ben was irritable. He said he'd been out in the boat the night before and wasn't up to hosting surprise visitors, making Lara feel even more uncomfortable than she already had been. Her anger-induced confidence had worn off as soon as she saw Ben in the flesh rather than as part of the imagined confrontation. Now she was inside his house, Lara wasn't sure how to raise the subject of Bella, but she told herself he would guess why she was there.

After an awkward few minutes, her attempts at small talk were getting nowhere so she showed Ben the photograph of the five friends on the night of the ball. Ben glanced at it before his focus returned to Lara. His expression suggested -*And!*

'Do you recognise the bangle Bella's wearing? It's silver with onyx stones.'

'Ben shrugged his shoulders. 'No. It's not mine.'

'There's no need to be sarcastic. I thought you might know how Chris got hold of it. He gave it to Hanna a few days after this photograph was taken.'

'Did Chris tell you that?'

'No. I haven't spoken to him yet.'

'And I don't recommend it either. He won't take lightly you spreading rumours like this. Chris is not a thief.'

'Hanna was wearing it on the night she died.'

'And!' This time Ben's expression did not sufficiently match his apparent confusion about her comment, so he articulated it.

'And he must have got it from Bella somehow.'

'Maybe he just bought one similar because Hanna told him she liked it. They did go out together you know.'

Lara hadn't considered Ben's simple explanation and she found herself floundering. 'Did you notice when Hanna began wearing it?' She guessed the answer before he opened his mouth.

'No, I didn't.'

Thankfully, bits of information came to the forefront of Lara's mind. 'Wait! That's not all. No bangle was found on Bella. It's not a coincidence. There was only one bangle.'

'So, Tom Bailey took it after he killed her. He was a real lowlife, Lara.'

That was the first time he had said her name and she felt a strange sensation running through her body. 'And gave it to Hanna?'

'It's not the same bracelet.'

'Bangle. It's a bangle.' But she knew she wasn't getting anywhere so prepared to change the subject.

'Was that the only reason you drove out here; to ask me about a bangle?' he asked, as though reading her mind.

Lara didn't answer immediately. It didn't seem the right time to bring up the stolen car incident. She racked her brain trying to think of something else she could ask Ben without offending him. However, he spoke first.

'You didn't come here to ask me about Chris and Bella, did you? It's about me.' His voice was intimidating.

Feeling herself getting angry at Ben's hostile manner, she bit the bullet. 'Yes, but I don't want you to get mad at me for asking. It's just that Bella got into trouble for riding in a stolen car when she was fifteen. The car crashed and the driver escaped leaving Bella to take the blame. Were you the driver, Ben?'

Ben half smiled before giving his answer. 'No, I was not the driver. I was the passenger. Bella was the driver. Anyway, she was sixteen, not fifteen when it happened. I was still fifteen. I was the youngest in the year.'

Lara wasn't sure whether to believe Ben but at least he'd admitted to being in the car. 'Did Bella threaten to tell the police you were in the car too?'

He nodded his head. 'A couple of years later she asked me for a loan of two hundred pounds. It was out of the blue.'

'Did you take that to be a blackmail attempt?'

'Yes, of course, I did. I'd just got a good position in the Navy and anything like that coming out might have ruined things for me. I hadn't a penny, but she told me to get it from my parents somehow.'

'Told or asked?'

Ben shrugged his shoulders. 'Okay, she asked me to get the money.'

'And did you?'

'No. She died before I had the chance. So I got away with it.'

Shocked by the bluntness of his confession, Lara wondered if she should be scared. What if he had no intention of letting her leave the cottage? Then she remembered her car was outside, so he'd be crazy to risk it. She remained calm.

'You're not scared, are you?' he said, putting her on the spot.

'Of course not,' she replied quickly. 'Why would I be scared of you.'

'Well, for a start there's just the two of us here. If I am a killer, like I think you're implying, would I let you leave?'

The tension in the room was more deafening than the silence. Lara's heart began to pound, and she could feel her skin tingling. But that was not how she was supposed to be feeling. She wasn't scared. 'I don't think you're a killer, Ben. Not for one minute. But I don't think Tom Bailey is either. At least, I don't think he killed Bella.'

The only sound was the wind battering the tiny wooden windows and Lara, knowing she had a long drive back, reached for her bag. Then she remembered about her keys. Ben was watching her searching for them and it made her nervous, so she gave up.

'I think I dropped my keys by the car. Would you come down with me while I look?'

'It's not a good idea to drive in this weather. It's only going to get worse,' he said.

She looked at him in astonishment. What was he suggesting she should do? Stay there? 'It's okay. It's still early. And I'm going to stop for something to eat on the way back.'

'It's half past ten.'

Lara was shocked at how late it was. They must have been talking for longer than she thought. But what exactly was he suggesting?

'There's a spare room upstairs. I think you should stay here.'

The thought of sleeping in her tight wet jeans did not sound any more appealing than driving in the wind and rain. And she was starving, not having eaten since early morning. But she was in a predicament. The other driver could still be out there and that scared her more than spending the night alone with Ben. For some inexplicable reason, she felt safer with him.

'Yes. I will stay, thanks.'

'I'm going to cook for myself, so you're welcome to have some too. It's freshly caught.'

An hour later, Lara was curled up on the sofa with a glass of brandy and an empty plate in front of her. Ben had cooked fresh fish and given her a large portion while his own was tiny. After handing Lara her plate, he admitted that he'd eaten earlier but didn't want her to dine alone. Lara was starting to wonder if he had a split personality but told herself he was just a moody guy.

It was nearly midnight and there was an elephant in the room. Moreover, she didn't know how she was feeling about that elephant. Somehow, she had to get upstairs into a spare room and Ben would have to guide her to it.

She caught him rubbing his eyes and remembered that she had upset his routine. After glancing at the wall clock, she said, 'It's past midnight. You look tired. I'll be all right on this sofa.'

He frowned. 'I told you there's a room upstairs. Come on. I'll lend you a T-shirt.'

As she followed him up the steep, narrow steps, Lara realised how drunk she was when she found herself swaying. She waited on the tiny landing while he disappeared for a few seconds returning with a black T-shirt.

'It's clean,' he remarked, as he handed it to her.

Instinctively, Lara took a step back, forgetting the stairs were behind her. Suddenly, she stumbled off the top step and, for a second, she thought she would fall down the stairs. He reached out and grabbed her around the waist. Then he pulled her towards him.

'Be careful. I don't want to be suspected of yet another murder.'

Their eyes locked and Lara found herself moving her face towards his. But he stepped away from her and pointed to the spare bedroom.

'Remember the bathroom is downstairs,' he said. 'And be careful.'

Then he walked into the other bedroom and shut the door behind him.

The road was unlit, so Chris struggled to see what was in front of him as he drove along the country road. He was tired and didn't feel that human urge to reach any destination as quickly as possible, so he kept to a sensible speed as he took one bend after another. The road really should be lit, he thought, as he wiped his tired eyes.

In the rear-view mirror, a car's headlights were quickly getting bigger until their reflection hurt Chris's eyes. Moving the mirror to the side, he steered the car as far to the left as possible, and the other car soared past. Chris made a disapproving gesture at the woman in the passing car and watched as it grew smaller. Idiot, he thought to himself. What's so urgent that you kill yourself to get there?

He glanced at the speedometer which read fifty miles per hour and considered that he might be driving too slowly. If he picked up speed maybe cars wouldn't be so desperate to overtake him. Then he realised that he didn't want to drive faster because he didn't want to reach his destination. Simone was waiting for him at her parents, and he'd agreed to drive there. Her father would definitely be there. The thought of what he had to say to them brought beads of sweat to his forehead. A heavy twig hit the windscreen and he forced himself to concentrate on his driving.

The speeding car had disappeared around a bend and the road darkened once again but then a faint glow became visible ahead, signalling the approach of another vehicle. Behind the dipped headlights, he could see it was the same car that had just passed him. What was it doing? Suddenly, he realised that the car was not just driving towards him but was driving straight at him. Then the other car's beam was switched on and Chris was momentarily blinded. In a desperate attempt to steer the car out of the way, he lost control. Suddenly, everything was in slow motion. He knew his car was going to flip over and he prayed it wouldn't catch fire. Hopefully, the other driver would help him out.

Just before the car turned over, Chris glanced out of the passenger window. The last thing he saw was the woman in the other car grinning.

Chapter Sixteen

Simone stared down at her husband. His once beautiful face was now bloodied and bruised. Paul put his arm around her shoulders and guided her out of the hospital room.

'The doctor said he's going to be all right, Simone. He's a lucky man.'

'Not to me, he isn't,' she said tearfully. 'What am I going to tell the children? They think he's on a football trip.'

'Why not tell them the truth? He hasn't done anything wrong. A witness saw a car forcing him off the road.'

If Paul thought that would reassure Simone, he was wrong. Her tears disappeared but were replaced with wide-eyed horror.

'What do you mean "forced him off the road"? I thought it was an accident.' She bit down on a knuckle as if to stop herself screaming. 'Have you got the other driver?'

Paul shook his head. 'No, but we have a description of her and the car. We'll get her, Simone. Don't you worry.'

'Her? I don't suppose she looked like Bella's sister, did she?'

Ignoring the question Paul pointed to the hospital room they had just left. 'I need to go back and sit with Chris. He could wake up any time.'

Simone watched him running down the white corridor and out of sight. She wasn't stupid. The person who killed Hanna and Tanya had now made an attempt on her husband's life. Well, she wasn't going to sit and watch over him. No. She wasn't hanging around waiting to be murdered too.

'Mrs Farmer.'

A nurse was standing next to her holding a white plastic bag. 'These are your husband's belongings. Could you pop some toiletries and clean clothes in? Tomorrow will be fine.'

'I shan't be in tomorrow,' Simone said quietly.

The first light of dawn was just becoming visible through the tiny wooden windows as Lara gave up trying to sleep. Her mind was still processing everything she'd learnt about Ben the night before. They'd talked for hours. He told her about his time in the Navy and how he'd sent most of his wages to his aunt who died three years ago. That's when he decided to leave the Navy. She hadn't left it to him, after all. He'd bought it from her with his own money, albeit at a discount.

His sisters had done well so there was no guilt on his part. So, he wasn't the scrounger that both Jenny and Mrs Parsons had accused him of being. He was just relaxing after "working hard at sea". It felt weird knowing he was lying merely a few feet away from her. The walls were thick and soundproof, so she had no idea if he'd got up or was still in bed. She suspected he was an early riser and, not wanting to outstay her welcome, she made her way downstairs.

In the early morning light, the downstairs of the cottage was larger than Lara had realised. To her surprise, the kitchen was clean and well-stocked. It wasn't what she was expecting to find after being served a meal consisting solely of fried fish.

After making two mugs of tea in case Ben came down, she tucked some ginger nut biscuits under one arm and began making her way to the sitting room. Suddenly, something struck her as curious, and she returned to the kitchen. Looking through the back window she found the answer. A makeshift conservatory was tacked onto the outside kitchen wall. That accounted for the absence of birdsong while she was making tea.

Glancing back in the direction of the stairs, she put down the mug and walked towards the kitchen door. The key was in the lock, and she gently turned it to the right. It was now unlocked. Glancing towards the stairs once more, she opened the door and stepped into the glass room.

In the middle of the conservatory stood a handmade easel draped in a paint-stained sheet. Too scared to uncover the hidden work, she walked over to a pile of canvases on a table. They were good. In fact, they were excellent. Each one captured the intensity of the colours of sunsets and sunrises. There must have been more than a dozen beautiful scenes of nature, similar, yet individual.

Then she noticed another pile, a pile that looked abandoned. Perhaps they were duds. Forgetting where she was, she reached out and picked up the cobwebbed paintings. The top one was not a landscape but a portrait of a young woman. The woman was beautiful. Lara brushed her fingers across the smooth, slick surface and tried to picture the scenario in which the painting was done. She felt an irrational surge of jealousy to know that Ben's eyes had once focussed on the woman's features, her pale skin tone, the strands of her black hair, painstakingly catching the light in her eyes.

Underneath were more portraits of the same woman. Who was she? An old girlfriend? Then she realised who the model was.

'What are you doing?'

Lara spun around to see Ben standing in the doorway. He looked angry. At first, she didn't know how to handle the situation and struggled to voice an apology. Then she became angry herself. How dare he keep such a thing from her?

'You painted my sister, not once, but several times, and you didn't think to mention it. How dare you be angry with me!'

They stared at each other in a standoff before Ben took one of the mugs of tea and disappeared into the sitting room. Lara followed him into the room, prepared to stand her ground but, to her surprise, he was sitting down holding his head in his hands. She was afraid of what he was about to say.

'My parents hated any mess, so my aunt let me come here to paint. Bella was my first model. She said it made her feel special having me watch her so carefully. But for me, she was just light and shadows and when I told her that she got angry and didn't come here anymore. The paintings were rubbish anyway.'

'So why do you keep them?'

'It was twenty years ago. I'd forgotten they were there. There is nothing important about those paintings, Lara. I was just a kid playing the role of an artist, but I knew nothing would happen outside of these four walls. And Bella just went along with it. She had no plans of her own. She just tagged onto my dream.'

'But that's not true, Ben. She did have her own dream and I think that dream ended up killing her.'

Ben looked up at her with a confused expression on his face. 'What are you talking about? What dream?'

Lara told him about the meeting with a record producer and how Bella needed money for the train fare and hotel room. 'I know it was probably false hope but for an eighteen-year-old girl, it was a huge break which would make her famous. I'm guessing that she asked several people to lend her the two hundred pounds she needed but nobody trusted her to give it back.'

'Why didn't she say what it was for?'

'Probably because she knew they would laugh at her.' Just like John did, she thought.

'You are just trying to defend her. You weren't there. Whatever her reason for wanting the money, she used blackmail to get it. She might not have said as much but she didn't have to.'

'Okay, but I'm sure she wouldn't have carried out the threat. It was just a shot in the dark and when it failed with you, she moved on to somebody else. But somebody wasn't prepared to take the chance and I need to find out who that person was.'

'I wish she'd told me. If she had, I would have helped her.'

The telephone rang, bringing them back to the present, and Ben reached over to pick up the receiver. After a few seconds of listening, he looked across at Lara and his eyes narrowed. 'I'll be there soon,' he said to the caller.

'What is it?' Lara asked nervously. 'Has something happened?'

'Chris is in hospital. He was driven off the road last night. Perhaps you passed him on the way here.'

'That's terrible. Is he okay? Hey! You don't think it was me, do you?'

Ben walked towards the stairs. 'I need to go to the hospital.'

'Don't mind me,' Lara said. 'I was just leaving.'

John didn't waste any time after hearing about the car crash. Chris, Hanna, and Tanya were all associated with Bella Young, as was he, and if they were targets, he might be too. Lara had told him that the former friends had all received anonymous letters and he wondered why he hadn't received one too. It must be because he didn't testify at the trial.

He looked at the computer screen in front of him hoping to see something that would stand out as wrong. First, he examined the testimonies of Bella's female friends. Their statements were very similar: the times, the locations, the conversations. Only Jenny's was different. She was drunk at the ball, therefore, had little memory of the later hours. Or at least, that is what she said. The girls' testimonies had described Bailey as angry after they'd turned down his offer of a lift. Then, after stopping the car again, he turned aggressive. They all watched him drive on towards the coastal path where Bella's body would be found shortly after. There was no obvious reason for him to go there as he lived in the opposite direction. As he was driving away, he shouted that he would get them when they were on their own. Bailey, of course, had denied saying that.

The prosecution stated that Bailey drove to the coast and parked up to have a smoke. Then he saw Bella walking alone. He then got out of the car and dragged her to the path where he intended to rape her. However, Bella fought back, and he killed her. Smears of her blood were found in Bailey's car. The friends' testimonies had been the icing on the cake of the prosecution case, but the substance was the DNA.

Of course, there was a defence, short as it was. Bailey had denied driving to the coast. He insisted he'd turned his car around and driven back towards his home which was on the edge of Weston. It was a fifteen-minute drive from the murder scene which would have put him out of the frame were it true. His family had testified that he'd got home at midnight and was his usual, laid-back self. Nobody believed them because most were criminals themselves.

One defence witness's name stood out - Ben Sutton. According to Bailey, after he'd left the girls, he saw Ben walking alone and offered him a lift home. This account was denied by Ben who insisted he'd been with his friend, Chris, at that time. Chris confirmed Ben's testimony. Both denied seeing Bailey at all that night.

John sat back in his chair, attempting to summarise the main points in his head. Hanna, Tanya, Simone, and Jenny had all testified for the prosecution. Ben and Chris were called by the defence but both of them denied Bailey's alibi. Hanna and Tanya were now dead and there had been an attempt on Chris's life. The others must be worried. Somehow he didn't think Jenny was in danger as her testimony hadn't in any way affected the outcome. There were two people left – Ben Sutton and Simone Farmer.

Ben handed a tissue to Simone which she held over her tear-stained face. Seeing Lara leave Ben's cottage that early in the morning surprised and confused her. Lara was not the person she was expecting to be with him. Simone had stayed in her car until Lara had left, then banged on Ben's door. She pulled the tissue away from her mouth to speak.

'I found it last night. It was in the pocket of his jeans. I'd put them in the laundry basket because they stank of smoke.' She looked at Ben with curiosity, wondering if he really did know about his only friend. 'All these years you've known, haven't you? You must really hate me.'

Ben pretended to look at the app on the mobile phone in his hand. He didn't need to.

'Of course, I don't hate you. I'm sorry, Simone, but I thought he'd changed. He told me he loved his family, you and the kids, and he wouldn't do anything to jeopardise things.'

'I should never have married him, Ben. I knew he didn't love me really. He just went through the motions. After the children were born, he didn't come near me. Mum insisted he was seeing another woman.' She laughed bitterly. 'You and he, were you …?' Her words tapered off as if she couldn't bear to finish the sentence.

'Friends. That's all we ever were, and still are. He is going to be all right, isn't he?'

Simone ignored his question. 'But you said you were together after the ball. Where did you go?'

'Why are you bringing that up now, Simone? We were just kids then?'

'Yes, and it would have been illegal at that time.'

'You need to talk to him,' Ben said softly. 'Maybe you can sort things out between you.'

Simone wasn't letting Ben keep anything else about her husband from her. 'Where did you and Chris go after the ball, Ben?'

Ben was silent for a while as if racking his brains for an answer. Finally, he returned the phone to Simone. '*We* didn't go anywhere. We weren't together and, as for where *he* was, it's about time he told you himself.'

Chapter Seventeen

Lara didn't go straight back to the hotel. The sound of bells ringing drew her once again to the local church. She knew she wasn't dressed appropriately but was sure that wouldn't matter. It was open to everyone not just those wearing their best clothes. As she walked inside, the musty odour brought back memories of Sunday school which she would attend while her parents gave thanks for their new daughter. But that church was always full to the brim. The church she stood in today was empty but for the few elderly volunteers placing prayer and hymn books on the pews. Lara sat in a middle pew feeling more self-conscious than ever before, wishing that more people would walk in so she wouldn't stand out so much.

After ten more minutes, the volunteers took their seats to listen to the service. She felt a tap on her shoulder and turned to see an elderly couple smiling. The wife asked if she wanted to join them, but Lara politely refused. She was in no mood for socialising. Just as the vicar was about to start, a latecomer arrived. Lara had seen her several times before. Still holding a carrier bag, the woman sat in the front row. Nobody else batted an eyelash so the woman was clearly a regular. Lara didn't feel so underdressed.

The service was long, and Lara tried to pay attention but found her mind wandering back to Ben. If he hadn't received that telephone call, she might still be there with him. She was beginning to think he liked her but now she wondered if he was just playing games. A rustling sound brought her attention back to the present and she watched as the woman in the front row began eating something she'd taken from her bag. Nobody seemed to mind.

After the service, the vicar walked to the church door to shake the hands of the few people leaving. When he saw Lara, he smiled and said he hoped to see her again. But she didn't want to leave.

'Could I speak to you in private?' she asked quietly so that nobody else could hear.

'Of course, my dear. If you'd like to step back inside, I'll be with you shortly.'

A few minutes later the vicar led Lara to a seat in the front row and they sat down at the front of the church.

'I suppose you want to talk about your sister?' he said kindly.

'Actually, I don't,' she replied. 'However, I think it might be connected to her.' She wasn't sure how to address a vicar in person, so she decided not to address him at all. 'When I was in the graveyard the other day, a young woman punched me for no reason. At least that's what I thought until I read the gravestone she had come over from. It was the grave of Tom Bailey, but not the one in prison. I wondered if you knew anything about her.'

'Oh, dear. You poor thing. I hope she didn't hurt you too badly,' he replied. He didn't sound shocked. 'How old was this woman?'

'Twenty-something. I'd seen her before. She was begging outside a local shop.'

'That sounds like young Connie Bailey, poor child. She has had a difficult life but that doesn't excuse what she did to you.'

'It was a shock but I'm okay. I want to understand why she hit me. How was she related to the Tom Bailey who's buried in the graveyard?'

'He was her grandfather. A good man by all accounts. He worked hard to keep a roof over his family's head and didn't deserve what happened to him.'

'What did happen to him?'

'After his son was convicted of your sister's murder, he lost his job at the factory he'd worked in since he was a teenager. There was no justice for him. Tragically, he took his own life not long after. He and his wife had looked after their granddaughter, Connie since she was a baby. Connie often spends time at his grave.'

'What about the father? Where is he?' Lara said, without thinking.

'In prison, of course. Tom Bailey Junior was still a teenager when Connie was born so it was the grandparents who brought her up.'

'And the grandmother. Where is she now?'

'She's just left. That's her donation,' he said, pointing to the rubbish on the floor. 'Mrs Bailey couldn't cope with the load she was left with. Unfortunately, she turned to drink and was no more used to Connie than her father was. It's an all-round tragedy.'

He stood up and then looked down at Lara. 'But not as tragic as what happened to your sister, of course.'

Jenny turned up at the hospital at the same time as Ben and they sat down together awkwardly as they waited for news on Chris. After waiting an hour, a nurse finally informed them that their friend was doing well but would not be able to receive any visitors. Jenny suggested having breakfast in the hospital restaurant and to her surprise, Ben agreed. He even bought the bacon rolls and coffee. The situation was bizarre - two people who hadn't spoken for twenty years now sharing a table and waiting for the other one to speak first. It was Ben who broke the silence.

'Did you have a letter too?'

She nodded her head. 'Yes. I think I must have been the first one to get one. I didn't take it seriously until Hanna died. Now it seems all of Bella's friends were sent one.'

'Yes. So, why is somebody sending us anonymous letters? What are they hoping to prove by that?'

'I don't know. Perhaps they are hoping to get a reaction from us. Ben, do you think Lara sent them?'

'No,' Ben replied.

The certainty in his voice surprised Jenny. 'How can you be so sure, Ben? You hardly know her. Or do you?'

'Not really. I just don't think she did.'

A suspicious Jenny wanted to ask more questions but wasn't sure if she would like the answers. She returned the topic to possible reasons for the anonymous letters.

'Lara thinks that Bella was blackmailing her friends. Did she blackmail you, Ben?'

He shook his head. 'Do you think I would tell you if she did?'

Jenny sighed. She felt that even with Ben sitting opposite her, he was as much a closed book as ever.

Then Ben began asking his own questions. 'Do you think Tom Bailey could be innocent?'

Jenny froze and turned white as if she'd seen a ghost. ''No, Ben. I don't think he's innocent. Why are you even asking me that?' she whispered, even though there was no one else in the restaurant.

'Why are you so surprised, Jenny? You must know that's what Lara thinks?'

'Yes, but that's different, Ben. Lara has been through a terrible experience and is using this as a distraction. She doesn't have a clue about what went on that night.' Jenny shivered and covered her face with her hands while Ben looked on with curiosity.

Before he could make another comment, Jenny changed the subject.

'I went to see Mrs Evans and she was angry about Hanna bringing shame to the family. I don't suppose you have any idea about that?'

'No. I can't imagine her doing anything naughty. Wait a minute! Didn't she disappear for a while? I remember she wasn't in school for the exams because she was my partner for a stupid speech in Drama. I had to do it by myself which made me look like a right idiot.'

'Yes, I remember now. Oh no! Suppose she was pregnant. That would explain everything. But who was the father?'

Jenny and Ben looked at each other as they thought of the same person.

When Lara got back to the hotel, she was surprised to find John sitting in the breakfast room.

'You're back!'

'Yes. I heard what happened to Chris. What's been happening here is no coincidence. We have to find out what's going on.'

'What's that?' she asked, referring to the pile of paper on the table in front of him. She tried to hide her thrill at being included in his last comment.

'I've got copies of the court records for Tom Bailey's trial. Do you want to know what I've found?'

Pulling up a chair, Lara took out her notebook and placed it in front of her. She didn't want to get too close to John as she knew how dishevelled she looked.

John recounted the testimonies made by the four female friends. 'They said that Tom Bailey threatened them after they turned down his offer of a lift. Then he drove towards the coastal path which was in the opposite direction to his house. The most significant part of their testimonies was that they saw his car driving away from the coast shortly after midnight. Besides putting him at the scene of the crime, it scuppered his alibi.'

'Do you think they were telling the truth?' Lara asked.

'Yes. Weston isn't quite Salem. It's very unlikely that all four of them would conspire to lie in court. Not for such a serious crime.'

'Unless they wanted him to take the blame for Bella's murder,' Lara said.

'That doesn't make sense, Lara. Why would they want that? Remember they all said the same thing in court. Well, three of them at least. Jenny was too drunk to remember anything. Hold on! It was a school ball with teachers present. They should have been monitoring everyone. And I seem to remember she wasn't that type of girl. Perhaps she is hiding something.'

Lara thought about John's words. Jenny had been the only person who seemed genuine. She was perfect – kind, attractive, successful, and popular.

The list was endless. Yet, Lara had suspected Jenny was holding something back.

'Even if the girls were lying, it doesn't explain why Chris was targeted,' John said. 'He *said* he was going on to a nightclub.'

'Don't you believe him? I heard they were close friends back then.' She was taken aback at the implication that Chris had lied. That would mean Ben was somewhere else too.

'Tom Bailey claimed that he saw Ben walking home and offered to turn his car around and take him back to Weston. Ben denied it and Chris backed up Ben.'

'Why would Bailey say that if it wasn't true? It doesn't sound important.'

'But it was important. The area in question was miles away from where Bella was found. If what Bailey claimed was true and he was with Ben at that time, he would be out of the frame for Bella's death.'

'And Ben too,' Lara said, before quickly adding, 'Were there any other witnesses?'

'Not of any importance.'

'What about you, John? Didn't they ask for your testimony?'

'No. Why would they? I was two hundred miles away.'

'And Paul Croft. He was here.'

'Yes, he was. The funny thing is, I can't find a statement from him, never mind a testimony. It seems he wasn't even interviewed.'

'You need to tell me everything you know, Dad.' Paul was sitting on a sofa opposite his father. The atmosphere in the room was as cold as the mug of coffee his hands were wrapped around.

'Don't talk to your father like that, Paul. He's not well.' Once again, Mrs Croft had taken on the role of spokeswoman for her husband.

'Why? It's on the records. You have access to them, don't you?' Gerald Croft said, finally.

'Not anymore. Not until we've heard from the Chief Constable. She's considering sending in another force.'

'Why? Are you all so incompetent that you need outsiders to tell you what to do?'

Paul was losing patience with his mother interrupting, and he tried to ignore her. 'As you already know, Dad, three murders suggest a serial killer is on the loose. Therefore, external assistance is a matter of procedure.'

Gerald Croft looked worried. 'But Chris survived, didn't he? Your mother told me he was okay.'

'Yes but clearly Chris surviving wasn't the intention. Someone out there is picking off locals who have a connection to each other.'

'And you have a connection to them too. You are all the same age,' said Mrs Croft.

'Yes. But I don't think it's just about us. That wouldn't make any sense because we have nothing in common anymore. It has to be linked to Bella's death.'

'But that's ridiculous. That was twenty years ago. Why would anything be happening now?'

'I don't know, Mum. Do you mind if I have another coffee? This one's gone cold.'

Paul knew his mother would not approve of what he was about to ask and wanted her out of the way. Reluctantly, she left the room and he continued.

'Dad, can I ask you about the investigation? There must be a record of all the witness interviews, those of Ben, Chris, Jenny, Simone, Hanna, and Tanya. That's all they talked about for days after Bella's murder.'

Gerald didn't take well to what he regarded as his son's impudence. 'Everyone connected to the girl was questioned. I knew how to do my job.'

'Except me. I wasn't questioned. Why not?'

'Because it was just a formality. A box ticked. A young couple found Bella's body half an hour after she left her friends. There was a narrow timeframe in which the murder was committed. Bailey had no alibi and was seen driving towards that area. I knew where you were at the time in question so there was no need to interview you.'

'Where was I?'

'What?'

'Where was I at the time of the murder?'

Gerald Croft's face turned white, and his hands were sweating. There was the sound of footsteps approaching the door and he looked towards it anxiously.

'You were here. We heard you come in. Why are you asking me this now?' His voice had lowered to the point of being barely audible.

Paul stared at his father. 'No, I wasn't. You lied, Dad. And now it's going to come out.

Chapter Eighteen

Lara and John stepped off the bus into a street neither of them had been to before. It was in a rundown area conveniently hidden from the view of the wealthier residents of Weston. John had refused to bring his car and strongly advised Lara not to either. He'd only agreed to go in the first place because he was worried Lara would go alone. She'd found out where the Baileys lived from the vicar who probably never dreamt what she had in mind. She wasn't sure she knew what she was doing herself.

'What exactly are we supposed to be doing here?' John asked, echoing her thoughts. In the eighteen years he'd lived in Weston, he'd not been to the spot where they were currently standing.

'I want to talk to them. I want to find out if they're behind any of this.'

'Anyone of what? The letters or the murders?' John asked.

Lara turned to face him. 'You're not being serious, are you? Do you honestly think one of those women could be the murderer? The grandmother can hardly carry a plastic bag while Connie Bailey is barely functioning.'

'Connie Bailey is a strong young woman who is more than capable of pushing two women to their deaths. Believe me, I've seen that amount of anger fuelled strength before.'

Lara made no comment. How could she argue with an expert on murder? As she looked around the tiny estate, she began to notice things. There was a line of green garages on which several children were standing. Situated at the top of a narrow path was a scruffy metal bench surrounded by empty beer cans and worse. Lara remembered the path but not that particular bench. No, the bench she remembered was wooden, not metal.

Flashbacks of sitting on the floor sobbing while a woman sat on the bench holding a bottle of something, filled her mind. Lara knew she was the child crying and that the drunken woman was her mother. Was that the night her mother died? These memories were new to her. They must have been hidden deep in the recesses of her mind.

'Are you okay, Lara?' John asked, noticing that the mind of his companion was far away.

'Yes, I'm fine,' she answered, relieved to be brought back to the present. 'Which house do you think they live in?'

'I have no idea, but I know a way to find out,' he said, before walking across to the garages.

The children pointed at the end house nearest to them, and the two visitors nervously approached it. John knocked on the half-boarded-up door and within seconds it was opened by a young man holding a bunch of keys. He looked surprised. Lara was the first to speak.

'Hello. I'm looking for Connie Bailey. Is she here?'

The young man looked back at her with curiosity. It seemed that he had no idea who either of the visitors were. 'She's not in, luv. She'll be in the village somewhere.'

'Are you her brother?' she continued.

'Yes. Why are you looking for her? Is she in trouble again?'

'Not really, but she did hit me, and I want to know why. Did she say anything to you?'

The young man laughed. 'She doesn't need a reason to hit anyone who goes near her.' Then he noticed the bruise on Lara's face. 'I wouldn't blame you if you go to the police but she's going through a bad time right now.'

'I don't intend to go to the police. I just want to understand why she hit me. Something tells me it was personal.'

'But we don't know that it was personal, do we Lara?' John sounded cautious. 'I think we've taken enough of your time. I can see you're on your way out.'

Lara scowled at John and tried to ask another question, but the man had already stepped outside and closed the door after him. 'Yeah. I gotta pick my old man up from the station. Sorry, I couldn't be more help.'

Lara and John began the short walk back to the bus stop in silence. She was furious that he had cut short what could have been a productive meeting. John knew he was in the doghouse but didn't make any attempt at peace-making. He was relieved that nobody important had been home. All through the journey there he was dreading Connie being home, or worse, Tom Bailey.

As they were waiting for the bus, a car pulled out of the estate and passed them. It was the young man they had just left, and he waved as he drove past in a battered car with a broken wing mirror.

The late afternoon sky was a typical autumnal spectacle. The darkening sky was streaked with the orange rays of the setting sun. High clouds were gathering above the boat as it left the tiny harbour and the temperature had dropped sharply. Ben pulled a thick jumper over his head and sat down facing the best view. Usually, at this time, he would light up a joint. He thought it helped him focus on the different shades of colour. But it was time to turn over a new leaf. Lately, rival drug runners from the nearest cities had infiltrated Copston and the surrounding villages making any purchase dangerous. Ironically, his home village of Easton had no such drug problem.

Eventually, his thoughts turned to Hanna. The only time he'd seen her happy was when she was going out with Chris. Everyone thought she was punching above her weight, what with Chris being the local heartthrob, but Ben knew that it was a convenient match for his friend. Hanna would be less demanding than the more confident girls. But Chris didn't know Hanna as much as he thought he did. He'd told Ben that she was as happy with their platonic relationship as he was. So, if Hanna was pregnant at one time, it wasn't by Chris. Initially, he'd thought of him, just like Jenny had, but on reflection, he realised it must be somebody else. Ben knew his friend well and would have noticed any tension or agitation that a teenage pregnancy would cause. But if Chris wasn't the father, who was?

He wondered if Hanna had told any of her friends about the pregnancy. Jenny hadn't known but she wasn't particularly close to Hanna. Perhaps Tanya knew but now she was dead, along with Hanna. He shook himself realising that Hanna's so-called pregnancy was just supposition. After all, there was no one who could be the father.

Lara hadn't wanted to tell John about the night before, but now it was clear she had to. She told him about the car that tailgated her on the way to Easton and how it had followed her down into the harbour. That car's wing mirror was broken just like the car that Connie Bailey's brother drove. At first, John tried to make light of it saying that half the cars in the area had broken wing mirrors. He asked her what the purpose of her visit to Ben was and she told him what his mother had told her about Ben and her sister.

'So, Ben was the mystery driver,' he said. 'I wonder if he was the instigator too. Ben came from a good family, so they probably helped hush things up.'

'Not for my sister, they didn't,' Lara said bitterly. She would never have guessed Ben came from a "good" family with his lifestyle. It seemed to her that everyone in Bella's circle had an advantageous start in life, except for her of course.

'Don't be bitter about the past, Lara. It won't do you any good. Bella was a strong young woman in spite of her background. She was determined to get on and if that meant borrowing money from her wealthy friends, then so be it.'

'You said she wanted to borrow not demand money from people. That means she wasn't blackmailing her friends. You refused to give her money, John, and she didn't do anything to damage you.'

'Yes, and I regretted it later. That's why I agreed to give her two hundred pounds to buy a new guitar.'

'And you told her to ask your mother for it until you got back. But your mother didn't know anything about that and refused to give the money to Bella.'

'I know. To be honest, I forgot all about it as soon as I settled into university life.'

'Why didn't you tell your mother afterwards? She still doesn't know.'

'Because I didn't want her to feel guilty. I shouldn't have brought her into it. If only I'd given Bella the money when she first asked me to.'

'Why do you say that? She would have gone off to meet a total stranger.'

'I don't know. If I'd given it to her, she wouldn't have needed to ask anyone else. Perhaps she asked the wrong person for money.'

Paul Croft was looking through the telephone records of Tanya Evans when Sergeant Brooks entered the room. He was carrying a pile of papers which he placed onto Paul's keyboard, much to the annoyance of the inspector.

'What do you think you're doing? I've lost my place now.'

But Brooks did not apologise. Instead, he pushed the computer to one side and held a sheet of paper under Paul's nose. 'You need to read this, Paul.'

Irritated yet again by Brook's refusal to call him Sir or Inspector, he waved the paper away. 'As you can see, I am busy, Sergeant.'

'I'm sorry for interrupting your work, Paul, but this is more important.'

Paul snatched the paper from his colleague and, instead of reading it, went straight to the bit underlined in red ink. He saw the name, Hanna Evans.'

'Okay. This is too long to read. What is it about?'

'It's about a report of a sexual assault in 1994. Hanna Evans, the alleged victim of the assault, withdrew her complaint shortly after. Guess who the accused was?'

'Tom Bailey.' Paul didn't have to be a mind reader. 'Do we know why she withdrew the complaint?'

'Most likely she was scared. It appears that she was found by the old canal. Her clothes were torn, and she was crying so the woman who found her brought her to the station by car. Hanna made a report about the incident but withdrew it the following day when she came back to the station with her mother.'

'How serious was the alleged assault?'

'The worst kind. She was examined and there was no doubt about it. She was raped.'

'Was Bailey questioned about it?'

'Yes. He said it was consensual and that he and Hanna were on a date. It sounds unlikely but Hanna did admit to going for a walk with him.'

'I can't imagine Hanna Evans going near that man, but we never really know people, do we?'

'No, we don't.'

'How on earth was she allowed to testify in his trial?' But even before Paul finished his question, he realised what the answer might be.

'You do know what this means, don't you? The conviction of Tom Bailey could be unsafe if it turns out that a major witness for the prosecution had a vendetta against him.'

'I don't think vendetta is quite the word I would use, Karl. If he did rape her, he deserved worse than a life sentence for murder.'

'A life sentence for a murder he may not have committed, Paul?'

'At least there was some sort of justice. And Hanna is dead so there's little use in raking over her past.'

'But we have two murders on our hands. What if someone is now getting justice for Tom Bailey? He's only just got out of prison so it's not him. I suggest we bring in every member of his family to interview.'

'I'm not sure about this, Karl. That family has got enough problems without giving them a worse name than they've already got. Anyway, I really don't think they can help us.'

'Most of them can't, maybe. But Tom Bailey certainly can.'

They were interrupted when a junior officer walked into the office and handed Brooks a sheet of paper. 'We've found another sighting around the canal at the time of Tanya Price's murder. It was taken from the other side so she must have climbed over the wall and walked through the trees.'

Brooks looked at the fuzzy image of what looked like a woman wearing jeans and a hoody. Her black hair could be seen dangling down in parts. 'Looks like we have another reason to visit the Baileys.'

Lara took out her notebook which was blank except for the first two pages. So much had happened lately that she hadn't had the time to write any notes. Now, she would use it for a different task. She ripped out the centre pages and placed them on the table in front of her. John looked bemused as she drew a large number of circles on the paper. Then, after counting them, she wrote a name in each.

'I've never found mind maps helpful, to be honest,' he said, as he watched her drawing lines out of each circle, then using different colours for the scribbled notes. He noticed his name was included.

She smiled. 'I don't know if I have either, but they make me feel that I'm getting somewhere when I add things to them. There are so many permutations but let's focus on the night of Bella's death. Who could have lied about where they were?'

'It seems I have the most lines,' he said. 'Am I the main suspect?'

Lara wasn't sure if he was joking. 'But you didn't receive a letter like the others so that's in your favour. Two of those who did are now dead,' she said, as she drew a cross above the names of Tanya and Hanna. 'And Chris is in hospital.' She drew a vertical line.

'So, they can be ruled out,' John said.

'Not necessarily. They were alive back then, weren't they? We can assume that they were punished for testifying against Bailey. Chris was too. That leaves Ben, Paul, Jenny, and Simone. They might all be in danger.'

John leaned back in his chair and looked at the woman leading the discussion. 'Who do you think sent the letters, Lara?'

'Isn't it obvious, John? One of the Baileys sent them to avenge their father's imprisonment. I spoke to the vicar, and he said the family were torn apart when Tom Bailey was sent to prison. His father lost his job and home, then died shortly after. The mother turned to drink, and just look at Connie.'

'That would make sense but for one thing. Paul Croft didn't testify so why did he get a letter? He had nothing to do with Bailey going to prison except for being the son of Gerald Croft.'

Lara stared at Paul's name on the paper. There was only one line coming off his name with the words "investigating officer's son" written at the end. 'He must be hiding something.'

'Perhaps we are all hiding something, Lara. I knew Bella as much as anyone so why didn't I get a letter too?'

She looked at his handsome face and hoped that he wasn't keeping anything from her. She hadn't told him about the bangle because he might have been the one who gave it to Bella. She was waiting for him to mention it. The tape of him and Bella arguing was still in her possession, which didn't seem to worry him. That suggested John wasn't worried about it surfacing.

John was waiting for an answer to his question. He asked another one. 'You're hiding something too,

Lara. What do you know that you haven't told anyone?'

John watched her intently and she felt as though she were on trial, sitting in the dock under oath, rather than in a cosy hotel with the owner's son - the son who could read her mind. She decided to tell him the truth.

'When Tom Bailey looked at me in the parole hearing, I knew I'd seen him before. It was the night of the ball while we were leaving this very hotel. I didn't tell anyone that I'd stayed here before. The plan was to see Bella all dressed up for the school ball but that didn't happen. She didn't want to see us, of course, and I was crying because I was eleven years old. My parents thought that she might have called in the hotel after the ball but by eleven thirty, they'd had enough.

We left the hotel without checking out because we'd already paid the bill. Then, as we were driving out of Weston, a car nearly ran us off the road. My parents didn't see the driver, but I did. It was Tom Bailey.'

'That doesn't mean anything, Lara. He could have driven there after killing Bella.'

'No, he couldn't have because the car radio was on when it happened. I was counting the pips at the hour and there were twelve. It was twelve o'clock when I saw Bailey laughing as he forced us off the road.'

There was a slight chill in the early evening air and Ben decided to call it a day. The water was too choppy for painting and so was his mind. He couldn't stop thinking about Chris. So much had happened in the last twenty-four hours that it was difficult to focus on any one event. When he first heard about the car crash his emotions were all over the place. Or course, he feared for his friend's health, but his immediate thoughts were towards the woman who he had only recently met. Lara never seemed to be far from people's misfortune, and these were people he knew well. He had to consider that she might be some sort of maniac.

A bird swept down towards him, and he waved it away. He turned back towards land and stared at the row of cottages standing alone and neglected. But something was wrong. An orange glow was coming from one of the larger houses. It was the Crofts' house. The glow was small but fluctuating in shape, and he knew that part of the house was on fire. He switched on the engine, powered the boat to the shore then ran up the cobbled lane leading to the house.

By the time Ben reached the fire, the small glow had increased to a dangerous size and some of the neighbours were shouting into the house. Others rushed around holding buckets of water. There was no sign of the occupants and Ben hoped that they were away. But then a terrified face appeared in an upstairs room. It was Gerald Croft. Everyone was shouting for him to jump out of the window, but he seemed frozen with fear. A neighbour brought out a long ladder and placed it against the wall, but the window remained closed. Without a second thought, Ben grabbed a wet rag, broke a downstairs window, and disappeared into the house. He placed the rag against his face and ran upstairs to the room Gerald Croft was in.

'Where's your wife?' he shouted to the man by the window who was clearly suffering from either shock or an episode of Dementia.

Ben grabbed Croft and pulled him towards the stairs where another man had appeared to help. While the other two men made their way to safety, Ben rushed through all the rooms looking for Mrs Croft before realising she wasn't there. She must have got out while he was with her husband. Suddenly, there was a large explosion downstairs, and he knew that there was no way down. The heat was becoming unbearable, and he had to get out before it was too late. He ran back into the bedroom and opened the window. It was a mistake. He should have shut the bedroom door first because the second explosion blew him out of the window.

Chapter Nineteen

As Paul watched Brooks knocking on the door, he was hoping no one was home. He knew that was ridiculous as Tom Bailey was on parole, so tracking him down would be as simple enough even if he was out.

But Tom Bailey was in, and it was he who answered the door. 'You didn't wait long, did you?' Bailey said, immediately identifying his visitors as policemen.

'Is Connie here?' Paul preferred to focus on the other reason for the visit.

Bailey's expression changed from irritation to suspicion. 'Why do you want to know? She's done nothing wrong.'

'We'd just like to speak to her for a few minutes. Is she in or not?'

'No, she isn't. I've barely seen her since I got out. I don't think she likes her old man much.'

'Seeing as we're here, could we have a few words with you?' Brooks said. He hadn't forgotten that Bailey was the one they had originally wanted to speak to before the news about the CCTV image of his daughter.

'What about?'

'It's better if we come inside,' Brooks answered, as a passing neighbour glanced over to them.

'Okay but make it quick.'

Both visitors were surprised as they walked through the hall and into the kitchen. From what they could see of the house, it was well-furnished with nothing out of place. The kitchen was spotless.

'Who does the cleaning?' Brooks asked.

'My son. It's his house. He's been looking after my mother and his sister while I've been inside.'

Not very well, thought Paul.

'Have you come here to ask me about this house?'

'Twenty-one years ago, Hanna Evans accused you of raping her. She withdrew the allegation for unknown reasons. Did you threaten her?'

Bailey grinned. 'She was a little tiger behind that woolly exterior. She'd had an argument with her parents, so I suggested a drink to cheer her up. Things happened and we made love.'

'Her clothes were ripped,' Paul said.

'It was very passionate,' Bailey said, smirking.

'You – '

Brooks stepped forward to shield Bailey from his colleague. Things were getting out of hand. Focussing on whether Bailey raped Hanna Evans risked bringing the visit to a premature end, so he moved the topic on one year.

'Why did your lawyer allow Hanna Evans to testify against you if she already had some grudge to bear?'

'Because he didn't think it would be a good look for his client if he didn't.'

'But it was her testament that helped put you in prison.'

'Not just hers though. They all lied. Even if she hadn't testified, her friends still would have. They had it in for me.'

'Why would they lie?' Brooks asked. He noticed that Paul was rubbing his hands.

'It's obvious, isn't it? That girl told them I forced her to go with me and they did it to punish me.'

'Your defence lawyer could have put that to the jury.'

'He decided against it. Said the jury might believe them anyway 'cos there was so many of them.'

'Why did you spend so long in prison?'

'Well, there are some very bad people in prison, and I had to protect myself. And I wouldn't admit to a crime I didn't commit, so they kept refusing me parole.'

'So, just saying you didn't do it, who do you think did?'

'One of her so-called friends,' he said, looking at Paul Croft.

Brooks looked at his colleague who had remained silent for most of the questioning. There was a moment of awkwardness until the sound of a mobile phone ringing broke the silence.

Paul answered his phone then looked at Brooks. 'I have to go to the hospital.'

The two detectives said their goodbyes and left. Just as they were about to drive off, they saw Connie Bailey walking into the estate. Brooks got back out and walked towards her.

'Connie Bailey I am arresting you for the murder of Tanya Price.'

It had been an accident. While his wife was taking a nap, Gerald Croft decided he was hungry so started making a bacon sandwich. The problem was that after he'd lit the frying pan, he forgot what he was doing and went back into the lounge, shutting the kitchen door behind him. The smoke alarms went off, of course, but they went off all the time, so the neighbours ignored them.

Ironically, closing the kitchen door had probably saved their lives because it shut in the fire long enough for them to be rescued. Former Chief Inspector Gerald Croft had suffered worse injuries than his wife. Whereas she had been led downstairs and out of the house by a neighbour, a confused Mr Croft had refused to leave before the fire had taken hold.

Watching his father lying on a hospital bed and attached to breathing apparatus, Paul was overwhelmed with sadness. To see his father, once strong and intimidating, now so weak and helpless he had to fight back the tears. Reluctantly, he left the room to join his mother in a side ward. She was sitting in a wheelchair, however, apart from minor smoke inhalation, she was uninjured. There was no house left to go back to, so Paul insisted on her staying with him and his wife until things were sorted out.

His mother was not happy about that though. 'I don't see why I can't stay in a hotel, Paul. You and your wife have enough to be getting on with without having to worry about me.'

'I would worry about you a lot more if you were on your own in some miserable hotel,' he countered.

'It wouldn't be miserable to me,' she answered.

Paul rolled his eyes. He knew his mother would rather be alone in a hotel than stay with him. And he wasn't particularly looking forward to it either. Yet he felt the responsibility on his shoulders. His parents had had little time for him since he reached adulthood. Sometimes he thought they actually disliked him. He knew they didn't approve of Rachel and in some ways, he understood that, but he felt that there was more to it than that.

As he steered his mother down the white corridor, he caught a glimpse of Ben sitting in the visitors' room. Apart from wearing hospital clothes, he looked like his normal self. Leaving his mother outside, Paul walked into the visitors' room.

'I can't thank you enough for getting my father out of the house. You saved his life, Ben.' He paused before continuing. 'I don't understand what happened. How could he forget he was frying bacon, for heaven's sake?'

255

Ben looked uncomfortable. He nodded in acknowledgement before saying only a few words. 'I'm sure he'll be okay, Paul.' He'd already told the doctors about Gerald Croft's confused state when they were together in the upstairs room. But he knew it wasn't his place to tell Paul.

'I'd give you a lift home, but my colleague is on his way, and he'll want to ask you some questions, Paul said apologetically. 'We need to rule out any possibility of arson. Don't worry though. You're not a suspect this time.'

Lara raced through the A & E wards, but it was too late. Ben had left the hospital immediately after speaking to Brooks. She was relieved to hear that his wounds were superficial but was disappointed not to see him. Would he have seen her anyway? Ben had implied she was the person who had driven Chris off the road. Or maybe he'd used it as an excuse to get rid of her. He was a lone wolf and perhaps she'd chipped into his world a little too much. Jenny and Paul had both seemed surprised at the close contact she'd had with Ben. That night in his cottage, it felt as if they were building some sort of connection, something special. Clearly, she was wrong. The door to his world had been slammed in her face.

She was about to leave when she noticed Sergeant Brooks leaning over the reception desk. He was alone and she took her chance. 'Can I show you something?'

Over a coffee, she told Brooks everything; from her first encounter with Tom Bailey to her insistence that Chris Farmer stole her sister's bangle. She even showed him Bella's diary. To her relief, Brooks listened patiently to her. Although he didn't say as much, she knew he believed her. Like her, he was an outsider and wouldn't be put off by locals telling her to leave things be. Locals like Ben.

Detective Sergeant Brooks had spent very little time talking to Ben. Domestic fires were not for him. He was more interested in finding out how a miscarriage of justice might have taken place. In the hospital café, Lara Campbell had told him about her real reason for coming to Weston; how she remembered seeing Tom Bailey in a place where he shouldn't have been. Where he couldn't have been if he had killed Bella Young. Brooks was surprised when Lara told him about the bangle. When he saw the photographs, he was convinced Bella and Hanna Evans were wearing the same one. Paul Croft really should have mentioned it in the last briefing. It was certainly a lead *he* was going to follow up.

Gerald Croft was in intensive care, but Chris Farmer had recovered enough to be transferred to a general ward. It was outside of visiting hours, but Brooks was not that sort of visitor. When he approached the bed, Chris was sleeping so he sat down on a chair and made some notes. An elderly man in the next bed was looking at Brooks with suspicion but Brooks ignored him. He was used to being looked at like that, especially in what he considered to be backwater places.

But the elderly man was not prepared to be ignored. 'Are you a friend?' he asked.

'Not quite,' Brooks replied loudly. Perhaps the conversation would wake Chris Farmer up.

'Well. What are you here for? Poor lad needs to recover. He doesn't need fans bothering him right now.'

Brooks looked confused. 'Why would I be a fan of his?'

The man leaned closer to Brooks before saying, 'Ah, yes. You're probably too young to remember him when he was playing. He had many fans back in the day.'

'Really. What did he play?'

'What do you think? Football, of course. He was a striker for Tabworth Town for a few years. Tipped to make the Premier League but was undone by injury.'

There was no response from Brooks. He didn't care what Chris Farmer nearly did or didn't do. But if he thought the other man would lose interest in him, he was mistaken.

'Where are you from, lad?'

'What do you mean by that?' asked Brooks, now so irritated he was tempted to wake his patient up.

'Is it east or south London? I used to be spot on with accents.'

'Hackney.'

'So, they finally brought in another force. Not before time. There's far too much corruption around here.'

'How do you know I'm a police officer? I'm not wearing a uniform.'

'You don't trust me, that's why. It's in your eyes and that's what all coppers are like?'

'Do you live around here?' Brooks asked, now asking his own questions.

'Right here in Copston. Born and bred I am, and proud of it.'

'Except for its police force?'

'Well, it's not that I've had anything to do with them, but Copston Station feels more like a sheriff's office. It could do with an outsider like you to shake things up.'

Brooks agreed but it was more than his job was worth to say. 'Do you recall a murder case from twenty years ago? A young woman called Bella Young was murdered.'

The man shook his head. 'No. I don't remember that name. Did they get the person who did it?'

'Yes. His name's Tom Bailey.'

'Tom Bailey. Yes, of course. I remember his father worked in the same factory as my brother. Poor man. He didn't deserve a son like that.'

'Is his father still alive?' Brooks asked.

'No. I heard he died shortly after his son went to prison. Lost his job. Lost his home. Lost everything. It was wrong.'

'Yes, that sounds unfair,' Brooks said, without conviction. He had yet to meet a parent who wouldn't lie to protect their offspring no matter how heinous the crime.

'Who are you?'

Both men turned towards Chris, now awake and staring at the detective sitting in the chair meant for his visitors.

'Nice meeting you,' Brooks said to the older patient quickly before pulling the curtains around Chris's bed. Seeing Chris reaching for the emergency button, he showed his police badge and sat back down.

'I'd like to ask you some questions about your relationship with Hanna Evans, Mr Farmer.'

Chris's expression was one of immediate confusion before changing to fear. 'Hey! I'm a married man. Why are you asking me about Hanna? We dated briefly but that was twenty years ago. I haven't seen her since.'

'Why did you split up?'

'What the hell are you asking me that for? That's none of your business.'

'Did you speak to her the night she died?'

'No. I've already told you I haven't seen her in twenty years. You're not trying to pin her murder on me, are you?'

'Are you sure about the last time you saw her?'

'Yes, of course, I am.'

Brooks noticed that Chris was sounding more nervous with every question asked. He was certainly guilty of something. 'A possible witness claims that she saw you and Hanna Evans talking to each other at the bar in The Royal Oak pub. It was the night she died.'

'Well, your witness is wrong.'

'Mr Farmer, I'm finding your attitude bizarre. A car just ran you off the road, almost killing you. The driver of that vehicle fits the description of the woman suspected of murdering Hanna Evans. You're not in any way suspected of that murder but please be honest with me.'

'If I was there, I must have been too drunk to remember. That's all I've got to say.'

Brooks didn't give up. 'There's a killer about and all the victims testified in Bella Young's murder trial. It is obvious there is a link.'

In spite of the seriousness of the claim, Chris's only response was to turn his head away. Thinking he was about to ring for the nurses, Brooks had one more go.

'Will you look at this photograph?'

Reluctantly, Chris took the held-out phone and looked at the screen. He took a deep breath when he looked at the image of the three women together like it could have been twenty years ago.

'That's a pretty bangle she's wearing,' Brooks said. 'I heard it was a present from you.'

'Yes. I guess she kept it all these years. She doesn't look as if she's enjoying herself. That's probably why she left early.'

Brooks raised his eyebrows at that comment.

'That's what I heard from Jenny and Tanya anyway. They said Hanna was upset and left early.'

'She did leave early, and she was upset. But I don't believe she was upset when this selfie was taken. I think she became upset after seeing this photograph.' He handed Chris one of the photographs given to him by Lara.

Now staring at the photograph of the five friends, Chris shook his head. 'What am I supposed to be looking at?' he asked impatiently.

'The girl at the end, Bella Young, is also wearing a bangle. Is it too small for you to see? You can use this,' he said, holding up a pocket magnifying glass.

But Chris didn't need the magnifying glass. He knew exactly what the bangle looked like. And how it felt after he'd wrenched it off Bella's wrist. It was finally too much to bear, and he dared Bella to tell his secret to anyone who cared. He was ready for the ramifications.

The following morning, he gave the bangle to Hanna despite knowing he was about to break her heart. He was planning on telling her the truth, but he had to tell his parents first. Of course, as it turned out, he didn't have to say anything. He would carry on as normal. His only regret was giving Hanna that bangle.

'Just one more thing, Mr Farmer. Was this the woman who drove you off the road?'

Chris looked at the photograph of Connie Bailey and nodded his head.

Chapter Twenty

It had been a quiet day and Jenny decided to shut up early. No customers came after five o'clock except during the holiday season, and she had better things to do than sit behind the till in an empty café. Starting the process of closing, she picked up the pole used to push back the canopy at the front. There had been too many days like this, she thought to herself. It was time to give up the ghost.

She'd been looking for the first excuse to pack up her things and return to the city she loved, and a failed business was it. It was an experiment which hadn't worked - coming back to Weston after so many years away. When she'd first considered the challenge of living once more in a place that terrified her, she'd forgotten one important factor.

The bell rang and, after putting down the pole, she walked back into the customers' area. There was only one customer. A man stood by the door with his back to her.

'Hello. What can I get you?' she called across to him.

He didn't answer. Jenny watched apprehensively as the man stayed still.

'Excuse me. What are you doing?' she shouted.

When he finally turned around, he was grinning. 'Hello Jenny. Long-time, no see.'

Jenny wanted to scream but no sound came out of her throat. It was her worse nightmare and now it was real. Finally, she found her voice. 'I'm sorry. I'm sorry. I didn't know what would happen to you. I swear, I didn't know. Please go away.'

'You're a liar. I know what you did and now it's time for you to be punished. The police know all about your scheming.'

She watched in horror as he turned around revealing that he'd turned the closed sign to face the outside. Then he walked towards her.

By the time Lara and John reached the café, the ambulance was leaving. When they went inside, two uniformed police officers were sitting at a table with a distraught Jenny. As soon as she saw Lara, she ran over and flung her arms around the surprised woman.

'I thought he was going to rape me,' she sobbed.

'It's okay. You had to do it, Jenny. It was self-defence,' Lara said. However, deep down she wondered why Bailey would risk raping anyone just after his release from a twenty-year jail sentence. She looked across at John who was busy talking to the police officers, so turned back to Jenny. 'Did he say anything to you?'

Jenny's tears suddenly dried up on hearing Lara's question. She looked angry. 'I can't believe you are asking me that now. Just leave me alone.'

On hearing Jenny's raised voice John walked over to join the two women. 'Leave her be. She's in shock,' he said.

'But, John, I just want to know what he said.'

Lara's frustration was greater than any concern for Jenny. This could be crucial to the mystery of Bella's murder. Why couldn't John see that too? But John looked different to the man who she'd befriended over the course of the last week. As if Lara wasn't there, he gently motioned Jenny to another table and then talked privately with her. He didn't even notice Lara leaving the café.

Lara ended up walking back to the hotel. Once he'd moved to another table with Jenny, John appeared to be unaware of anyone else in the café. Perhaps he was now acting as Jenny's solicitor and didn't want to talk to her right now. Could a judge act as a solicitor? She had no idea but the way he'd shielded Jenny from the police suggested he'd taken that role regardless. He wouldn't even let her speak to Jenny once he'd ushered her to another table. She was glad that Jenny had managed to protect herself against Bailey. It was lucky that the pole was available to use as a weapon against him. However, John had been a huge help to Lara, and she worried that he would now close her out. At least Brooks seemed to be on her side.

There was nowhere left for her to go. No one left to talk to. Her next move should be to go home and leave the mess behind, the mess that some would say she'd caused. But according to Brooks they had arrested someone for the murders of Hanna and Tanya, and he insisted that it was not related to Lara showing up in the village. Brooks wouldn't say how he knew that or even who they'd arrested but Lara worked out that it must be Connie Bailey. She felt sad for the arrested woman and hoped she would be released without charge, despite the detective's confidence. After all, the police had made a mistake before. But that was for somebody else to find out. Her job was done.

It was certain that her sister's case would be reopened now, and an outside force would probably be called in to investigate. Bailey might be a despicable sexual predator, but he had not killed anyone, at least not Bella. She also had a nagging doubt about the incident with Jenny. Was he really intending to assault her just after getting released from prison? Perhaps he was just trying to intimidate Jenny and she panicked. Whatever happened, Lara knew he didn't kill her sister. Hopefully, the real killer would be found soon but she wouldn't be here to see it. However, before she left there was one person that she hadn't spoken to. She didn't want to leave any loose ends so the next day she would visit Simone.

'You can't arrest someone on the back of two similar-looking bracelets,' Paul shouted to his Chief Inspector.

'Bangles not bracelets,' muttered Brooks. 'Like the pop group.'

'Bangles! Bracelets! What the hell is the difference? They are all made in their millions so it's not unusual to have two women with the same type'.

'What is the difference between a bracelet and a bangle?' asked the Chief curiously.

'A bracelet had a clasp, Sir. Bella Young had a mark around her left wrist which could have been made by someone struggling to pull it off. The clasp of a bracelet would have snapped with that much pressure. This mark was assumed to have been made by Tom Bailey in an attempt to bind her wrists but that probably didn't happen. And no bangle was found at the crime scene.'

'Because it was taken by Bailey,' Paul said. 'Why is that such a problem for you, Karl?'

'It's a problem because that same bracelet turned up on Hanna Evans's wrist a short time after the murder,' Brooks replied. He was determined to make his case even though Paul was doing his best to stop him. 'Look, Paul, I know Chris Farmer was a close friend once, but killers have friends too.'

'What does that mean? Are you implying that I'm covering for him?'

'Not consciously, no. But who would want the local celebrity to be a murderer? Chris Farmer is not above the law.'

'Perhaps he took the bangle earlier that night which would mean she didn't have it when Bailey killed her,' the chief suggested.

'Are you suggesting we arrest him for stealing a bracelet twenty years ago?' Paul asked sarcastically.

'No. I'm suggesting we arrest him for contempt of court, an action that possibly led to a miscarriage of justice. But we could throw in the bangle theft. Look, Sir, Hanna Evans got upset when she saw the photograph showing Bella Young wearing the same bracelet the night she was murdered. Okay, we don't know for certain that was the thing that upset her, but I think we should assume that it could be.'

Paul Croft scoffed but inside he was beside himself. While he was busy dealing with his parents, this pain of a policeman had the presumption to take over the investigation. It was bad enough that Brooks had been interviewing witnesses without him there to lead. Now he was making wild guesses about Bella Young's murder. The mention of contempt of court had chilled him to the bone but he knew the Chief Inspector well. That man wouldn't listen to the rantings of Sergeant Brooks over him.

The Chief Inspector was listening carefully to his sergeant's surmising but was leaning towards the view of his inspector. It was not that simple, however. There was a risk of another force taking over the new murder investigations, so he didn't want to leave any stone unturned. It was obvious why Paul Croft would be against anything that would taint his father's name. Gerald Croft had led the original investigation almost single-handedly and was rightly hailed for his success. But there were some doubts. Bailey had never admitted his guilt even though it lengthened his sentence. And some officers were all too happy to get him off the streets knowing that he was probably behind the attacks on young women.

'I just don't see where the contempt of court comes into it, Brooks,' he remarked while glancing at Paul.

'Because it put him somewhere he shouldn't have been. He said he was in Easton with Ben Sutton. The two men said they had taken a shortcut through the fields. He was either in one place or the other. He couldn't have been in both.'

'Maybe he took it in Copston,' the chief said. 'That's assuming he did take the bracelet.'

'Bangle, sir. There's another photo showing her wearing a bangle while leaving the ball. It's not clear enough to see it in detail but it is certain to be the same bangle. She was with the other girls until she reached Weston.'

'Well, that means they both lied,' the chief said. 'It's time you had a chat with Ben Sutton too,' he continued, looking at Brooks.

When Simone answered the front door there was a flicker of resentment in her eyes as she saw Lara standing on the doorstep. 'What do you want?' she asked. Her tone was unfriendly and far from welcoming.

'Hello, Simone. I know this is not a good time, but I really need to talk to you. It won't take long as I'm leaving Weston tomorrow. I might even leave tonight if I can see you now.'

Simone looked at Lara with suspicion but allowed her inside. 'I suppose I should offer you tea or coffee?'

'Tea would be lovely, thanks.' Lara hoped the atmosphere might mellow over a hot drink.

'So, what do you want to ask me? Is it about Jenny?' Simone asked when the two women were sitting at the kitchen table.

'No, it isn't, actually,' Lara replied. 'Well, first I'd like to say how sorry I am about your husband. But it's good to hear that he's going to make a full recovery.'

Simone pulled a face. 'He'll be making his recovery far away from me.'

'Oh, I'm sorry. I didn't realise you were having problems,' Lara lied.

'Of course, you did,' Simone said. 'You've spent enough time with Jenny to know he's been staying there.'

'Yes, but she didn't tell me anything, Simone. She's a loyal friend to you.'

'I know. That's something I used to be grateful for but now I realise it never made any difference.'

Lara was in a dilemma. She really didn't care about the couple's marital problems, but it seemed that Simone wanted to offload so she kept on topic. 'He clearly loves you, Simone. A man doesn't marry lightly.'

'Yes, that's true. Not even Jenny managed to pull that off as fabulous as she is. Living with a man just gives him what he wants without commitment. She never got anyone to marry her.'

'Perhaps she's not ready,' Lara replied. Despite wanting to keep Simone on side, she couldn't stop herself defending the woman who had been good to her. 'She's still a young woman.'

'Yes, and so am I. Anyway, you haven't told me why you're here.'

'I've been piecing everything together and there are a few things that don't fit. One of them is why your husband may have lied about his whereabouts that night. I don't think he was with Ben when he said he was.'

Simone knew that Lara was correct. Ben had told her that he and Chris weren't together at all after the ball even though they'd both testified to the contrary in court. Neither of them knew where Chris actually was at the time he was supposed to have been with Ben. At that moment in time, she hated her husband, however, any trouble would affect her and her children so she would keep her own counsel for now. 'You do know that Chris and I weren't a couple back then, don't you? I have no idea if he lied because I wasn't with him.'

'The reason I believe he lied is because he got an anonymous letter, just like Tanya and Hanna.'

'And me,' Simone replied.

'Yes. And you. But I'm not here about your letter, Simone, even though I guess you got it for testifying against Bailey. But you were all together at that time so it's clear that you didn't lie. But Chris wasn't where he said he was, so he lied to the police and then lied in court. He must have had a reason to lie, and I think it might be that he killed my sister.'

On hearing that last comment, Simone spat out her coffee and laughed. 'You can't be serious. It seems that I don't know much about my own husband, but I do know he's not capable of killing a fly, let alone a human being.'

Simone's reaction confused Lara. She was expecting Simone to be shocked at the possibility of her husband being a murderer, but she just laughed it off. However, Lara kept to her script. 'Did he like Bella?'

'No, I'm sure he didn't but that doesn't mean he would risk everything by killing her.'

'Do you think Bella tried to blackmail him, Simone?'

'Yes. I'm sure she did try. It was her hobby.'

Lara sighed. She was tired of hearing so much vitriol about her sister. 'Why did you even bother with her if she was blackmailing all of you?'

'We bothered with her because she was Jenny's friend. And she didn't blackmail me but I do think she was blackmailing somebody.'

'Why do you think that?'

'Because she talked about going to London and becoming famous. How could she even afford the trip? She must have known she was getting money from someone.'

'Okay. Well, I'm sorry if she did that. I'm sure it was a stupid way of feeling superior to those who were better off than her.'

Lara was beginning to reject the idea that her sister had been blackmailing her friends as not one of them would admit to having been a victim themselves. Except for Ben. But Ben wasn't sure, was he? She then told Simone about the bangle and why it had convinced her of Chris's guilt.

After a few moments of thought, Simone nodded to herself. 'I remember that bangle. When he gave it to Hanna, I hated her so much. How could Chris choose her over me, I thought? Of course, Hanna told herself that was it and the next thing would be a ring. But it didn't happen. To think she kept it all these years.'

'Don't you remember Bella wearing that bangle at the ball?'

'No, I can't say that I did. To be honest, I didn't see her much that night, apart from the journey there and back and I'm sure you know all about that.'

'Yes. Can I ask you why you hated her so much when she didn't blackmail you?'

Simone lowered her head before answering Lara's question. 'I suppose I was jealous of her. She was poor and she was bad news, but the boys loved her, especially when she played that cheap guitar at school. They thought she was the next Susanna Hoffs. I used to think Chris secretly fancied her too. That's a laugh.'

Chapter Twenty-one

The visit to Simone had been more productive than Lara could possibly have hoped it would be. Not so much in terms of finding out the truth about Bella's killer as she didn't share Simone's conviction that her husband would not harm a fly. Rather, Lara was pleased to find out that her late sister had some admirers even if she did also have serious faults. Who knows, perhaps she would have returned the money if she'd made the big time. Of course, that's if she really had blackmailed anyone.

Lara's eyes began to well up as she thought about leaving Weston. It would be unlikely that she would return for a long time so Bella's grave would remain uncared for. That thought prompted her to drive past the hotel with the intention of visiting the grave for the last time. As she passed The Royal Oak, she noticed a solitary motorbike parked outside. It was Ben's bike.

After parking down a side street, Lara walked into the pub. At first, she thought it was empty and was about to walk out again when she spotted Ben sitting on his own at a corner table. He was holding a half-empty pint of lager and staring into space. Lara wondered if the glass had been used more than once.

To the surprise of the young barman, she ordered two coffees then held her breath as she carried them over to Ben's table.

'You don't have to drink it if you don't want to,' she said, as she placed the cups on the table, 'but I got you one just in case.'

Ben glanced at the cups and then back into space. His only response was to take another swig of his lager. Unperturbed, Lara sat down next to him.

'I came in to say goodbye and to thank you for helping me when I was attacked by that man. And for giving me shelter that night of the storm.'

'They've arrested Chris.' Ben had not looked at Lara once since she came into the pub, and he continued to look in front of him even when speaking.

'What for?' Lara asked awkwardly. She was worried that Ben would tell her to leave him alone.

'For lying about that night. The thing is, Chris said he was with me, and I said I was with him. If he was lying, so was I. Looks like I'm going to prison.'

Lara sat in silence. This was not how it was supposed to end up. All she wanted was for the real killer to be found, but instead, several innocent people could end up in prison. She had opened a can of worms. Suddenly, without speaking, Ben picked up his empty glass and went to the bar leaving Lara alone with her thoughts. Now it was she who stared into space. Without warning, a pint of lager appeared on the table in front of her and Ben sat down next to her once again.

'Do you want to join me?' he asked, holding his glass in the air as if making a toast.

Lara politely refused. 'Thanks. I would but I'm driving.'

'So am I,' he replied.

Not if you drink those two pints, she thought to herself, as he moved the glass over to him.

'Look, Ben, the last thing I wanted was to get you into trouble, but the truth must come out. You do see that, don't you?' But she wasn't sure that he did.

He didn't reply.

'Why did you say that you were with Chris when it was not true?'

Ben remained silent.

'Was he with someone else? Was he with someone he could never admit to being with?'

For the first time since she arrived, Ben was now looking at her. 'What do you mean by that?'

'He was a football player in the nineties when homophobia was rampant throughout the game. If the person he met was a man, and he had to admit that in court, his career might have been over.'

'How do you know Chris is gay?' he asked.

'An educated guess,' she answered.

Ben rolled his eyes. 'So you didn't know.'

'I'm not interested in local gossip, Ben, but how do you know he was really with another man?'

'That's what he told me. He said he'd have to give up everything if the truth got out. I wanted to help him, so I said he was with me.'

'And where was that?'

'I went straight home like a good boy. The walk back took ages because I kept to the road hoping to hitch a lift. As soon as I started the walk home, Tom Bailey stopped his car even though he was going in the opposite direction. He offered to turn around and give me a lift home, but I said no.'

'Why?'

'As I told you before, he was bad news.'

'Oh, Ben! What have you done? You didn't just give Chris a false alibi, but you also refused to back up Bailey when he said he offered you a lift. You could have prevented his conviction.'

'I know. I made a choice between saving him and protecting my friend. Bailey wasn't worth saving.'

'Ben, listen to me. The reason Chris has been arrested is not just because his alibi is now considered to be false. It's because he wasn't with some secret boyfriend. He was with Bella.'

'What! How would you know that?'

Lara cringed. She knew she'd exaggerated the evidence putting Chris at the murder scene, but she would have to keep her nerve. But was Ben beginning to doubt she was telling him the truth?

'Finish your drinks, please. We need to close. You can come back at seven.' The barman was clearly fed up with staying open for a few pints and a couple of coffees.

Lara was desperately disappointed. She had so much more to ask Ben, but he was already leaving.

'Hey! You can park your bike in the back for a few hours. I don't want any trouble leading back to me.'

'Come on! How am I meant to get home?' Ben said.

The barman was not to be persuaded so Ben did as he was told.

'I guess I'll have to kip on this wall for a bit.' Then he looked at Lara. 'On the other hand, could you give me a lift to Easton?' Then he opened his wallet and held out a ten-pound note.

'No. I haven't got time but come back to the hotel and you can sleep it off in comfort.'

'Okay. Let's go.'

Within ten minutes they were inside the hotel, and, to Lara's relief, Mrs Parsons did not appear to be in. Flora must have taken her shopping. To Lara's dismay, Ben began looking around every room downstairs as if he were about to rob the place. She ushered him upstairs and into her room.

'I'll leave you here to have a sleep. Try not to make a noise because the landlady might be back any minute. I'll be downstairs.'

Ben nodded and then began walking towards the bed. Suddenly he staggered to one side and nearly fell. He must have been drunker than she thought. Grabbing him by the arm, she steered him to the bed and pushed him gently onto it. Then she realised he was holding onto her arm too and she fell on top of him. When she lifted her head, he was staring at her. Then he smiled and pulled he even closer to him. And she didn't resist.

Dark clouds had formed in the sky above and several parents and children were leaving the children's park, but Simone was sticking it out. Her children needed wearing out and she had company for once. She'd moved back into her house because Jenny was staying with her. Now, sitting together on a narrow bench, the two women were sharing their sorrows while wondering if the latest events were some sort of Karma.

'I wish my parents had moved away from that awful place earlier,' Simone said. Her eyes were fixed on her oldest child, but her words were addressed to the woman sitting next to her.

'Why do you say that?' Jenny answered. 'They only moved because of what happened to Bella. That old house of yours was fabulous with its sea views. I used to love staying there.'

'I never did like the sea,' Simone replied. 'The seagulls are noisy and the beach smells of fish. Give me a river any day.'

Jenny shivered as she thought of returning to her seaside home. She would have to, sooner than later. Her mind was made up. As soon as she pulled herself together, she would put the property up for sale.

House prices were rising in the area as news of a possible redevelopment of the village circulated. She'd have to be there for the valuation, and it was sensible to get everything done before Tom Bailey got out of the hospital.

On reflection, she knew she'd overreacted, and he only meant to torment her over probable criminal charges coming her way. But, given what he'd tried to do to her before, she wasn't taking any chances. She'd told everyone she was fine about the attack back then, but really, she thought about it every night. To this day she couldn't walk anywhere alone at night. All because of Tom Bailey.

At first, she thought she'd killed him when she slammed the steel pole into the back of his head, but the paramedics told her he was only unconscious. She should have hit him harder.

She heard a child crying her name and she waved to the little girl she barely knew. Wasn't it strange how trusting children are, she thought?

'Another five minutes, Edie,' Simone shouted to her daughter. She needed that time to bring up the topic they'd avoided for so long. 'Jenny, do you think Chris could have killed Bella?'

'You've been listening to Lara, haven't you? And no, I don't think Chris killed Bella. Why are you even asking such a stupid question? We know who killed Bella. It was Tom Bailey. We all saw him coming from the coastal path.'

'You didn't see him though, did you, Jenny? You were too drunk.'

'But the rest of you saw him - you, Tanya and Hanna.'

'And they are both dead. We all testified at the trial and now someone is killing us. Listen, Jenny, I'm really scared. I think I'm going to be next.'

'But why? Why would anyone want to kill you for saying the truth?'

Simone looked back towards her daughter, pleased that the child was still engrossed in the sandpit. She took a deep breath before she made her admission. 'I didn't see anything, Jenny. Tanya rang me the next day. She told me that Bella had been murdered on the coastal path and that she and Hanna had seen him driving away.'

'So, why did you say you'd seen him too?'

'They blackmailed me.'

'What? I don't understand. What are you hiding, Jenny?'

'When I was seventeen, while my parents were out, I borrowed the car. My mother had left salad for dinner, but I wanted pizza.'

'So, you borrowed your dad's car. That's not a cardinal sin.'

'I hit someone.' Her voice was unemotive as if she had disassociated herself from the words coming from it.

Jenny gasped at the confession. 'And you didn't stop?'

'Of course, I didn't. You would already know about it if I had.'

'What happened to the person you hit?'

'He recovered eventually. He was drunk so couldn't identify the car that hit him. My dad's car wasn't damaged, so my parents never knew.'

'How did Hanna and Tanya find out about it?'

'Bella told them. She saw me crying after parking the car in the drive. Her foster home looked down on our house. Tanya said Bella had told her that I wasn't so high and mighty after all. I had no idea that they knew until that day. They told me that Bailey had raped Hanna, and this was a chance to punish him for it.'

'Bailey raped Hanna! I can't believe it. So that's why she had an abortion.'

'Apparently, she didn't have an abortion. She had it adopted.'

'Simone, that means I was involved in a conspiracy to jail Bailey for Bella's murder.'

'Yes. I'm sorry but it didn't seem so terrible. When the other evidence came out about him, I think we convinced ourselves he was guilty anyway and our testimonies wouldn't matter too much. He is a monster as you well know, Jenny.'

Jenny's mind was in turmoil. She was stunned by Simone's admission that Bailey's attack on her was a lie. That lie had traumatised her for the past twenty years and, if Tanya and Hanna weren't dead, she would hate them. But what about Hanna? Bailey raped her. Or had he? She would never know.

'What are you thinking about, Jenny?'

Jenny looked at her broken friend and felt sad for her too. 'What shall we do about it? If you admit everything, you might go to prison.'

'I know but at least I won't be dead.'

Lara was happy for the first time in over a year. Ben was asleep but his arm was still wrapped around her, and she could hear his heart beating under her head. She wanted to stay there until he woke up, but she knew Mrs Parsons was downstairs and might wonder what she'd been doing alone in her room for all this time. More than that, she had something important to do. She got up quietly and tipped out her bag to find her phone then left the room. She found an empty bedroom, sat down on the bed, and pressed her most used number.

'Hi Mum,' she whispered.

'Hello, Lara. Is everything okay? Why are you whispering?'

'I don't want to disturb anyone. Listen I know I said I'd be leaving today but I've changed my mind. Something's happened.'

'Oh, dear. I don't like the sound of this. Do you want us to come down?'

'Mum, I've met someone who I really like, and I think he likes me too.'

'Think! That doesn't sound very promising.'

'But it is. We talk for hours, and I feel a real connection to him. He's in my room now that's why I'm whispering.'

'Some men are more than happy to talk their way into a woman's bedroom. I'm happy for you, Luv, I really am but please don't do anything hasty.'

Lara didn't tell her that it was already too late and that she had dived into bed with the drunk man who she claimed liked her as much as she did him. Trust her mother to throw cold water over her happiness.

'I don't care what you say, Mum. He likes me. I know he does.'

Feeling like a scolded child, Lara made an attempt at a friendly goodbye and then marched back to her room. She hated herself for feeling that her mother might be right, as she usually was. Perhaps she would play it cool when Ben woke up if it wasn't too late.

When she opened her bedroom door, she wanted to run back home and never set foot out of the door again. Ben was awake and he was standing by the dressing table. In one of his hands was a diary, the diary with her handwriting in. The other hand was stretched out with one finger pointing towards her.

'It was you all along.'

He was looking at her the way he had back when they first met … when he hated her. She tried to explain but he wouldn't listen. He picked up his keys and walked out of the door ignoring her as she pleaded with him. Then the front door opened, and John came in.

Ben turned to him. 'If you've had any anonymous letters lately, she's the culprit.'

Chapter Twenty-two

'That's why I didn't get a letter, isn't it? You didn't know I existed until you came here.'

'I didn't know any of the men existed until I got here. It took a few more days to find out about you, though.'

'How did you know where everyone lived?'

'Premium 192. It was too easy.'

'Why did you send them?'

'To ruffle some feathers. When I decided to come here, I didn't know what I would find so I wanted people to be interested in my arrival. I knew they'd suspect me of course, but it would be better than nothing happening at all. As it turned out Jenny was so helpful, introducing me to Tanya and Hanna, and telling me their side of the story. There was no real need for the letters. But I sent Paul one anyway.'

'Why didn't you send me one while you were at it, even if it would have been late?'

'Because you were so good to me. Unlike Paul who was rude and dismissive. You made me feel like I could confide in you, and I did, eventually. I wish I'd been more open with you earlier.'

'I'm glad you weren't because it would have put me in an awkward position.'

'But you know now. What are you going to do?'

'It might not matter about my actions. Ben was very angry and might well have gone to the police already.'

Lara remembered the expression on Ben's face when he was pointing at her in the bedroom. Instead of asking her for an explanation, he just stormed out. If he liked her, he would want to understand her motive for sending those letters, not ignore her pleas. She realised that her feelings for him were not reciprocated. Then a thought struck her. Did he think she was a killer? John didn't though. Or did he?

'John, what if they arrest me for more than the letters?'

'You don't have to worry about that for now,' he said. 'They've arrested Connie Bailey for the murder of Hanna and they're sure to add Tanya's murder onto any charge.'

'But that makes no sense, John. Why now after so many years?'

'Don't forget she was a small child when he was convicted and she's only in her mid-twenties now. She probably blames her miserable life on her father's imprisonment, and seeing you was the catalyst. It brought things to a head.'

'I still don't see it.'

'You don't have to, but it looks like this whole thing will be wrapped up soon.'

Throughout the long, one-sided police interview Connie Bailey was using her right to remain silent. However, Paul wondered if she was even able to speak so they allowed her brother to be present while she was being questioned. Brooks had not agreed with the decision but was overruled.

The interview was tedious. Every question was responded to with silence from the accused then her solicitor's "no comment" on behalf of his client. Jack had given up trying to answer for his sister after being threatened with removal from the overcrowded interview room. Unlike his father, Jack Bailey had no experience of the type of situation in which his sister now found herself.

Before he was silenced he'd insisted that his younger sister was incapable of such a crime as murder, particularly one that had an element of planning. Paul Croft tended to agree with him. However, the figure in the CCTV footage, what could be seen of it, did bear a resemblance to Connie. Also, she had a motive. The two murdered women had helped send her father to prison, setting off a chain of events that led to her current state of near insanity.

She appeared to be in a world of her own. The only acknowledgement of her surroundings was to take sips of water from the plastic cup she held in one hand. But just as the interview was about to finish, she looked up at Paul and began to cry.

'I think we're done here,' the solicitor said abruptly. He'd never been part of such a pointless interview in his thirty-year career. 'You have no evidence against my client and a blurry CCTV image does not change that.'

'It does if she cannot explain where she was at the time the image was captured,' Paul insisted. Despite his own doubts, he wanted Connie Bailey to be guilty because that would put an end to rumours circulating about a possible miscarriage of justice regarding Connie's father. Tom Bailey would still be known as the murderer of Bella Young and the last couple of weeks would soon be forgotten. But he knew they didn't have nearly enough evidence to convict Connie, even if it were proved that she was indeed the person on the CCTV image.

'If there are no more questions, I suggest we end this interview now,' the solicitor said. He had a dinner engagement and would need to change his clothes after an hour in the stuffy room.

'One more thing,' Brooks said. He'd been quiet up until that point but was getting frustrated at his colleague's lack of attention to detail. 'Where were you at ten thirty on Friday 8th October?'

Connie Bailey made no reaction to the question, but her solicitor gave a loud sigh at the new area of questioning.

'What has this got to do with my client's arrest?' he asked, hoping that the new line of questioning would not take as long as the first one had. He was hopeful when he heard an answer to the question.

'She was with me,' Jack said.

'Don't get yourself into trouble,' said Brooks. 'You don't want to make the same mistake as your grandparents.'

'Don't you dare bring them into this,' Jack replied. It was the first time he'd raised his voice since the start of the interview.

Brooks was not taking any stick from someone who shouldn't even be in the interview room. 'They gave your father a false alibi and duly paid the consequences. So I'd shut up if I were you.'

'I'll shut up once I've finished what I was trying to say. At seven o'clock in the evening of the date in question, I took my sister to A&E after she tried to cut her wrists. We were there until midnight. You can check that CCTV.'

After Connie Bailey was released without charge, the two detectives sat slumped at their desks. They had suspected three different people for at least one of the murders. Chris Farmer was in the frame for Hanna's while Ben Sutton had been the main suspect for Tanya's until Connie's name came into the mix. It had been assumed that the same person committed both murders, but the Bailey woman was definitely innocent of at least one. Chris had no known motive for killing Tanya and the same was true of Ben regarding Hanna's murder. They were back to square one. Brooks said that he and Paul must look like idiots to their colleagues, as well as to the various suspects. It was time, he said, to bring in the only person, other than Connie, who had a motive for both murders. It was time to seriously consider Lara Campbell as a suspect in the murders.

Chris winced as he picked up the crumpled black t-shirt from the floor and was surprised to smell perfume on it. He took it downstairs and put it in the washing machine. He hated seeing dirty laundry around the house. It was one of the many things Simone did that irritated him, along with just being his wife. But now that she knew the truth was out, she wouldn't be his wife for much longer. He imagined her convincing anyone who would listen that he should not be granted joint custody given his lies and deceit. But he would fight for it, nonetheless. It was not a crime to be gay anymore.

He heard the sound of a motorbike from outside and braced himself for any news that Ben might bring him. Ben knew that he'd lied to him about that night. He had to lie because he knew Ben wouldn't have given him an alibi if he'd told him where he really was – arguing with Bella. But Ben had forgiven him and given him somewhere to stay until things were sorted out. Then the front door opened to reveal his friend, dishevelled and smelling of beer.

'I can't believe you drove home in that state,' Chris shouted.

'Give it a rest, Chris. I'm not in the mood. And you should be resting.'

'What's the matter? You look awful.' Chris's instinct told him that Ben's bad mood was nothing to do with him.

'Never mind. Will you make me a coffee while I have a shower?'

Minutes later, the two men were drinking coffee and discussing how they were both suspected of murdering two of their old friends. Chris related his experience with Detective Brooks whose ramblings about a bangle sent Chris running straight to a lawyer. The detective had actually suggested he'd murdered Bella after taking her bangle. Then Ben spoke of his horror when he'd realised that the police might have a case against him regarding Tanya's murder. Although Chris mentioned the anonymous letters, Ben did not disclose his discovery of the writer's identity. He didn't know why. The conversation moved on to the future.

'Are you sure this is what you want out of life?' Chris asked while staring at the cracks in the surrounding walls.

Ben was aware of every tiny fault in his home but wasn't the type of person to seek perfection unnecessarily. 'This might not be the most glamorous house in the area, but it'll outlast yours.'

Chris laughed. 'You're probably right but I wasn't talking about this house. I meant living on the edge of a cliff. You must get bored seeing the same thing day after day.'

'Maybe. I've been thinking about renting this out for a couple of years. There's a company up north that's looking for people with my experience, so I've made enquiries.'

'You never have told me what you did all those years in the Navy.' Chris shook his head because he knew Ben wasn't about to enlighten him.

'And what about you, Chris? You could still come to some arrangement with Simone. Lots of couples have fake marriages.'

'You mean actors and politicians. It's different for a man working in sports. It was bad enough pretending before, but now squeaky-clean Simone knows too much.'

'The bangle?'

'Yes. And don't worry, I'll make it clear to the police that you knew nothing about that. I'm sorry for not telling you the truth, Ben.'

'Why did you take that stupid bangle anyway? And what were you doing down by the coastal path?'

'At the ball, Bella was bragging about being signed up by some record producer in London. I asked her how she was going to get there, and she said she was getting the money later that night. She was meeting someone at the coastal path at twelve. When I asked her why anyone would give her money, she laughed and said they had no choice. Then she said if they didn't show up, she'd ask me instead. After drinking a few lagers, I got so mad that I went straight to the path to have it out with her. She just laughed at me. Then I noticed the bangle on her wrist and assumed she'd bought it with money she'd got from blackmailing some other poor sod. I forced it from her then left.'

'Didn't she scream? There must have been some people around.'

'No. I think she was in shock, to be honest. The next morning, I gave it to Hanna. Then I heard that Bella had been found dead and I was terrified I would be blamed.'

'Did anyone see you?'

'No. I saw the girls walking home but they didn't see me.'

'What about Bailey? He must have been around there somewhere.'

'I didn't see him, but I did see a car driving towards the coast. It was too expensive to be Bailey's.'

'So, all this time you knew Bailey wasn't there.'

'His car wasn't there. It doesn't mean he wasn't there.'

'But the girls said that he was in his car. That means they lied in court too. Your wife isn't as squeaky clean as you think.'

Detective Sergeant Brooks was sitting in the corner of the office he shared with Paul Croft. In front of him was a pile of old photographs and a scanned copy of Bella Young's diary. Underneath these were pages and pages of records from the investigation and court case regarding the murder of Bella. It had not taken long to break the childish code that Bella had used to write her diary entries with. That was just as well because there was little that was significant in the tiny book.

Bella seemed like a typical teenager, bitching about female friends while wondering about the attentions of male friends. It was clear that she had feelings for John Parsons but knew they were unrequited. Towards the end of the diary, the language was more positive, and Bella mentioned that she would win Parsons' heart when she was famous.

It was sad to read the words of a girl filled with naïve hope, but Brooks felt that they were not important to the current investigation. The only words that mattered were those that foreshadowed her murder. In the last entry, Bella referred to the person who would later kill her. But who was that person?

Connie Bailey was undoubtedly innocent, but Brooks was disappointed that Chris Farmer had been released. Everyone involved in the investigation agreed that the bangles worn by Bella and Hanna Evans in the three photographs were one and the same. However, it would be impossible to prove that without a confession from Chris Farmer and that was unlikely, especially after his top-notch lawyer made an appearance. No. He would have to find more evidence than that.

He picked up a magnifying glass and slowly moved it around each photograph, looking for any images of the young footballer. Chris Farmer was in almost every picture. Most images showed him laughing and joking around with the female students while they gazed at him adoringly. But the last photograph showed a very different Chris. He was scowling and the direction of his anger was at the female figure standing amongst a small group of boys. It was Bella, but she didn't seem to notice Chris because she was looking towards the bar. Brooks followed the direction of Bella's gaze until Paul Croft's teenage face appeared through the magnifying glass. The young man's arm was half draped around the shoulder of the woman standing next to him. But she was too old to be a student. Brooks recognised the silky dark hair and olive skin of the teacher trying to push her student's arm away. It was Rachel Croft.

The conservatory was the place where Paul liked to relax when he'd had a bad day at work - just like today had been. But tonight, his mother was sitting on his chair making endless phone calls. Within a couple of hours, she'd arranged for a hotel room close to the hospital and all paid for by the insurance company. Paul just hoped that his parents were insured against setting fire to their own house.

Rachel put her arms around Paul while he stood in silence. 'Come and sit down. You need to relax.'

'I can't relax, Rachel. There's so much going on at the station. We're bringing in Lara Campbell tomorrow morning. We'll see if it's possible to charge her with the murders.'

'I thought you'd arrested the Bailey girl for them.'

'She has an alibi. Hopefully, we've got the right one this time. I've got a feeling she knows far more than she's said so far.'

'Why are you suddenly focusing on her?'

'I'm not so sure but Brooks has done a U-turn after believing everything she told him about her reasons for coming to Weston. Now he thinks she could be insane.'

'What were her reasons for coming here?'

'Something about knowing that Bailey was wrongfully convicted of Bella Young's murder. She claims to have seen him miles away from the murder scene, but I don't know the details yet.'

'Okay but try to forget it for tonight. You've got enough to worry about,' she whispered.

Mrs Croft emerged from the conservatory and joined her son and daughter-in-law in the sitting room.

'You really shouldn't be on your own tonight, Grace.'

'Thank you, Rachel, but that's precisely where I need to be. There's so much to sort out.'

'But that's precisely why you should stay here, Mum. You can use our phone and the computer.'

'But I shan't be able to concentrate being in someone else's house.'

Paul and Rachel exchanged wary looks at his mother's reference to their home. They were hardly "someone else". Paul picked up his mother's bag which contained several items of clothing that her neighbours had donated. She would not accept any of Rachel's things.

'Come on then, Mum, if we're going to get you to that hotel before midnight. I need to get back too, remember.'

Once in the car, Paul turned on his mother. 'Why do you always have to be so rude to Rachel, and to me for that matter.'

Mrs Croft didn't answer her son which made him angrier. He slammed on the brakes.

'I know there's something wrong. You've been like this for years. Is it really because I married Rachel? Won't you finally accept that we love each other and always will?'

'She was your teacher. It's not right.'

'It might have been wrong back then, but we've been married for fifteen years so something must be right about us.' Then he shook his head. 'But it's not just that, is it, Mum? You were like this before we came out as a couple. It's not even Rachel that you hate, is it? It's me. Tell me why.'

His mother shifted in her seat while her son stared at her. Then she turned to him with tears in her eyes. 'Not while your father's still alive.'

Paul was more confused than ever when he saw his mother's eyes. He couldn't remember seeing her cry, not even when her parents died, or his sister gave her grandchildren. He felt his heart sinking as he realised his mother had been hiding something from him. His childish remark about his mother hating him and not Rachel had worked too well and now he was scared. But he had to know.

'If you don't tell me now, after I drop you off at the hotel, I'm driving to the hospital. I'll ask Dad what's going on.'

His mother's eyes widened in horror at her son's words. 'You can't. It'll kill him, Paul.'

'So, tell me.'

Turning her face towards the side window, Mrs Croft spoke quietly as if someone else might hear her voice.

'He took your tie before anyone noticed. You left it there.'

'What are you talking about? What tie? Where?'

She turned back to face him. 'The tie you killed that girl with. You must have been off your face with some drug you got from that awful girl because you clearly didn't even remember murdering Bella Young. He covered for you, and he's had to live with it ever since.'

'You think I killed Bella? I don't believe it.'

'But your tie was there, the one we bought you especially for that night.'

'Mum, I lost my tie at the ball. Anyone could have taken it. And I've never taken drugs in my life. Is that why Tanya wasn't prosecuted? Dad thought it would lead back to me?'

She shook her head. She wouldn't, couldn't believe what her son was telling her. That would be too much to deal with. 'Now, will you start this car again?'

But another question was on Paul's mind, and he wouldn't be able to concentrate on driving until he had the answer.

'Did Dad frame Tom Bailey for Bella's murder?'

Chapter Twenty-three

Lara was trying to sleep but she kept waking up from the same nightmare. In her dream Bella's body was lying on the ground in front of her and Lara could hear the waves crashing close by. The faces of Bella's friends flashed before her and she was screaming at them, accusing each one of murder. But they all laughed at her. Then there was the sound of someone walking towards them, and one by one the friends disappeared, leaving Lara alone. Then Bella got up and hugged her before she disappeared too. The footsteps got close. They were noisy as if walking on gravel and Lara yelled at the invisible person before waking up once again.

She decided to give up on sleep and got out of bed. She'd settled her bill before going to bed and her bags were packed ready. Deciding there was no point in lying in bed waiting for morning, she dressed and slipped out of the hotel. No one saw her leave. Mrs Parsons was in bed and John had disappeared earlier following a phone call from Jenny. He said it was important and Lara wondered if Jenny had found out about the anonymous letters. Given his anger, Ben was likely to have told everyone else who had received one, those that were still alive anyway. Lara was scared that she might be arrested for sending them, but more than that, she was disappointed in Ben for not caring about her as she cared about him.

As she walked across to her car, the sound of her shoes on the driveway reminded her of the footsteps in her dream. She'd thought that it might have been John coming back but his car wasn't in the drive. She shivered as she thought of burglars stalking the area, looking for weak door locks, and then began to feel guilty about leaving Mrs Parsons alone in the house. Perhaps she should wait until morning. Then she noticed a truck parked on the pavement outside and looked up at the bedroom windows. There was a light on, and she realised there must be other guests which would account for the footsteps she'd heard on the gravel. That made up her mind.

She got in her car and started the engine. A faint light fell on her as someone pulled back the curtain from the lit upstairs room and she glanced up to see a male face looking down on her. The curtains fell back, leaving her in darkness once again until she switched on the car lights. Then she drove away.

John was surprised to find plenty of space in the driveway. Where was Lara's car? Was that it he'd just seen driving away? He went upstairs and knocked on her room even though he was certain that she wouldn't be in there. When there was no answer, he opened the door to find an empty room. She had left. He knew he should have stayed with her after Ben's

306

outburst about the letters, but the trip to Simone's house had been worth it. She and Jenny had confessed to lying at the trial of Tom Bailey and, in the process, helped ensure his false conviction.

But John wasn't so sure that their testimonies had been crucial, not when there had been DNA evidence placing Bella's blood in his car. In itself, that would have been enough to get a guilty verdict. But that didn't alter the fact that Simone committed perjury even if, as she insisted, she thought Bailey was probably guilty anyway. She could well be looking at a prison sentence. Jenny, however, was guilty of nothing other than believing her friends' story about Bailey trying to attack her. She only found out about the alleged rape of Hanna from Simone a few hours earlier but insisted she would happily have lied in court too if she'd known.

He thought of the moment he'd heard about Bella's death. It still pained him to think of the last time they were together, the day she slapped him across the face for implying that she would sleep with the mysterious record company scout. He hadn't meant it, of course, because he was aware of Bella's feelings towards him. She hadn't told him as much, but he could see by the way she smiled at him, as though they were a couple. Then she wrote the words down in a letter which reached him the day she died.

Written in that letter were the silly romantic words of an innocent teenage girl, a girl who never had the chance to be appreciated. He still had the letter. He'd thought about passing it on to her sister, but that would be betraying Bella. Her words had been intended for him only. Anyway, Lara had left without saying goodbye, probably scared of being arrested for sending the anonymous letters.

Suddenly, he heard a mobile phone ringing, and, after fumbling between the blankets, he found it. It was Lara's phone. In her haste, she had left without it. There was nothing to be done so he took it downstairs and left it in the kitchen. She'd probably ring once she got home. He doubted she'd come back for it.

There were no cars on the road except for Lara's and one other driving someway behind her. She was tired so turned up the radio and forced herself to listen to the late-night play. The voices made no sense and she thought about switching stations, but then the play ended so she waited for the news to come on. After countless bends, the road ahead was straight for at least half a mile, so she picked up speed while the road was clear. The car behind had fallen further back which pleased her. She remembered the car that tailgated her and then followed her down to Easton. With a shiver, she realised that it might have been Tom Bailey driving that car. But the car behind did not have a broken wing mirror so she relaxed.

As she came to the next bend, she eased her foot down on the brake. She could feel no pressure from the pedal. She pushed her foot down further, but the speed of the car remained constant. Finally, she slammed down hard on the brake pedal until she could feel the floor under her foot. But still, the car did not slow down. Her heart began racing as she realised she was heading straight for the bushes along the side of the bend ahead. She frantically changed down to first gear to force the car to slow down then pulled up the handbrake. But it was too late to stop the car ploughing into the bushes. Suddenly she was pinned to the seat by the airbag, but knew she was okay.

She squeezed out of the car and, after grabbing her bag from the other side, searched for her mobile phone without success. Why didn't she check her bag before leaving the hotel? Now she was stranded miles from anywhere and faced with a long and dangerous walk to either Copston or back to Weston. Then she saw headlights and she remembered the car that had been behind her until she'd speeded up. She ran to the side of the road waving her hands in the air and the car flashed its lights and slowed down.

Lara was relieved to see that it was a woman driver at the wheel as the car came to a stop. 'Thank you so much for stopping. I don't know what's wrong with my brakes, but I couldn't get the car to slow down. If you let me borrow your phone, I'm sure I can get someone to come out here.'

Lara waited for the woman to pass a phone through the window, but instead, she got out of the car. Immediately Lara recognised her.

'Oh, hello. I thought I was the only mad woman driving at this hour.' Lara was trying to sound light-hearted but there was something about the woman's expression that made her feel uneasy. Why wasn't the woman answering her? Then she noticed the woman was carrying something. It was a hammer.

'Why are you holding that?' Lara asked nervously.

But the woman still didn't answer. She started walking towards Lara who by now, was sensing danger. The woman was only a few feet away when Lara turned and ran into the field behind the crushed hedge. She didn't look behind her for fear of losing her ground. The other woman was at least ten years older, so Lara felt confident she could outpace her. She knew there was nothing ahead of her, but she had to keep running. But then she was on the ground and the other woman was on top of her.

'You can't beat me in a race, Lara. I was a games teacher, you know.' But she was exhausted and could hardly hold the hammer.

'Why are you doing this?' Lara cried. But she already knew. 'You cut my brakes.'

'Yes, and it worked out better than I expected when I saw you leaving just after I got back into my car.'

"So, it was you who killed my sister. Why?' Her face wet with tears, Lara tried desperately to play for time, telling herself she might be able to fight back.

'Why do you think? She tried to blackmail me, threatening to ruin my career when it had just started. She told me to bring the money to the coastal path, a stupid place to make such demands.'

'It was only two hundred pounds. Was it really worth killing someone over?'

'Oh, she would have come back for more. Blackmailers always do. There was another victim with her when I first arrived, Chris Farmer. I don't know what he had to hide, but he wasn't giving in either. That must have been when he took the bangle.'

'Why did you have to kill Tanya and Hanna? Surely they weren't blackmailing you.'

'Hanna came over to me in The Royal Oak, asking me if I'd seen Chris. She was upset so I asked her what was wrong. Then she told me about the bangle and how she needed to speak to Paul about it. I couldn't have that.'

'Why not?'

'Because he might look into the case. He's always wondered why his father lied for him, saying Paul was at home when he was with me.'

'And why did he lie?' Lara asked. So much remained unexplained but, as she looked into Rachel Croft's wild eyes, she knew time was running out.

'He probably found Paul's tie at the scene. Paul took it off at the ball and I picked it up off the floor and put it in my bag. I must have dropped it when I left the path. Then it mysteriously disappeared.'

'So, you used the tie to strangle Bella?' Lara remembered how Gerald Croft had reacted to her question about the murder weapon.

'Yes. She had no chance against me. Neither have you.'

In an attempt to distract Rachel Croft from her murderous intent, Lara returned the subject to her other victims. 'How did you know where Hanna would be so that you could kill her?'

'I didn't know actually. That was just luck. As I was driving that night, I gave my friends a lift home. On my way back I saw Hanna walking towards the bypass. I stopped and went up on the footbridge to wait for her. I was wearing Paul's hoody that he'd left in the car. It gave Hanna a shock, I can tell you.'

The more Rachel was talking, the more Lara realised that she was dealing with a deranged woman. She also knew that she had little chance of getting out of the situation alive. 'What about Tanya? Why did she have to die too?'

'Because she started ranting on and on about that photograph while she was serving me. I was behind Ben in the queue and had already heard them arrange to meet later for some criminal transaction. Then she told me she was going to speak to the police about Chris. I couldn't let her do that so after she finished her shift, I followed her to the canal but sneaked through the bushes so that I wouldn't be seen. It was too easy.'

'You won't get away with killing me, though. This won't work, Mrs Croft.' Lara shouted the words out in the hope that someone passing would hear her, as unlikely as that would be.

'I have no choice, Lara. You have ruined everything for me. If only you hadn't come here.'

Lara could tell that the other woman had got her breath back and was ready to strike. All she could do was scream. If she was going to die in such a brutal way, she didn't want to know when the first blow was coming.

'Rachel! Is that you?' A man's voice came from the near distance.

Rachel spun around to see her husband walking towards her. 'Hi, Darling. Please don't be angry with me for not waiting for you to come home, but I couldn't let her ruin everything for us.'

'Rachel, what are you doing with that?' He pointed to the hammer which was still in his wife's hand.

'We need to get rid of her, Paul. She's trying to destroy us. It's lucky you're here. You can help me get rid of her body.'

'I was on my way back from dropping Mum off when I saw your car.' His voice was monotone, showing no clue as to what he was thinking at that time.

The terrified Lara was now paralysed with fear. Of all the people she'd wanted to hear her calls, her attacker's husband was not one of them.

But Paul was almost as terrified as she was as he watched his wife about to commit murder in front of his very eyes. After hearing his mother's revelation, he thought that nothing would ever shock him as much again. But this was worse. He had to act before it was too late.

Rachel turned back to her captive and, once again, raised the hammer high above her head. But it stayed there. Someone was holding her arm back. Paul.

'It's no good, Rachel. When I saw the cars, I thought she was attacking you. I phoned Brooks and he's on his way. It's over.'

John brought coffee and sandwiches over to the couple sitting in the breakfast room. He'd given up on trying to persuade them to stay for one night as they kept insisting that they had to get back.

'We've got a long drive ahead of us,' said Mr Campbell, as he stared at the microwave on the sideboard. 'As it stands, we won't get home till the early hours.'

'Wherever is she?' sighed Mrs Campbell, hearing the grandfather clock strike seven times.

'I'll go and check.'

John climbed the stairs and walked across the landing until he reached the back bedroom. He tapped on the door. 'Lara, are you nearly ready?

Your parents are getting anxious about the drive home.'

'You can come in, John,' Lara shouted.

Inside the room, Lara was sitting on the bed. Her case was packed, and the bed was made. John went over and sat down on the bed next to her. Then he put his arm around her.

'You've had one hell of a holiday,' he said. 'It might be worth writing that book.'

Lara smiled. 'What book? Seriously, when I first got here, I never really believed I would find out the truth. Maybe the whole plan was just an excuse to visit Bella and apologise for going away and leaving her alone. That's why she died, John. She didn't have anyone to take care of her.'

'You found her killer, Lara, and nearly died in the process. I think you can put that guilt to rest now.'

'Did you know Rachel Croft much, John?'

'No. She joined the school a couple of years after I left.'

'I can't believe she killed three people to protect something that wasn't even a crime. She would have got the sack, that's all.'

'But she was an ambitious woman, Lara, and she thought Bella was going to ruin her career before it had hardly started. And once she'd killed her, she felt she had to kill Hanna and Tanya to prevent the truth from coming out.'

'Poor Hanna. If she hadn't met me that night, she would still be alive. Tanya too. Then again who knows what Tom Bailey may have done to them. He must know they lied at his trial.'

'Yes, he does. And he's been making quite a lot of noise about it too. He'll be getting a hefty compensation package. There'll be a few questions that will need answering once the new police force has caught up with everything.'

Lara felt sad. She hadn't come to Weston to cause chaos amongst decent young men and women. 'At least you're in the clear, John.'

'Even if I had the most lines coming from my name,' he laughed.

The sound of the front door opening brought them back to the present.

'That'll be Jenny,' John said. 'Are you sure you don't want to join us? The restaurant we're going to is on your way.'

Lara laughed. 'We don't want to gate crash your first date.'

Downstairs Jenny was talking to Lara's parents, but on seeing Lara, rushed over and hugged her. 'I can't believe you're leaving. It feels as if I've known you for years.'

'Well, you won't be here much longer either, Jenny.'

'Yes. I guess I'm a city girl at heart. London is in my blood.'

'And closer to Cambridge,' Lara whispered.

Jenny blushed. 'I'll be up to see you as soon as all this is finished with.'

'You'd better not leave it too long,' Lara replied, fighting back the tears. She looked over at her parents who were half outside the door. 'See you soon.'

'Lara, there's someone here to see you,' Mrs Campbell said.

Ben was standing in the driveway. He was holding a large object wrapped in brown paper. 'I brought this for you. I'm sorry for being mean,' he said, handing the parcel to her.

Lara took the parcel, without showing emotion. 'Thank you, Ben,' she said, without looking at him.

'We need to get going, Lara,' her father shouted.

Ben stood back to allow Lara to get into the car. They pulled out of the drive and started the long journey home.

Lara unwrapped the brown paper and looked at the gift.

'What is it, Lara?' her mother said, from the front seat.

'Just a little memento,' Lara said, before putting the portrait of her sister back in the wrapping.

Two weeks later

It was cold but at least it was not raining. Lara sat down on one of the empty benches in the station. There was a strong breeze which almost snatched away the letter, so she held it firmly in both hands. It had not been a surprise to receive yet another letter from Bella's foster mother, given all the press reports about the miscarriage of justice regarding her foster daughter's murder. Mrs Baxter was shocked to hear that the local headteacher was now charged with three murders but insisted that she'd never liked her anyway due to her "always picking on my kids". The words that did come as a surprise, a welcome surprise, were at the bottom of the sheet of paper.

"It was nice to get my bangle back after all this time. I always thought that it was taken by that Bailey man, but a Sergeant Brooks sent it back to me. Bella was so pleased when I lent it to her. She said that it made her feel like a rich girl."

For the first time, Lara realised that Bella had not been alone all those years. She'd had loving foster parents who had done their best for her, guiding her through her later childhood and school exams. Perhaps Bella was as happy as any young woman, with hopes and dreams of a glamorous future. And maybe she would have achieved those dreams.

'Sorry, I'm late. The train was delayed.'

Lara put the letter away before looking up. She smiled. 'Better late than never. Perhaps you should bring your motorbike next time.'

Forget Me Not

Marie Sibbons

Prologue

The narrow stairs creaked at every third step taken as if they were telling her to turn around. Although alone in the house, she winced at each sound she made as she climbed towards the attic room. White silvery clouds were lending a shimmering glow to the otherwise dark room. Her reflection appeared in the cracked windowpane as she took the final step onto the ragged carpet. Taking off her glasses as she moved closer to the image, she could see the blotches under both eyes. They reminded her of the disappointment she had experienced a few hours earlier. And yet the day had started so hopefully. Maybe it wasn't over yet. No. It is over and she must accept it.

Crouching to open the tiny cupboard door, she looked down to see a teardrop splashing onto the wooden box that she was holding. She recalled her conversation with that old woman in the nursing home which had made her feel so ashamed. It was time to move on with her own life and not dwell on someone else's past. Tomorrow would be a new day, different from all the others. She placed the box inside the cupboard and closed the door for the last time.

Then she heard the stairs creak.

Forgetful Waters

Marie Sibbons

The brightness of the sky is wondrous tonight. Every star in the universe must be making an appearance, radiating a myriad of dying glows through the darkness of space and time. It is said the stars visible on Earth no longer exist and are merely the remnants of a life long gone. Just like a person in a photograph. But she doesn't want to believe something so beautiful is not really there.

Even the moon appears so much closer than usual. She reaches out to touch the vast golden ball in the hope she will be energised by its cosmic rays. But of course, it is an optical illusion. The moon isn't really golden. Rather, it is a lump of dull rock many thousands of miles away, a giant version of the one she is sitting on, the one that is now digging into her skinny legs.

What is she doing up here alone? That's right. She's meeting someone. But she can't remember who it is. The inside of her head feels like the sea below, tossing and filled with froth. What was she drinking back there?

An unseasonal brisk breeze sweeps across the headland causing a moment of soberness and she trains her ears to listen out for footsteps between the lapping of the waves. There is something. Someone. She can hear

323

shuffling … yes, footsteps. The steps are getting louder, and she wonders if she should be afraid. Seagulls are cawing loudly, and for a moment, she loses track of the other sound. There it is again, stronger this time.

Ahead of her, the outline of a person begins to emerge, and her heart misses a beat. It disappears into the sea mist, and she thinks she may have imagined it. Then it reappears and steadily grows larger as it comes towards her. It is him. He is here and is smiling at her, his eyes glistening in the near darkness. She cries out with relief, running towards him before suddenly stopping. She can see something else glistening like the stars so far above them. As the steel slices her arm, she cries out in pain. The blade rises up again and she steps back to avoid it, falling into the dark water below.

Printed in Great Britain
by Amazon

35924521R00185